"When I reached the last page of  ri-
enced an overwhelming sense ol ks
are not the only ones whose hea ;e;
Penelope Wilcock's legion of reac d,
as well. Mercy, grace, and forgiv ... ...ven throughout the
story with a deft hand, as we meet a community of God's faithful
servants who are genuinely flawed yet always sympathetic. The
descriptive passages are poetic, and the medieval details evoca-
tive, with a rich sense of time and place. I offer my highest praise
and most heartfelt recommendation: you will love this novel!"
> **Liz Curtis Higgs,** *New York Times* best-selling author,
> *Mine is the Night* and *Bad Girls of the Bible*

"Penelope Wilcock has written a novel as deep and contemplative
as the monks whose stories she tells. Her intimate knowledge of
medieval monastic life sweeps you into the past, yet the struggles
she chronicles are timeless. This book is not toss-away entertainment; it's literature that pours from a poetic soul. Putting it down
at the end of the day was the hardest thing to do."
> **Bryan Litfin,** Professor of Theology, Moody Bible Institute;
> author, *The Gift, The Sword,* and *Getting to Know the
> Church Fathers*

"Beautiful, profound, moving, and spiritual. . . . As the readers
are drawn to live in the ancient monastery of St. Alcuin and to
share the daily challenges of the community struggling to receive
the grace of God and bring it into their world, each one of us comes
to ask: 'What is the hardest thing to do?' and, 'Can I do this, with
God's help?'"
> **Donna Fletcher Crow,** author, *Glastonbury: The Novel of
> Christian England* and *A Very Private Grave*

"James the apostle wrote that 'mercy triumphs over judgment,' but some of the brothers of St. Alcuin's Abbey find vengeance more satisfying than forgiveness in Wilcock's delightful tale of medieval monastic life. *The Hardest Thing to Do* is wonderfully accurate to time and place, and perceptive in its treatment of the strife which can afflict even the people of God."

Mel Starr, author, *The Unquiet Bones, A Corpse at St. Andrew's Chapel,* and *A Trail of Ink*

THE HARDEST THING TO DO

4

The Hawk and the Dove

The Hardest Thing to Do

A NOVEL

PENELOPE WILCOCK

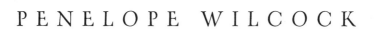

:: **CROSSWAY**

WHEATON, ILLINOIS

The Hardest Thing to Do

Copyright © 2011 by Penelope Wilcock

Published by Crossway
    1300 Crescent Street
    Wheaton, Illinois 60187

Cover design: Amy Bristow

Cover illustration: Shannon Associates, Glenn Harrington

First printing 2011

Printed in the United States of America

ISBN-13: 978-1-4335-2655-8
ISBN-10: 1-4335-2655-7
PDF ISBN: 978-1-4335-2656-5
Mobipocket ISBN: 978-1-4335-2657-2
ePub ISBN: 978-1-4335-2658-9

Library of Congress Cataloging-in-Publication Data
Wilcock, Penelope.
   The hardest thing to do / Penelope Wilcock.
      p. cm. (The hawk and the dove ; bk. 4)
   ISBN 978-1-4335-2655-8
     1. Monks—Fiction. 2. Monastic and religious life—History—
Middle Ages, 600–1500—Fiction. 3. Historical fiction, English.
4. Christian fiction, English. I. Title.
PR6073.I394H37   2011
823'.914—dc22   2011001938

Crossway is a publishing ministry of Good News Publishers.

BP		20	19	18	17	16	15	14	13	12	11
14	13	12	11	10	9	8	7	6	5	4	3	2	1

FOR
FATHER TOM CULLINAN

who is quite unforgettable
whom I love dearly
who bound my Bible for the ridiculous sum of 10 £
whom I respect profoundly
whose house is full of loving-kindness
whose wisdom and gentleness humble me
who cares for the earth and serves Christ most faithfully
whose flint has struck my flint at times
who lives in the most beautiful simplicity
whose experimental soup whizzer—made with razor blades
and a coat hanger attached to his drill—was a total failure
whom I revere absolutely
whose bicycle is the oldest I have ever seen
who sees almost every imaginable thing differently
from the way I see it
whose face and house and friends and voice and chapel
and garden are lodged in my memory
for ever

For I am become like a bottle in the smoke;
yet do I not forget thy statutes.
How many are the days of thy servant?

PSALM 119:83–84 KING JAMES VERSION

What we need is people who are capable of loving;
of not taking sides, so that they can embrace
the whole of reality as a mother hen embraces all
her chicks with two fully spread wings.

THICH NHAT HANH

The word of God is very near to you,
already in your mouths and in your hearts;
you have only to carry it out.

PARAPHRASE OF DEUTERONOMY 30:14; ROMANS 10:8

Reconciliation can be initiated in an instant.
It's also a process.

ALICE WILCOCK

All life is but a wandering to find home.

SAMUEL BECKETT

Contents

THE COMMUNITY OF
ST. ALCUIN'S ABBEY

(Not all members are mentioned in *The Hardest Thing to Do*.)

Fully professed monks:

Abbot John Hazell	*formerly the infirmarian*
Father Chad	*prior*
Brother Ambrose	*cellarer*
Father Theodore	*novice master*
Father Gilbert	*precentor*
Brother Clement	*overseer of the scriptorium*
Father Dominic	guest master
Brother Thomas	*abbot's esquire, also involved with the farm and building repairs*
Father Francis	*scribe*
Father Bernard	*sacristan*
Brother Martin	*porter*
Brother Thaddeus	*potter*
Brother Michael	*infirmarian*
Brother Damien	*helps in the infirmary*
Brother Cormac	*kitchener*
Brother Richard	*fraterer*
Brother Stephen	*oversees the abbey farm*
Brother Peter	*ostler*
Brother Josephus	*has acted as esquire for Father Chad between abbots; now working in the abbey school*
Brother Germanus	*has worked on the farm, occupied in the wood yard and gardens*
Brother Mark	*too old for taxing occupation, but keeps the bees*
Brother Paulinus	*works in the kitchen garden and orchards*
Brother Prudentius	*now old, helps on the farm and in the kitchen garden and orchards*
Brother Fidelis	*now old, oversees the flower gardens*
Father James	*makes and mends robes, occasionally works in the scriptorium*
Brother Walafrid	*herbalist, oversees the brew house*
Brother Giles	*assists Brother Walafrid and works in laundry*
Brother Basil	*old, assists the sacristan—ringing the bell for the office hours, etc.*

Fully professed monks now confined to the infirmary through frailty of old age:

Father Gerald	once sacristan
Brother Denis	scribe
Father Paul	once precentor
Brother Edward	onetime infirmarian, now living in the infirmary but active enough to help there and occasionally attend Chapter and the daytime hours of worship
Brother Cyprian	porter

Novices:

Brother Benedict	assists in the infirmary
Brother Boniface	helps in the scriptorium
Brother Cassian	works in the school
Brother Cedd	helps in the scriptorium and when required in the robing room
Brother Conradus	assists in the kitchen
Brother Felix	helps Father Gilbert
Brother Placidus	helps on the farm
Brother Robert	assists in the pottery

Members of the community mentioned in earlier stories and now deceased:

Abbot Gregory of the Resurrection	
Abbot Columba du Fayel (also known as Father Peregrine)	
Father Matthew	novice master
Father Aelred	schoolmaster
Father Lucanus	novice master before Father Matthew
Father Anselm	once robe-maker

Members of other religious houses resident at St. Alcuin's:

Fr. Wm. de Bulmer	prior of St. Dunstan's Augustinian Priory near Chesterfield

LIGHT ✠ FIRE ✠ ASHES

Scribed with care on finest vellum, illuminated magnificently with consummate artistry, bound in leather and clasped with silver, the beautiful Gospel lay closed on the lectern, waiting. Tomorrow, Ash Wednesday, would be the first day of Lent.

THE
FIRST DAY

*B*rother Thomas sat impassively in his stall in the choir: he felt irritated nonetheless. The air was astir from Father Chad's bustling as the prior made his way with exaggerated purpose to the abbatial seat. The energy of his going generated a crack and flap of robes that grated on Brother Thomas's nerves.

Why can't he just tread quietly? Why does he have to exude this self-importance every blessed time someone gives him something to do? Oh, ye saints and archangels, just sit down, Chad—whatever it is I bet we've heard it all before.

Ash Wednesday. The smell of the burnt palm crosses mixed with chrism pervaded the chapel.

Prime, then the morrow Mass and imposition of the ashes: "*Memento, homo, quia pulvis es, et in pulverem reverteris. . . .* Remember, O man, that dust thou art, and to dust thou shalt return. . . . Turn away from sin and be faithful to the Gospel."

Tom rose to his feet, his brow marked with ashes by the prior's thumb. He returned from the altar rail to his stall, where he sank down to his knees again, wanting to repent about Father Chad and not finding it possible to rid himself of baser thoughts: *His voice is annoying. His face is annoying. That little nervous laugh is annoying. The way he says "homo" sets my teeth on edge.*

There exists nothing that God has not made. *Is God annoy-*

ing? Did Chad spring fully-formed from some irritating, half-baked little crevice unacknowledged in the mind of the Divine?

Lent is hard. Cormac's bread is hard, but in hard Lent the bread is even harder: just flour, salt, and water, no leaven. No eggs, no meat, no cheese, no butter. Beans and roots and cabbage; cabbage and roots and beans. There are no alleluias in Lent. But the hardest thing to do is to take away every comfort, every grace note from the daily round, and *still* remember not to look at Chad as if you wished he'd crawl right back under his stone.

Come soon, Brother John. This place needs you. I need you.

The community filed through into the chapter house to hear the reading of the Rule, the superior's homily, and the daily discussion of community concerns.

"Brothers, there has come unsettling news of a tragedy." Father Chad's voice resonated with the frisson of awful tidings. "One of our guests who was with us on Monday night brought word yesterday of a great fire that has broken out, he said, in a monastery but a few days' ride from here. I pressed him for more detail, but he had heard only rumors—talk of complete destruction, of ashes floating on the wind across the neighboring country, and many lives lost. When I hear tell of what community has suffered this dreadful calamity, I will bring you news: for now, dear brothers, please keep those stricken in your prayers.

"Please pray, of course, also for our brother who is traveling home to us and will be with us any day, we hold good hope. We beseech God of his great kindness that our brother may be kept in safety from danger, disease, wild animals, and violent men, that he may soon be received under our roof with all charity and rejoicing.

"And we keep in our prayers before God all who are sick and frail, especially Brother Cyprian, whose health is failing."

Father Chad turned to the Rule of St. Benedict and the

chapter for the observance of Lent, exhorting the brethren to keep their lives pure and to wash away in this stretch of extra effort the creeping negligences that gradually attached themselves through the rest of the year. The chapter urged each man to seek out some extra offering of his own self-denial—some item of food or drink, another hour of sleep, forbearance from conversation—to deepen the penitential journey of Lent and heighten the joy of spiritual desire for Easter.

Tom noted the enriched timbre of Father Chad's voice as he read from the Rule: "Let each one, however, suggest to his abbot what it is that he wants to offer, and let it be done with his blessing and approval. For anything done without the permission of the spiritual father will be imputed to presumption and vainglory and will merit no reward. Therefore let everything be done with the abbot's approval."

Tom considered the possibility of humbly asking Chad's permission to keep out of his way for six weeks—for the good of his soul. Then he felt a sudden stab of shame at his lack of charity.

Father Chad had proposed that the admission of their new abbot be incorporated into the Easter festivities as a grand and joyful occasion. Brother Thomas had seen things differently. "It's not for show; it's not about the pomp and ceremony!" he had wanted to say, but had stood in silence, biting back the flood of criticism that had wanted to tumble out, until the prior asked him, "Yes, brother?"

And with an effort he had kept his words honest and simple. "Father, I think Brother John likes things done quietly. I think the receiving of our new abbot is a private, family thing. I beg to offer that we do this simply, just among ourselves, and let Easter have the glory that belongs to it, without us trying to gild the lily."

Father Chad had nodded thoughtfully, alert to the quiet stir of assent that reached his ears.

"That sounds like wisdom, dear brother," he conceded.

He hesitated, then added, "We shall be empowered to do this because the bishop has given us permission to admit our new abbot as soon as he arrives among us. *I* am permitted to act as the bishop's commissary."

Tom nodded, keeping his eyes lowered. He understood what he was hearing. Chad had no confidence in himself, no natural authority. He swung between the paralysis of hopeless inadequacy and preening himself on account of borrowed authority. He was not the abbot of this community and felt the deepest relief to know he never would be. He entertained not even a fantasy of becoming a bishop. Responsibility frightened him, administration confused him, and pastoral ministry frankly terrified him, but to pull borrowed rank occasionally restored his self-esteem.

That was settled then. Their new abbot would be installed privately, quietly, simply, as soon as he had come back home to them.

✠   ✠   ✠

"Brother Conradus, you're late."

This was undeniably true and not atypical, but Father Theodore understood how to soften the rebuke. Only recently clothed in the habit of the Order, still relying on friendly hands to steer him into the right place at the right time, the short, plump, young novice clung to his name in religion and the right to be a brother of this house as a consolation amid chronic weariness and bewilderment. *Brother Conradus*—the words brought exultation, even when they were normally a mere preliminary to correction.

He fell to his knees before the novice master seated in the teaching circle. "I confess my fault of tardiness, my father, and I ask forgiveness of God and of you."

It never felt hard to ask Father Theodore for pardon. Even

as Conradus kissed the floor in penance, the gentleness of the novice master's voice—"God forgives you, and so do I, my son; I do know you are trying your best"—brought comfort and the feeling of being understood. It was not impossible to make Theodore angry, but that happened only when deserved. Theodore could see the difference between human weakness and human sin. He was ready with a hand to lift you up when you stumbled, which was very often in Brother Conradus's present reality. It was not easy to get used to plain food made awesomely plain in Lent. It was almost impossible, having tossed and turned on the lumps of a straw mattress on a February night and having finally fallen into an exhausted sleep, to waken at the clamor of the bell, then leave a blanket still barely warmed and join the subdued line of tired men stumbling down from the dorter at 2 A.M. for Matins, to pray for the king and the dead—the situation of either seeming infinitely preferable. The silence, the work, the unquestioning obedience—Brother Conradus thought everything was as difficult as he'd been warned and maybe more so. But he thought the hardest thing to do was holding it all together, trying to remember everything he'd been told and asked, where everything was and where he was meant to go.

Eager for Father Theodore's morning lesson, Conradus took his place in the circle with the others, and peace settled upon him. Conradus did not know that when Theodore had passed through the novitiate the novices had sat in rows facing their master at the front. He did not consider Theodore's reasoning in arranging the stools in a circle; even so, he was not insensible to the atmosphere of community in this room. Here was a place where people learned together, and everyone felt included.

The young monks and their novice master, all now gathered, sat without speaking in the circle—another innovation of Theodore's. Invariably late to almost everything as a novice himself, his memories were of lessons begun and half missed:

he used to miss the start because he was late, miss the next bit because he was overcome with bitter humiliation and self-rebuke, and miss most of the rest because he couldn't quite make sense of it, trying to imagine what the bits he had missed might have been.

So he initiated the practice of starting the time together in silence.

"In silence we enter the room, brothers. In silence we take a place in the circle—*any* place, not *my* place or *your* place, not the same place always, for place is nothing to be possessive about. We sit quietly then and take in where we are. Sit with your eyes open or shut, it matters not; but be aware. Know that being a monk is not about withdrawal but about community, and feel the community here. We listen to our brothers . . . see them . . . smell them . . . [that usually brought a laugh] and we stay open to what else we can notice. Restlessness? Weariness? Friendship? Peace? Every day is different in community, and we are made more sensitive to the differences because every day is the same."

Conradus liked to sit with his eyes open and rest his gaze on the circle of his brothers, because he had noticed that this was what Father Theodore usually did. Sometimes, like today, a deep sigh escaped from somewhere deep in his body, as he began to relax in this accepting circle. He looked at the smudges of ash on the faces of his brothers. The acceptance belonged to every day; but this was the day of ashes, and that set it apart.

Into the silence Theodore spoke quietly about miracles of transformation.

"A miracle alters the normal course of things, turning what comes naturally into something new. In the everyday world, we take a flint and a rag, or take a taper to a candle, and we make a light. We take the light to the hearth and start the fire. When night comes down and we cease to feed it, the flames die away, the embers grow cold, and all that is left is ashes.

"A vocation can be like that, or a marriage, in the everyday. Someone sets alight something new, it flames up warm and bright. But with time and neglect, it dies down, dies out. As the years go by while you walk this way, you will sense among your brothers those of whom this is true.

"The psalmist says, '*Quia factus sum sicut uter in pruina, justificationes tuas non sum oblitus. Quot sunt dies servi tui?* For I am become like a bottle in the smoke, yet do I not forget thy statutes. How many are the days of thy servant?'

"And when it is like that—as it can be for any of us at times—the going is so arduous. As you walk this path, my brothers, if you see that . . . if you see that your brother has become like a bottle in the smoke, just the used remnant of what must once have been a vocation, oh, do not judge him. One day it might be you."

Brother Ced lifted his head, his face troubled. Father Theodore caught his eye, his face kind.

"But the miracle starts here," he said, and he sounded so certain that Brother Cedd felt reassured. "A miracle is not the everyday way of things—*light, fire, ashes*. A miracle changes everything, challenges the order we know. In a miracle God smiles and says, 'Try this for a change: *ashes, fire, light.*' Inside a soul, when all is ashes—when a brother has become as grubby and unattractive as a bottle in the smoke—the secret fire of the Holy Spirit arises out of the kind desire of God, burning away the dross and the sin, kindling again the precepts, the statutes, the rule of life. Fire is painful, oh, God, it is painful; there is nothing warm and cozy about the mercy of God as it burns away coldness and indifference. But the flowering of the miracle is luminous; there comes light that is evident to everyone who has eyes to see; the inner light of peace betokening the house where Christ lives again: resurrection, I suppose.

"That bottle in the smoke—the empty, clouded, burned-out vessel—you notice the Latin word for it is *uter*—something we use, a useful container—but growing also into the word for a womb, the place where new life begins. The jar lying forgotten in last night's ashes can be the womb of a new beginning.

"So the slow, painful journey of Lent takes us from ashes, through fire, to Easter light: reversing our tendency to fall asleep and neglect the flame, to let the fire go out."

Theodore stopped speaking. His novices, shifting a little on the uncompromising wooden seats, glanced up to see what might follow and traced his quizzical, amused gaze to Brother Robert, who furnished a helpful illustration as he nodded off to sleep.

THE
SECOND DAY

*J*ohn sat up, frowning. The house was quiet. He had slept longer than he meant. Kicking off the woolen blanket they had given him, he looked down at his shins covered in flea bites and gave thanks that his stay did not extend to a second night, for his hosts knew of a carrier's wagon traveling north this day, if he didn't mind a delay at Chesterfield.

John stretched his body free of stiffness. Everything ached. This damp weather had got into his bones. Tired of unfamiliar places and hospitality begged of strangers, he longed for home. A slight sound caught his attention. He looked up to see Goodwife Jenny in the doorway, watching him.

"Good morrow, Father. You have slept well."

"I've slept late, Jenny, but I've a bone to pick with you. I have three sheepskins here for a bed, keeping me warm and comfortable. Now, I'll wager someone in the family has gone without, so I could sleep soft. Am I right?"

Her face illuminated in her sudden wide grin. John counted one, two, three teeth missing.

"You have my fur there, and my man's, but that's no matter after all you've done for us. Father, I have some gruel on the fire when you are hungry, and the carrier is nigh on ready for off. But, my lord . . . "

"What? Don't call me 'my lord.' I'm not anyone's lord. I'm a monk, Jenny, poor and simple. Say straight out what you want, and I'll help you if I can, only I have no money."

"Nay, Father, it's not that. And we know you tell truth about the money, for Robin went through your bag while you were sleeping. It's for Janet, my neighbor. She's been throwing up and had the trots this five days, and the babe's not well, his eyelids are all swollen. I only thought, if you might make haste in rising now you're awake, you could maybe take a look at her and tell us what to do: what physic she needs and how we must take care of her, like you did for the rest of us."

John stood up. "Take me to her, Jenny; I'll see what I can do. While your mind's on herbs, a handful of lavender and bed-straw wouldn't come amiss in here. You have the fleas."

"Fleas?" She frowned, puzzled. "Everyone has fleas."

"They do not. There are no fleas in our abbey infirmary; I give you my word."

Jenny shrugged. "Well, I expect it's a big place with room to shake things out and brush everything down. What can I do here in all this cold and wet? We've all to keep in this small house and the five of us with the goats and all at night. Do you room in with your goats in your infirmary?"

John nodded, resigning himself to reality. "I hear you. It's not that you're careless; I didn't mean it so. Lavender. Lady's bedstraw. It'll help."

In Janet's house, which was even more cramped and dark than Jenny's and full of smoke and the sour smells of flatulence and vomit, John squatted by the bed of Jenny's friend.

"Put out your tongue. Just four drops, there. That's myrrh; it'll stop this in its tracks and give you a little rest, but not for long. Jenny, you must clean the house up for her. Wash out any bowls where she's been sick, and stand them outside in the fresh air. Shake out her bedding, and strew some herbs; rosemary will do, or anything you can beg. If there are any nettles at all starting in the hedgerows yet, make her a tea with the tops. Janet, have you a bowl I can use—a *clean* bowl?"

He took from his bag a square of linen and spread carefully on it his little packs and phials of herbs and oils. Janet sat up in her bed, and Jenny stood over him, the two watching as he mixed, in the bowl Jenny washed and brought him, wormwood, mint, and aloe, with oil of roses. The odor of the house began to improve. Jenny sniffed appreciatively as John carefully dripped his precious rose oil into the small pile of powdered herbs. "That smells so lovely," she said.

"I have no more linen strips to spare. I am so sorry. I must just spread this on your belly, and you'll have to keep it in place as best you can. It's all I can do. It'll help anyway. And, Janet, when you must relieve yourself, do it away from the house, away from your beasts, and away from the place you get your water, or the sickness will return and spread in your household. Now, where is the child?"

They brought him the baby, a poor little scrap with red eyes swollen shut, and John made a tisane of chamomile and lavender, having heated water over the fire until it boiled.

"Let this cool now. Bathe his eyes with it, three or four times in the day. Keep him clean; keep his eyes clean. If you have a cloth that will serve, lay him to sleep in a hammock slung from a stick; not on the floor where it's dusty, and—if you can help it—not in the drift of the smoke. God bless you, God keep you, good ladies; peace be upon you, peace and healing to your house."

So it was that John made his way slowly up-country, finding lodging wherever hospitality was offered him, traveling with whoever could take him another day's journey north.

He had spent a year at Cambridge, preparing for the greater responsibility of the abbacy, under commission of the brothers' unanimous vote, and now priested and educated he was making the long, patient journey back home. He had no horse and no money, but his healing skills and small store of herbs and simples earned him gratitude and goodwill enough to supply his needs for food and shelter, friendship and transport. The most direct route was not always available, and at this time of year, after the hard rains and slow-melting snows, some roads were mired beyond passing. Delays were commonplace. But he had made it to Nottingham in ten days and had high hopes of seeing the moors north of York within a fortnight.

✠   ✠   ✠

Tom surveyed the wood yard balefully. Brother Germanus looked apprehensive. Tom had been Father Peregrine's esquire and helped out wherever a wall had tumbled down or extra help was wanted with the beasts or a rick needed building. Now, waiting for their new abbot to settle him to the obedience that would occupy his days, Brother Thomas had far too much time on his hands for Brother Germanus's liking. Tom still grieved for Father Peregrine. He continued to tend the abbot's lodging, and the work of the farm and the building repairs, along with any number of odd jobs around the place, kept him busy, but he had a space in his heart for something to care about. That left him restless, and irritable.

"The hand ax is rusty as well as blunt. The kindling's got wet. Were you hoping to start a fire with this lot? Brother, who's been looking after this woodpile? Is it you?"

Brother Germanus said nothing and dropped his gaze.

"How could you let it get in this state? Everything here is a sleazy, slipshod mess! The fire won't catch, and when it does, it will smoke. Oh, for heaven's sake, you don't need me to tell you all this!

"Sharpen the ax and rub it down and oil it. Don't leave it out in the rain like this. Take the kindling under cover. What's the matter with you? Is that so hard to do? How could you do such a shoddy job as this?"

He stood glaring for a moment at Germanus's discomfited silence, then turned on his heel and walked away. The care of the wood yard was not Brother Thomas's obedience, but he had offered as a favor to get the firewood up for the novitiate that day.

He took the basket of soggy kindling up the novitiate stairs and dumped it by the fireplace. The supply for the warming room and the abbot's lodge had been brought in ahead of time and dried before a fire already lit; it was only the novices shivering.

Tom found Theo alone in the novitiate, his charges having been turned out on a walk for their health, the rain having given way to sunshine for a wonder. He had directed them toward the river: "Let the clarity of the water and the strength of the great trees find a place in you, restore your souls."

"I have your kindling here, and split logs will follow, when I recover my good humor and the incompetent Germanus is out of sight of the wood yard."

"Good afternoon, brother. What has Brother Germanus done to upset you?"

Tom snorted, indignant. "Have you not seen the state of the wood yard?"

"No. Is it bad?" The news set Theo more on alert than Tom had expected.

"Bad? Shiftless! Untidy! Neglected! It's a god-awful shambles, a total careless mess! Don't grin at me like that!"

"I see. Well, thanks for our kindling. I could fetch the logs, in truth, because I've a little while to myself now before None. But what's Brother Germanus got to do with all this?"

"Isn't he caring for the wood yard?"

"I don't think so. He's been working in the kitchen with Brother Cormac since Advent, hasn't he? Brother Conradus has been overseeing the wood yard, but if he's been doing it badly I shan't fall over in amazement. He's managing his passage through the novitiate as neatly and gracefully as you did or I. Living on bread and water and leniency at the moment for his daily fare."

"Not Brother Germanus? Germanus is in the kitchen?"

Theodore nodded.

Tom ran his hand over his tonsured head in a gesture of embarrassment and uncertainty. "Why didn't I know this?"

"Brother, I have no idea! Would you normally know everything?"

Tom gazed at him hopelessly, shaking his head. "I shall have to go and ask his pardon for what I said. Oh, Theo, we're in such a mess! The left hand doesn't know what the right hand's doing. The wood yard's not a big deal, but it shouldn't just be left to the care of a novice! Not in the winter! Oh, come *soon*, Brother John, before we slump into complete chaos!"

Theodore smiled. "You tore Brother Germanus off a strip for his mismanagement of the wood yard?"

"I did."

"And he didn't correct your mistake?"

"That's right."

"He may even have been sheltering poor Conradus from your wrath?"

"I guess so."

"Well then, my brother, it seems we have not forgotten everything we've learned. Things may not be so bad as you fear."

Tom nodded slowly. "I'll bring your firewood up as I promised, Theo. And I'll do a little tidying up down there, maybe sharpen and oil the axes. I'm sorry I was so hasty."

THE

THIRD DAY

*T*he road from Nottingham to Chesterfield showed treacherous even at a glance. The weather had taken its toll. No matter that the biting and relentless northeasterly winds of the last week had dried up the puddles now, the frosts had done their work and left the ways more uneven than ever. At least now the dry potholes lay in plain sight, giving some profit to wariness. As they climbed out of the river valley toward the hills, the road grew less swampy but no more level.

Sitting beside the carter who had taken him on board, John contained his impatience and set himself to courteous pleasantry. Fifteen miles covered only half the distance he had hoped for, and their road took him farther west than he had planned on his journey north. Even so, he had been grateful to find a man with a horse-drawn wagon willing to take him; the pace of an ox would have driven him crazy.

They carried a mixed load on the wagon: seven casks of good ale, a carved alabaster panel bound from the mason at Nottingham to be painted and gilded before going on to its destination at the manor, three live geese, and some bundles of fleece. Once they completed the climb up from the vale of the Trent to the trade center of Chesterfield, John would help unload at their various destinations; he would seek a night's lodging among the common people and give a hand with the next day's load, which was already promised and would see them over the border into Yorkshire at last. Tomorrow they were bound for Sheffield. There John and his kindly wagoner would part company, for John's way lay north while his companion would load up again in Sheffield and make his way back down to the woodlands and fields of Nottingham.

John huddled down into the folds of his woolen cloak, grateful for the protection its thick weave offered against the wind. He reflected that for all the simplicity of holy poverty, the monastic life did not neglect the practical care of the brethren.

As the cart rolled and the sun poured down in a pale gold flood, enjoying the steady, reassuring power of the great horse's haunches in front of him, John felt suddenly immensely happy. This was a beautiful day, a beautiful world, and the way ahead lay beautiful because it was the way home.

"We'll see what the fire's done, mayhap." John's companion broke the easy silence.

"Fire? Where? A big fire?"

The carter laughed. The shrewd little eyes in the weather-beaten face appraised John sharply, ascertaining the authenticity of the question.

"You must be a good monk, brother. Here's all the sign I need to know you have naught to do with wagging tongues and gossip! 'Fire? What fire?' Aye, 'what fire' indeed! And, yes, *big* is the word for it!"

This interesting conversation lapsed abruptly as the man put his mind to avoiding some of the deeper holes in the way. Wheels, wagon, and horse were all precious to him; they won his daily bread, and the money to replace them came scarce and slow once his rent had been paid and his children and poultry fed.

"St. Dunstan's Priory," he volunteered at last. "Did you truly not hear tell?"

"St. Dunstan's?" John frowned, trying to place it. "That's an Augustinian house, is it not?"

"'Is it?' No. Was it? Yes. There's not much to show for it now but a shell of stone, and from all I hear even the stones have come in handy for the villagers' household repairs before ever the timbers had finished smoldering and the lead ceased to drip."

John sat in silence, taking this in. Everyone dreaded fire. You stood helpless and saw the labor of earning and crafting, the patience of years, consumed in a night when fire struck, sick at heart to begin over again.

"I'm sorry to hear of it," he murmured, grieved for this community, not known to him but brothers nonetheless.

"Sorry, are you?" His companion chuckled. "There's further proof you're a good monk, my friend, for you're the first I've met to say anything more than 'good riddance and serves 'em right.'"

John's lips parted in bewilderment, the puzzlement in his eyes seeking enlightenment. The man looked back at him, laughing. "You really don't know, do you? This is not you just having me on!"

"The house is not loved, from what you say?"

"'Not loved'? That's delicate! That's rich! Nay, loved they were not! Will I tell you then, or does gossip offend you?"

John grinned. "Friend, I aspire to holiness, and I'm bound not to gossip myself. But how can I intercede for my brothers if I do not hear their trouble? Tell me all you know."

The carter was laughing outright now. "Eh, that's more like the monks I'm used to, at least as wily as good! If you'd said no to a juicy tale, I'd have set you down in Chesterfield and left you there: a saint would be too weighty for my old cart! Heh heh! Settle down and hear tell of St. Dunstan's then, good brother. Hey up! Just a moment—branch in the road!"

The weight of fallen wood always surprised John. Even this modest-sized bough took the strength of them both to move aside, and after the heavy snows in December and January, such obstacles were not uncommon. "What d'you do when you're on your own?" he asked as they climbed back into the cart.

"I'm never on my own, brother. I have old Dobbin here with me everywhere I go and always a rope and a chain somewhere in back. But thanks for your help. You have some sturdy muscle: not spent all your life chanting prayers and painting little flowers around the Psalms, then?"

John smiled. "I'm an infirmarian."

"*Are* you so? I'll thank you to take a look at my gout when we pull up for a bit to eat!"

"Gout? I don't need to look at it. More beans, less sausage, no beef; more water in the ale, and pass up the wine. And some nettles and mustard to draw away the heat and soothe the pain. I'll give you some herbs mixed for a warm compress before we part. Eat apples and blueberries. Go easy on shellfish and mushrooms and cream. And when the summer comes, eat lots of cherries."

The carter grimaced admiringly, impressed.

"St. Dunstan's?" prompted John.

"Oh, aye. It's flat country, but they lie in the folds of where the hills just begin and the land slopes away down to the river—plenty of good forest well stocked with deer, plenty of fish in the river. Our road looks across to the priory; we shall see it as we go by.

"The fire caught late one night within this last week. You wanted gossip, and this is gossip you're getting, you understand. There are rumors, but common sense will keep silent on the facts."

"So what are the rumors?"

The carter paused.

"They say the fire was started a-purpose, while the monks slept inside. Killed they was, mostly. That's what I heard."

Something in the way he stopped speaking alerted John's

ear, practiced in listening, to hesitation, reticence. There was more. "Go on," he said.

But the man replied, "Nay. I think I've said enough. What you don't hear you can't repeat. And what you don't repeat will bring nobody any trouble. There's a kindred spirit between all of you monks, I imagine. 'Tis wiser to leave it there."

The grim story drew the chill of the day deeper into John's body, and he shivered. He pulled up the hood of his cowl from beneath his cloak, against the wind, and he withdrew, subdued, into prayer until, making good time along the road, the carter's pointing arm stretched across his vision. "It's yonder."

In the clear, pale February sunshine, the ruined house stood out plainly. Black and charred and derelict, everything had gone; the gatehouse that stood at some distance from the main buildings was burned out also. In all the sprawl of buildings John could see nothing left intact. Here and there people moved about, clambering in the ruins, doing things with handcarts; he could not make out what. He strained to see if any of the figures moving about wore the black outdoor habit of the Augustinians, but across the valley it was too far to tell.

"That's horrific," he murmured. "God have mercy. Did none survive?"

"That I can't say," responded the other. "I've not heard that any did."

John shook his head slowly, in sorrow and disbelief.

"How can this have come about? Did no one help them or raise the alarm? Did no one show any pity? Have they had a decent burial?"

He turned to his traveling companion, indignant and distressed. He saw the veil of wariness draw over the man's eyes and sensed extreme caution and retreat. "What? For the love of God, man, what?"

The carter drew breath, weighing his words carefully before he spoke.

"They were not kind men, good brother," he said at last. "They were greedy and ruthless and cruel. They lived deaf to the pleas of the destitute; they laughed at the poor; they cared nothing for the sick. They demanded rents from the orphaned and the widowed as mercilessly as they took from strong young men. Their coffers and their barns and their prisons were full to overflowing. Their hearts and their prayers were empty. Where they saw wealth, they stripped it out for their own store chests. Where they saw poverty, they turned it away to fend for itself. There was not a peasant or a serf or a knight or a stray dog but hated every last one of them to the heart's core. That fire? Maybe it was lightning. Maybe it was an act of God. And maybe it was not before time."

They traveled on in silence. After a while, his voice heavy with sadness, John said, "I have held people who were beside themselves with terror, sat with people who felt frightened and traumatized and trapped. And I have nursed men with burns. When you're confronted with agony, it's not hard to feel compassion. An infirmarian does not ask who you are or what you have done; he looks for how best you may be healed."

Silence fell between them again. A while passed before the wagoner replied. "That's just it, Brother Infirmarian. Those callous hypocrites in St. Dunstan's—they saw people frightened and troubled often enough. They saw people at their wits' end. They had bounty to share and could well afford mercy, but kindness was never their style. They had no regard for anybody's sorrow—too busy putting safeguards around what was their own to hoard up and gloat over. They never looked upon what they had with gratitude or saw the hope and help it could bring. All it meant to them was power—and that was the thing they liked best. To turn a blind eye when a man whose children are starving takes a deer from your wood or a hare from your field or a fish from your stream—is that so hard to do, would you imagine? Nay! But they couldn't bring themselves to it. I wouldn't have set their place afire, but I'd not have run to put it out too quick neither!"

☩　☩　☩

Brother Conradus followed beside Brother Mark through the long grass of the orchard, their habits kilted up into their belts free of the wet.

"It's good of Brother Theodore to spare you, and good of you to help me, brother. God reward you, I am grateful!"

Brother Conradus liked Brother Mark's soft voice. It had a kind of furry buzz to it. And he felt encouraged by the appreciation and glad of the sunshine.

"We need to heft the hives, brother, to be sure their stores are adequate. It's important to take care of the bees! When Lent is over, and you can have some honey and butter with your bread again, bless the bees in your heart, bless the sunshine and the cow.

"The signs are good this year—all that bitter cold we had encouraged them to cluster, and the sunshine in this last week or so has brought the first few out to forage.

"Ivy and shrub willow they go for at this time of year. And there's the winter jasmine and winter honeysuckle too. The bees like that.

"We got to look at the combs, brother; bee husbandry is all about reading the combs. We can heft the hives, and they feel heavy and full; but what if it's all ivy honey, eh? What then?"

Mystified, Brother Conradus hoped the question would turn out to be merely rhetorical. "Is there something wrong with ivy honey?" he ventured.

"Aye! There you have it!" Brother Mark nodded vigorously in agreement, beaming at him as if Conradus had offered profound wisdom. "Exactly! If they do make all ivy honey, it will crystallize right there in the comb! If we heft the hives, they weigh full heavy; if we look no further, ah, then our brothers the bees may starve! They can't get at the honey, d' you see? Not when it's all sugary like that. So we got to read the combs. And check all is well with the mouse guards and see that the woodpecker hasn't been near!"

Brother Conradus thought it sounded complicated and said so.

"Nay, nay, it's a simple thing for simple people, looking after bees. If you're at peace in yourself, and you have a sharp eye, know what to watch for, you can do well. We keep the mold away. We feed them in the winter. We defend them against the cold and the foe. We see they have water to drink. We keep their doorways clean and the air flow free. We listen, and we watch, and we tend.

"The candles, the honey, the propolis—bee treasure is sweet and fragrant, feeds us body and soul and heals our diseases. The bees are our brothers; it isn't complicated. The hardest thing to do is live with myself when I lose a colony—due to disease or storm or pests breaking in—or the wax moth tunneling, now *there's* a serious thing!—or simply my own mistakes. But hush now, my brother, here we are. Speak soft if you speak at all now; we mustn't disturb the bees. Speak soft, speak low."

His face brown and wrinkled from a lifetime working out in the abbey gardens, and not far from toothless now, he smiled up at Brother Conradus. The novice followed him, entranced and delighted by the old man's gentleness and sense of unity with the bees. They never stung Brother Mark, he'd been told; they knew and trusted him. Like most legends, this did not bear too close examination, but there was truth in its substance somewhere.

As they inspected the hives together, Conradus thought that it was not so much the aspects of monastic life he had expected— the prayer, the devotion, the rhythm of life—as the small bright shards of vivid personality set into this surprising mosaic of community that fed his soul and made it all seem so worthwhile.

THE
FOURTH DAY

John picked his way through the crowds past the cacophony of squealing and urgent bleating arising from the cattle market on Swine's Green. The going was much impeded since all roads led to Chesterfield Market, and the world and his wife seemed to be in town for the lord of the manor's Saturday market.

Keeping close to the buildings, to avoid the splash and filth of the gutter, he made slow progress along Beetwell Street into St. Mary's Gate. The crooked spire of the church made an easy landmark, and John wanted to hear Mass before setting out on the road again. Having had no success in finding a bed for the night, he had shared the stabling of the cart horse, which he found warm and pleasant enough. Such small store of money as he had been given sufficed for bread and ale each day and for replenishing his stocks of herbs if he made frugal choices, but he had to manage it with care. It occurred to John that trying to eke out slender resources while surrounded by mendicant paupers, with his belly rumbling with hunger on a cold winter day, probably furnished good practice for stepping into the abbot's shoes at St. Alcuin's. Making the money stretch there had its challenges too. Their finances had limped along the whole time John had known them, and it took all the ingenuity the abbot and cellarer could bring to it to make what substance they had wind around the year.

"Father, can you spare a coin?" As John paused, pressing

back against the wall of the bakehouse to avoid collision with an exasperated mother shepherding her four children out of its crowded doorway, he heard the low-spoken words of the beggar. Looking around for the source of the voice crouched in the mouth of the adjacent alley, he was startled to see a man well-fed and clothed in the woolen habit of a monk—once the white of the Augustinian indoor habit, but filthy now—his garments torn, his head and beard not recently shaved, his hands bound in dirty rags.

The two looked at each other, and John read exhaustion, desperation, fear in the other man's eyes. Forgetting the press of the crowd and the noise of the street as if it had vanished entirely, forgetting all thought of going to Mass, he sank to a squat beside his destitute brother.

"What has happened to you, my brother?" he asked, gently.

Often enough in the infirmary he had seen this same look on a man's face—recessed from present reality in a pit, a cave, a prison. Drawing a soul out of that place into the light of day was work he knew well. The bedraggled vagrant said nothing in reply, but a convulsion of emotion passed briefly across his face, swiftly brought under control.

John looked up at the bakehouse just close by and rose to his feet again.

"I have no sufficiency to clothe you or buy you shelter. I cannot take you with me, for I am relying on charity, where I can find it, to make my own journey. But if you are content to share bread and ale with me, we can dine together before I must be on my way. Wait for me, I'll make all speed and see what provisions I can get."

John had three apples left in his bag, and the ale-wife had replenished his flask at the tavern in Low Pavement. He purchased a small, dense barley loaf that he thought would fill their bellies well and struggled back out of the shop to the man waiting in the alley close by. John smiled at him.

"Let's get out of the way of all these people. We can sit on that step yon, you and I together."

In the relative privacy of the narrow alley, the two men sat together on a doorstep. John broke the bread in half. With the knife that every brother carries in his belt he cut one of his apples in two. He held out a half share of what he had to this destitute stranger. His new friend took the food eagerly but awkwardly into his bandaged hands, then paused to mumble a blessing and leave a split-second of silence before beginning with difficulty to cram the bread into his mouth, wasting never a crumb.

They ate together, and John offered the man his flask of ale. "Drink it, my brother. Drink it all, there's not overmuch there. I can get some water at the conduit, and who knows when another meal will come your way."

John finished his half of the apple, seeds and all, and part of his share of the loaf, folding the remains in his food pouch for his supper. He waited, while the beggar drained his flask, then sat slumped, expressionless, closing his eyes.

John took back the empty flask and stowed it away.

"Have you hurt your hands?" he asked, quietly.

"They are burned . . . and bruised," the man replied without opening his eyes.

"May I see? I have some comfrey with me here and a little powdered alder bark. I've no clean linen, but we may be able to use your bandages again."

The man said nothing, did not move, but did nothing to hinder John from beginning to unwind the bandaging cloths. They would not come off. The serum from the wounded flesh glued the layers firmly together.

"O *mater Dei*, this needs time, and I have so little time," said John softly. "I'll go fill my flask with water, see if we can't get these free. Wait for me here."

He ran to the pump and then, commending the rest of his

journey to divine providence, spent the last of his money on more bread, oil and wine, and a kerchief from a young woman selling linen in the market. For the kerchief he had to both haggle and flirt; he needed it for less than the price she was asking.

Dodging through the cheerful Saturday crowd, John found his way back to the alley. The man sat without moving, perfectly still, exactly where he had left him. He allowed John to bathe the bandages free from his burned and abraded, swollen, dirty hands. John made no comment but worked silently, tearing the new kerchief into five long strips: one to clean the wounds and two to bind each hand. In the little wooden cup he carried in his bag to share soup and pottage where he was offered hospitality, he crumbled dried comfrey leaves ("I'm sorry, brother; I wish I had these green") and powdered alder bark, mixing them with oil and wine into a runny paste that he dabbed with infinite care and gentleness onto the damaged skin of the hands. He bandaged them again and rolled up the dirty cloths he had removed to wash and use for someone else's need. Glancing up, he saw the man had opened his eyes and was watching him.

"My name is John," he volunteered. "I am far from home. I am the infirmarian from St. Alcuin's Abbey high in the hills above York. It is a house of St. Benet. And you, I think, are an Augustinian?"

The man's face twisted into a sour and humorless grin. "Oh, aye," he muttered bitterly, "from St. Dunstan's. But I am learning it's not always best to make that known."

The church bells began to ring the Angelus. With a pang of alarm, John realized he had to make haste.

"I am so sorry. I have to leave you. Here—there's another apple for later, and I bought you another little loaf: think of it as manna! May God keep you safe and Christ watch over your way. I will pray for you, my brother. But I do have to go."

The man nodded. He took the bread and fruit into his freshly bandaged hands, his expression hopeless with self-pity.

But he raised his face to look at John, saying, "God reward you, good brother. You are not the first brother of that house I have admired."

John paused, perplexed, on the verge of inquiry, but the man turned his head aside and gestured him to go. "It's an old story and a long one. It'll keep. God speed you. I shall in my turn pray for you."

Before the wagon rolled north, John washed out the soiled bandages he'd saved, pounding them with stones in the well water of the stable yard until he judged them clean enough for use.

He packed them away to dry later, rinsed out his pottage cup, stowed everything neatly in his bag, and gave a hand to load the cart with the bundles and packages bound from Chesterfield Saturday market to customers in Sheffield: hemp cloth and goatskins, incense and pots, eggs and wine and shoes.

Finally the reins snapped against the horse. The cart heaved forward. The carter was in a jolly mood, full of stories of acquaintances met and good trade accomplished. He had ribbons to take home to his wife and daughter and a new knife, very stout and sharp. John held his peace and listened, his own thoughts wandering irresistibly back to the monk he had left in the alley; troubled and intrigued, he wished he knew the full story. Why was he adrift in his trouble? Why hadn't the priest taken him in, if not the people? What about the other religious houses? How could he have been left so to fend for himself, injured and hungry and alone?

But the wheels rumbled, and the cart jolted along the north road as the sturdy horse kept a steady pace. Despite his uneasiness and perplexity, John's heart lifted as, the sun setting glorious, luminous in the cold, damp air, they continued to climb into the western hills, crossing the boundary from Derbyshire into the West Riding of Yorkshire.

THE
FIFTH DAY

Cormac leaned against the doorpost of the abbey kitchens, watching the rain streaming relentlessly from the massy gray blur of the sky, rippling and running in rivulets as big as small brooks across the stone yard at the back of the kitchen down toward the orchard and the river.

Though the day presented as dreary a prospect as bleak February could muster, Cormac's soul basked in the quiescence of profound contentment—not his habitual frame of mind. For Lent offered him remission from the preparation of dead bodies: his brothers and sisters the trout, the goose, the cockerel, the wood pigeon, and the duck. Some people ate sparrows, song thrushes, and finches, but here Cormac had long ago drawn the line.

In his early days in the abbey kitchen, newly professed, he had been required to pluck and gut, for the table, larks caught in traps mounted on poles set on the hillside. His abbot of those days, Father Columba—named for the dove but known by his baptismal name of Peregrine, the hawk, a bird he better resembled—had been hard at work in his lodging, frowning in concentration over the pleas of his tenants against necessary increases in rents, meticulously aggregated and listed for him by Brother Ambrose, his conscientious cellarer. Suddenly his door flung open to reveal Brother Cormac, tears streaming down his face, advancing without a knock or a by-your-leave across the abbot's atelier, holding out to his superior in both his shaking hands the cradled corpse of a lark.

"Look! In God's name, look!" For a moment Cormac had stood unable to speak further, shaken with terrible grief. His eyes, compelling wells of outraged sorrow, transfixed his abbot's attention. Then Cormac crumpled, sinking down to his knees on the stone floor, his body gradually succumbing to complete prostration.

Father Peregrine, eight years lame, reached down for the wooden crutch that lay beside his chair and got to his feet, coming around the great oak table spread with precious books and the records of administration, to console if he might his tempestuous, grief-racked brother. He opened his mouth to speak, but before he got a word out, Cormac jerked up onto his knees, still holding in both hands before him the mute, broken body of the dead bird.

"LOOOOOOOOK!!!!" Cormac howled at him, like an elemental entity unleashing a storm of possessed compassion, his face contorted with emotion, flushed with rage, wet with weeping, his mouth gaping in an awful stretched black rectangle of sorrow.

Peregrine had drawn breath in the beginning of an involuntary sigh but stifled it at its inception as insensitive. "Brother Theodore, will you close the door please, but you can stay," he said. Theo, newly professed himself in those days, arrested by the intrusion, was scribing letters at a work-desk under the window.

Theodore did as he was bidden and closed the door. The abbot limped across the spacious room to the two chairs that stood near to the fireplace. He seated himself in one of them. "Brother Cormac, bring the bird to me here please. I can't get near you when you're crouched down on the floor."

Scrambling to his feet and stumbling across the room, Cormac had delivered the little corpse into his abbot's hands, searching his superior's face for affirmation of the outrage.

"Sit you down." Cormac perched on the edge of the other chair—tense, trembling, wire-taut. Father Peregrine did not speak then but held the fragile feathered body of the small brown bird in his left hand, allowing his gaze to rest upon it with complete attention, his right hand delicately stroking the pale feathers of its breast, tracing the white edges of the tail and the smaller wings of the female kind, the crest upon the head, the fine, pointed beak, the sturdy little legs, feet curled, clawed in death.

Peregrine's own hands were clawed and twisted, scarred and maimed, and a fresh agony of grieving racked Cormac's soul: for cruelty and pain, for all that is suffered and ignored, for the legacy of indifference and the failure of compassion, for hope snuffed out and life wiped away without being given a chance.

His abbot said nothing, did not look at him, only held the bird in his hands and in his gaze and let his brother weep. He sat in complete quietness and stillness, until eventually Cormac's distress subsided to a shuddering and sniffling that Peregrine thought he might be able to work with.

He glanced up at the young monk. "Tell me what you see," he said simply.

"What d' you mean?" Cormac's voice, shaken and uneven, quavered as vulnerable as a child. "'Tis a skylark."

Peregrine nodded. "I know. I see her. What I mean is—tell me why you are torn to pieces and I am not: make me see, my good brother, what I am missing."

Cormac sat in silence—all the earth's wretchedness and misery gathered in the haggard grieving of his face—shaking his head at the hopeless task of trying to put anything into words. But his abbot waited.

And at last Cormac said, "Father, what is a lark but its song? The exultation of blue summer, the heady joy—ah, it effervesces and bubbles over with sheer gladness in life. Sweet, wild song, tossing free above the meadow, winging up into heaven in a cascade of trilling rapture, until your eyes can see but a dot against the blue. That's what a lark *is*. That's what we have killed for a poor bundle of draggled feathers and a mouthful of meat gone in an instant that anyway we don't even need! If the scrap of food you can get off a lark is all we have between us and starvation, in God's name we'll be dead by morning in any case! Plucked and boned for the pot it's just a nothing, just a scrap of *nothing* hardly tasted and then gone.

"But left to be, it is a delirium of joy in glory, the soul's delight arising to Christ's heaven in sweet transport of bliss. You can't *eat* what a skylark is—though you can kill it sure enough. But when we kill the songbirds, we choose brute-blind violence over everything that makes life worthwhile.

"The wild birds, Father . . . the songbirds . . . they are God's picture of the freedom of the soul." His voice trailed away, choked in tears.

Brother Theodore (not yet priested then) got up from his stool by the window, crossing the room to where the two of them sat. He reached down, and Peregrine gently gave the lark into his hands. "We'll not eat this one, any road," said Theo with complete finality. "I'll take her and lay her to rest, Brother Cormac, in the burial ground with the blessed dead of our community."

Father Peregrine glanced at him, nodding his permission. He privately weighed, only for a moment, the cost of incurring the wrath of Andrew, the kitchen brother, over what he felt moved to do. Then he gave his promise to Brother Cormac. "Tell Brother Andrew," said the abbot, "we will not eat songbirds in this house anymore."

And that was years ago.

Now Father Peregrine lay in the burial ground where the little skylark lay, and Brother Andrew too. Brother Cormac held the obedience of cook, and the oversight of the abbey kitchen was his responsibility. And for the forty days of Lent, the monks ate neither fish nor fowl—nor butter nor milk nor eggs. The milk went to the calf, the eggs stayed under broody hens, the geese grazed in the orchard at their ease, the trout poised and drifted in the eddies of the brook. And Cormac couldn't have been happier, for that was how he thought the world should be.

Devout Christian noblemen scarcely knew how to get through Lent with the monotony of fish, deprived of ox roast and suckling pig bathed in sweet honey. They rarely visited the abbey in Lent, giving a wide berth to its ascetic table of dry bread and mushy peas. To fast on a vegetable diet the whole forty days seemed nigh on impossible, but for Cormac the hard thing to do was to break fast after Holy Week and welcome Christ risen with the resurrection of suspended carnage.

But today, only the fifth day of Lent, what others struggled to bear without complaint sang sweetly in his soul.

He leaned against the door frame, watching the rain fall, filled with peace.

"*Sicut ablactatus est super matre sua, ita retributio in anima mea.*" He murmured the words from the Psalms: "Like a weaned child on his mother's breast, so I am satisfied in my soul."

He'd kept a bag of pine kernels for a treat, to toast on a griddle and sprinkle on the baked split-pea patties he had made the brothers for their midday meal. He thought they'd like that. It was Sunday, after all, even if it was Lent. Pine kernels kept it special.

THE
SIXTH DAY

Though the February sun rose the best part of an hour before the morrow Mass, the sky hung so heavy with cloud and the rain fell so interminably, buffeted into squalls by the persistent northeast gales, that England seemed buried in unbroken twilight. Daybreak barely lifted the gloom in the chapel at all.

Brother Clement squinted close at the Gospel page before him, trying to make out the words. Brother Michael, who had oversight of the infirmary now that John had left them to prepare for the abbacy, noted Brother Clement's difficulty with a twinge of sadness. For as long as Michael had known St. Alcuin's, Brother Clement's benign presence, graceful illumination, and exquisite lettering had molded and encouraged the endeavors of the scriptorium. If the days of his artistry drew to a close now, and Theodore's days were filled from Lauds to Compline with the novices, who among them could do justice to the beauty of the Gospel? Mediocre scribes abounded; a fine hand and a discerning eye came less frequently. Michael needed no one to tell him that such a turn of events would break Brother Clement's heart, and while he could, working right under the light of the window, he would bring to life the beautiful Gospel in vellum and ink and gold leaf.

Still, for now all Brother Clement really needed was to find on the page the start of the lesson. Beyond that, the words served only as a prompt for passages of Scripture he knew almost by heart.

" . . . *et respondens Iesus dixit eis videte ne quis vos seducat multi enim venient in nomine meo dicentes ego sum Christus et multos seducent.*"

The morning's reading added its own grim cast to the already somber day.

"And Jesus answered and said unto them, Take heed that no man deceive you. For many shall come in my name, saying, I am Christ; and shall deceive many."

Michael hated listening to the texts that followed: "Ye shall hear of wars and rumors of wars . . . but the end is not yet. For nation shall rise against nation, and kingdom against kingdom: and there shall be famines, and pestilences, and earthquakes, in diverse places."

Like the dead beat of a drum, the words knelled in his head: *famine . . . pestilence . . . war . . . but the end is not yet.*

Sometimes, since Brother John had departed for Cambridge, Michael had started awake at night sweating from a recurring nightmare that haunted his sleep. It had many different beginnings, but it always ended the same way: with Michael left solely responsible in a world that had succumbed to a terrible plague. In his dream, people moaning in pain—people with emaciated faces invaded by terrible tumors, people overtaken by fevers and ulcers and boils—reached out to him, skinny, convulsive claws grabbing the skirts of his habit as he passed. They called out to him, pleading for attention, for comfort and relief from pain. And there was only him, the lone survivor in a community overwhelmed by horrible diseases.

Michael could cope with the nightmares, and he understood the cost of infirmary work. He had Brother Damian to help him, Edward to advise him, and Brother Benedict from among the novices, but without John's knowledge and experience, the burden was heavy, the work sometimes lonely, and the days and nights sometimes blurred into relentless stretches of toil. Brother Michael's passion in life was the care of the sick; but even so, when he heard these prophecies of the Scripture, it was all he could do to sit there with his hands folded, still, in his sleeves. What he wanted to do was put his fingers in his ears and scream.

". . . *haec autem omnia initia sunt dolorum.*" The words continued mercilessly: "All these are the beginning of sorrows."

As the prophecy pursued its theme, leaving no ghastly eventuality excluded, Michael felt as if he could drown in its prospect of horror: hatred and betrayal, men turning upon one another and killing each other, the faithful delivered up for torture and affliction, confusion sown by false prophets everywhere—"*et quoniam abundabit iniquitas refrigescet caritas multorum.*" The instinct for charity would turn to ice in everyone's heart.

To his consternation, Michael felt a tear trickling down his cheek; for the first time in his life as a brother of St. Alcuin's, he experienced profound relief in the reflection that it was no longer Father Peregrine but Father Chad whose homily must open the Scripture to them. Chad had the unfailing ability to lead his brethren forth from any deep water onto ground they could expect to be reliably dry.

So it proved today. Chad reminded them not to lose heart. "We carry in mind that Jesus said—I can't remember where, but he did say it . . ." Michael saw Theo's eyes close in despair at this pronouncement, which shook him out of his horror and left him suppressing a smile. ". . . that nobody knows the day or the hour when all this is to take place, so there seems little sense in worrying about it. Worry is a useless emotion and contributes nothing of profit to our life in community."

Michael relaxed as the anodyne flow of clichés soothed his harrowed spirit. Released from the grip of terror into a new drift of thought, he prayed that Father Clement might be given the grace to bear the dimmed eyesight of old age and that by

God's grace his own capacity for compassion would never, never be among those that gradually grew cold.

✠   ✠   ✠

After Chapter, Father Theodore detoured by the kitchen. It took him a while to find Brother Cormac, who had gone outside to gather herbs and fetch water.

"Oh, there you are! Brother, I have come to beg a kindness."

Cormac looked wary but set the pail down and laid the herbs on the chopping block, turning back to Theo as he wiped the rain from his hands with his capacious apron.

"Go on then. What can I do for you? No—don't tell me. I know it. Your novices have had enough of Lent already and need a few morsels to help them get through the day."

"As did we," responded Theo, smiling.

"Aye, but for the most part ours had to be stolen, if my memory serves me right. Take them these little bannocks. I made them with honey, so they're a bit more palatable than they might have been. I had a feeling this request would be coming my way before long. Sorry—no butter, no leaven, but it should keep them alive."

"God bless you, brother!" said Theo happily as Cormac folded the bread-cakes in a linen cloth, placing them into his hands. He hastened across to the novitiate then, taking the stairs two at a time.

As Theodore hurried into the room, he found all eight of his novices assembled, sitting in self-possessed and recollected silence, solemn composure, on the circle of low wooden stools. His heart swelled in a moment of delighted pride in them as he walked quietly around the outside of the circle to take his place among them. It seemed he had taught them well. Each sat with his eyes closed, his hands folded into the wide sleeves of his robe, rapt in peace.

Theodore took his place among them, unobtrusively sinking onto his stool, laying the linen bag of bread-cakes beside him on the floor without a sound. He closed his eyes, joining his brothers in the contemplation of holy silence.

Then "Father Theodore!" chorused eight voices in well-rehearsed unison, "You're *late!*"

As the circle dissolved into laughter, Theo knelt and prostrated himself in the midst of them. "I confess my fault, dear brothers, asking forgiveness of God and of you."

"God forgives you, Father," volunteered Brother Cedd loftily.

"And so do we!" added Brother Conradus.

"Good," said Theo, resuming his seat. "I thought you might when you saw what I've brought you from Brother Cormac."

The bread-cakes were eagerly received and swiftly dispatched.

"I remembered how hungry I used to be in my novitiate days," Theo told them as they ate. "When I stopped by the kitchen to beg a morsel to stave off starvation, it turned out Brother Cormac had the same set of memories. Our abbot brought us all pies (it wasn't Lent) one afternoon when he had reason to believe we'd reached desperation point." Theo smiled, remembering.

"He was special to you, wasn't he?" ventured Brother Boniface.

"Yes. I loved him very much. He lifted me up, taught me to live when I had lost hope that life was worth anything. He did so much for me. I shall never forget him."

"I wish we had known him," said Brother Conradus.

Theo felt inclined to agree but suddenly bethought himself that this line of reminiscence hardly opened a constructive welcome for John's arrival among them later in Lent.

"He was dear to me, but," he continued carefully, "of all that he did for us and taught us, I think what meant the most was that he showed us what we ourselves could be—if we were willing to trust each other, to be gentle and generous, and willing to forgive. And of course we still have that, don't we? Have you finished eating? To our lessons then!"

Theodore wanted to go back to the words Brother Clement had read from the Gospel of Matthew. Listening uneasily to the ominous words, a new thought had come to him.

"The Gospel says," he began, after ascertaining his novices had been paying attention—at least two of them remembered part of what they had heard, "that we shall hear of wars and rumors of wars, that nation shall rise up against nation, kingdom against kingdom, everyone falling to fighting one another. There'll be famine and horrible diseases and earthquakes—all the things that make life unbearable, breaking out all over the place. How does that make you feel? Peaceful? Secure?"

"Terrified," said Brother Placidus in a low voice. "If those words are true, I don't even want to think about it, and if the Scriptures are not true, I don't want to think about that either."

His fellow novices nodded, the cheerful spirit that had buoyed them up earlier beginning to dissolve.

"The Scriptures are true," Theodore reassured them, "but finding in them the truth that sets us free, the Holy Spirit's truth, is a matter of how we live as well as how we listen. What caught my attention in Mass this morning was that bit saying, 'all these are the beginning of sorrows.'

"Every time I've heard this text before, I've thought it meant, 'Ha! Just you wait! You think this is bad—wait for the rest!' And maybe it does, but that never helped me. Christ's word to us, 'see that ye be not troubled' has been meaningless to me—but I thought I saw a glimmer of light when I heard it today. So much of what Christ says is taken for pronouncement—'Thus saith the Lord,' you know? But I wonder if some of what he says isn't more *observation*—'This is the way the world is made; this is the reality we work with.'

"Listening to it again this morning I thought, how could we

possibly not be troubled when we see these things coming to pass? I know myself too well. I can try to be faithful, but I never shall be brave. And the faithfulness doesn't go so well either the bulk of the time.

"But then I began to gaze upon that thought, 'all these are the beginning of sorrows,' and I realized, oh yes, so they are! 'Tis when we fall to fighting each other, when people are divided against each other in suspicion and fear, when natural disasters sweep away our homes and ruin our crops, when disease lays waste the community and the beasts on the farm—these are the beginning of sorrows. When the young men are devoured by war, and the gold reserves of the country are poured into preparing an arsenal, and the women are ravished and the children trampled by the boot of the invader, and the implements of the farm forged into weapons—these are the beginning of sorrows. Of course they are. How could they not be? When it's put like that you can see it for yourself.

"Maybe what we can take from these sayings of Christ is, don't live like that then! Do the things that bring healing; don't do what brings diseases. Save your resources to rescue each other in the face of storm and flood; don't use it all up making trouble. And above all, don't fight each other; find ways of reconciliation, and learn to work together. If you could do all that, you would truly 'see that ye are not troubled' because you'd be on top of the situation when it hit; you'd be standing in the very center of heaven's peace.

"But then our Lord goes on to say that they (whoever 'they' are—the enemy, the people who hate us, I guess) will deliver us up to be tortured and kill us; and everybody will turn against us. And he says then it all begins to disintegrate—brothers falling out with one another and turning upon each other; hatred and betrayal and indifference. False prophets crop up in that climate, whisperers who tell important people what they want to hear, people with an ax to grind who need the name of God undersigning the petition of their particular interest instead of sticking with the simple, humble truth.

"And I had taken the betrayals and disintegration of community to be the second wave in a sequence of tribulations: first you got famine, war, and disease; next you got torture, false prophets, and betrayal. But this morning I wondered if we can see it as being not sequential but consequential.

"So what we can take from it into our lives, for the purposes of living this Lent in St. Alcuin's Abbey novitiate, I would see going something like this:

"Where there is dissension, don't you get all worked up about it. It's bound to happen, but you have a Rule to follow and a faith to uphold, so don't get distracted by joining in the argument.

"War and division, sickness and natural disaster begin human sorrow.

"Consequent upon those calamities are dissension and blame: we get suspicious of each other and start saying, *it's all your fault!* We forget the debt of love we owe each other, under pressure of the times in which we live—we forget to be spacious and generous and understanding, begin to be resentful and antagonistic, giving never an inch, insisting on our rights and our own way. People start getting all visionary about their own point of view, denouncing one another, pointing a trembling portentous finger of blame at any vulnerable individual who dares contravene the party line of what's right.

"Are you with me so far? Somebody give Brother Robert a prod. Somebody put a few sticks and a log on that fire. I've nearly said my piece; stay with me, my good brothers.

"For now we come to the end of the passage Brother Clement read us this morning; mind you, it goes on. Father Chad drew our attention, you remember, to the verse later on in the same passage where Jesus speaks of the end of all things, saying that only the Father knows the timing of these events. He set it in context nicely, but let's us stick for now with the passage we heard today.

"In the last part of that, Jesus says that because iniquity shall abound, the charity—compassion, loving-kindness—of many will grow cold, will fail and die. But 'he that shall endure unto the end, the same shall be saved.'

"So what my heart is holding in its hand is this thought: sickness and natural disaster, but above all war are the beginning of times of sorrow. In such difficult times communities that normally hold together begin to disintegrate into factions, blaming and attacking each other. Betrayal and torture, the two ugliest choices the human race can make, begin to abound, and self-serving lies. In such a climate compassion can no longer flourish; people grow coldhearted, seeing 'the other' as 'the enemy.' People stop helping each other.

"And when Christ says, 'the love of many shall wax cold. But he that shall endure unto the end, the same shall be saved,' I don't think he means, just hang in there, see if you can get through it; last man standing gets to heaven. He means that the nature of salvation is when, regardless of what anyone else may be doing, a man chooses the way of compassion every time.

"When your crops have failed, when your flesh is consumed with the plague, when your sister has been raped and your brother run through on the battlefield, when they turn on you and torture you, when they hate you and tell lies about you, when even your own brothers are divided against each other and you find yourself in the middle of a vicious tug-of-war— what you are fixing your eyes upon is not survival but compassion. The whole way and example of our Lord is not survival but compassion. Salvation is not only knowing that, but having the guts to live it. Glory, there's the bell for Sext! How can that be? How long have I been *talking*?"

THE
SEVENTH DAY

*A*bove the frater where the brothers ate in community, in the room adjacent to the scriptorium, sharing the same good morning light of the eastern wall, Father James held the obedience of making and repairing robes, shoes, and belts.

Mostly working on his own, he managed his working environment in the robing room with meticulous calm. When nobody brought him any repairs and no new robes had been requested, he directed his attention to his other occupation next door in the scriptorium, where he fashioned the intricately worked silver clasps and corners for the leather-bound volumes of sacred Scripture and liturgy. Before he came to his profession as a Benedictine brother, James had learned from his father the craft of the silversmith. Nothing had been wasted in the life of the abbey; all that the brothers could offer—their life experience, their trades—the abbot put to good use.

Today he was finishing Brother John's ("Tsk! *Father* John! I mustn't forget that—*Father* John now!") new habits and scapulars and cowls, two of each, for the whole community relied upon their abbot to look humble but neat and presentable before guests of every station in life, from lords to lepers.

James laid his work out on the bench and eyed it critically, checking again that the seams lay flat and the lengths all looked correct. He had John's old, patched habit for a template.

He privately resolved to send it back to the infirmary to be finally worn out on the senile and the incontinent, so stained the front had become and so threadbare the sleeves.

Father James felt the woven black wool of the new cloth between finger and thumb appreciatively, pleased with the choice. The last lot had been too rough and scratchy, and a habit lasted a long time. Holy poverty must be ever at the forefront of his mind, that Father James knew; but if their cellarer could nail a good bargain by concentrated haggling and being willing to walk away from a trade, James saw no reason to step down further into holy discomfort.

He had made a new belt. He had no idea of the condition of John's belt but thought it likely to be extremely shabby if it belonged to the same man as the old habit—and, serviceable or not, he judged it fitting that no one stepping into the role of superior should be let down by the brother in the clothing room neglecting detail. He would not offend against the customs of frugality: John could keep the old belt as a spare in his chest of clothes in the abbot's lodging—or, if he preferred, leave it to hang in the clothing room for whoever was in need.

Father James put the final stitches into the hem of the second cowl, then folded everything up with a peaceful sense of satisfaction, a task completed with skilled craftsmanship and loving care. He carried the bundle down the stairs, along the cloister to the abbot's lodging. Father Chad had moved out yesterday, back into the prior's snug cell built cozy above the warming room, against the wall with its chimney.

In the abbot's lodging James found Brother Thomas, polishing the oak table with beeswax, having swept and scrubbed the floors and aired the mattress and blankets in the chamber.

"We're ready for him then," Tom remarked as Father James emerged from the clean chamber into the atelier, where the fragrance of Brother Mark's beeswax infused with lavender scented the air.

The scribe's desk stood neat and emptied under the window. Everything was waiting to begin.

"'Should we light a fire, d' you think?" wondered Father James.

Tom gave it some thought and shrugged his shoulders. "It's not as though it's stood unused. Father Prior has kept it warm all through the winter. Leave it, I think. I'll lay the kindling ready and fetch in some wood. Oh, brother, if it's not too much trouble, would you beg some candles from Brother Ambrose for the sconces?"

When Father James returned, he found Tom admiring the finish like glass on the ink-stained, well-worn surface of the table.

The two men simultaneously glanced around: all was trim, everything poised for a new beginning, the air full of expectancy.

"God speed him home," Tom said, "and God sustain him in the work he comes home to do."

THE
EIGHTH DAY

*f*rustrated by the inactivity of the Sabbath, John had walked from Sheffield as far as Rotherham after Mass on Sunday. Famished and weary, wet to the skin, and out of money entirely, he asked directions from those he met and headed down into the wooded valley of the beck at Maltby, to seek food and shelter with his Cistercian brethren at Roche Abbey. They received him kindly, refreshed him, and offered him a bed for the night. He hesitated to accept, because the journey seemed to be taking forever; his lifts north had taken him so far to the west, prolonging everything. He looked out at the teeming rain, wondering if he could try the nine-mile walk to Doncaster, maybe finding shelter before sunset, and found himself without the push to make the attempt.

His cloak and habit mired and sodden, he shivered as he held his hands to the almshouse fire. The Cistercian almoner took in his plight as he brought him chamomile tea and a hunk of bread. "Let me set these down here, my brother, and fetch you something dry to wear. Wherever you're bound, you'll get there faster without taking a quinsy."

It felt odd to be clothed in the gray-white unbleached wool of the Cistercian habit and strangely immodest to be offered no undergarment. But John accepted the kindness of hospitality with profound gratitude, and well-being crept back as he crouched by the fire with his bread and tea.

"You put honey in this." He smiled at the almoner. "God reward you for your charity."

The Cistercian nodded appreciation of John's thanks and hurried away with the bundle of wet, dirty clothes.

"Have you come far, Brother Traveler?" he asked conversationally on his return ten minutes later. "And have you very far to go?"

John shared little of his personal history with those he met on his journey. His vocation expected self-effacement; the focus of his thinking must be directed outward to the charitable service of others. But he also knew that, though gossip was never permitted, any monastic community took keen interest in the news and doings of brother monks passing through.

"I've come from Cambridge—a long and tedious, roundabout way from Cambridge too! And my way lies north of York, to St. Alcuin's in the hills yonder."

"Ah!" The Cistercian nodded. "I knew your good Abbot Columba, whom they called Father Peregrine. He was ever welcome in this house; we loved him right well. He is gone now, I think?"

"A year ago last November," John affirmed.

The almoner nodded thoughtfully. "God rest his soul. So who is your abbot now?"

John paused. Apart from those who had formed him at Cambridge for this ministry, he had not discussed this with anyone, not even the brothers of his own house. He had accepted the call, but with a certain blankness of shock that left it feeling unreal. Before leaving them he had immersed himself body and soul in the work of the infirmary, ensuring that by the day of his departure nothing had been left undone, no loose ends, not the smallest task outstanding: all toenails trimmed, everyone shaved and medicated, every vessel cleansed, and every rag washed and rinsed and hanging neat to dry. The almoner's friendly inquiry forced him into a territory he had not dared to let his heart explore.

"Well," he said cautiously, "at present we are without an abbot."

The Cistercian shook his head, tutting in sympathy, "Oh, aye, that's a difficult passage to weather! Have you none among you who could fill Father Columba's shoes then? Oh, that would not astonish me! Are you awaiting the discretion of the bishop?"

"No." John felt suddenly shy. And then his brother saw.

"Is that why you were at Cambridge?" he demanded, a beam of understanding and admiration lighting up his kindly face. "They have elected you?"

"Yes." As he said it, John felt very alone and very afraid. "They did."

"God bless us, what an honor to have you in our house! The abbot elect of St. Alcuin's! Glory, why didn't you say so before? I mustn't keep you here! You must eat with Father Abbot tonight. By our Lady, what an honor for us!"

John had not allowed himself to project his imagination forward and imagine how all this would make him feel. And now he felt disturbed at the surreal contrast: a humble infirmarian spending his days coaxing senile old men to eat their gruel and wiping up the consequences after they had, a simple monk rooming in with a carter's horse because he had no money for a bed at the inn, sharing what he had with those he met who were even more destitute than himself, now ushered forward as a guest of honor to eat at Abbot Robert's table. How could he hold these reversals together and still have any idea who he really was?

"I beg your pardon; did you ask me a question then? Oh! Yes, I'm sorry. John—my name is John."

He found that the knowledge of his appointment worked a transformation. Not only was he fed as well as the strict Cistercian observance of the Benedictine Rule permitted in Lent, but he was also given a bed in the guest house, and he found his clothes rinsed free of mud and dried by the fireside after Mass in the morning. On top of that, Abbot Robert sent his prior to ride with him as far as Doncaster; the prior would lead the horse back home when they parted company. They inquired if his purse needed replenishing and gave him money for his food and lodging the rest of the way.

Grateful, and slightly unnerved by all this attention, John stood in the rain at the market cross in the center of Doncaster, waving a farewell as the Cistercian prior turned back on the Rotherham road. Everything looked more possible now, but the power of his new status felt unsettling.

He was offered lodging by some Franciscan friars proclaiming the way of humility in the pouring rain right there in the middle of Doncaster, in the market square. Finding that John did not know the way to their friary, the street preachers seemed glad enough for a reason to call it a day with their damp and thankless occupation. They escorted John back to the simplicity of their house, where they fed him and made him right welcome. After some discussion among themselves, they came up with the name of a cloth merchant, a Franciscan tertiary, traveling to York on the very next day. One of the brothers volunteered to run across the city and arrange a lift for John. In thanks for bed and board and all their kindness, John helped in their infirmary the rest of the day and well into the evening, containing his impatience to be back on the road in the morning.

Not long after sunup and first Mass, he was away on the cloth merchant's wagon, with a view of dappled haunches instead of chestnut, rumbling along the Tadcaster road toward York. The rain eased off, and they made good time despite the weather, doing the whole twenty-five miles before the sun sank below the horizon. Even if he had to walk the rest of the way to St. Alcuin's, John knew he could be home by tomorrow or the next day.

In the low-lying land of the Vale of York, floodwater stood

everywhere in the fields. The dappling of pale green and orange lichen clung bright against the dark, soaked bark of the trees, some with their roots in lakes of rainwater; all with bare branches stood stark against the pearly gray of the sky. In folds of the landscape, low clouds hung in pockets of mist, and the swollen streams gurgled turbulently in flood.

Enjoying the ride despite the bone-shaking jolting of the cart on roads broken up by frost and rains, John watched the flight of a crow and glimpsed a line of raindrops hanging like jewels from a red, slender branch: new growth. He looked at the bright cushions of moss and the first tentative shoots of green plants in the black tangle of the hedgerow, the emerald spikes of grass growing through the dead remains from last year. Everywhere was raw cold still, but in those moments when the rain stopped, it gave his soul a chance to connect with the beauty of the sun's return and the first signs of the greening of England as the winter gave way to the spring. Not dour, but a taciturn man, the wagoner had little to say, and John enjoyed the peace of his silent company, until at last they passed through Tadcaster, near their journey's end.

The road from the south came into York through Micklegate Bar, and there John said his thanks and made his parting from the merchant who had brought him, promising at the man's request to say a Mass for his soul. Looking about him, John saw any number of inns where he might find a meal and a bed for the night. Grateful for the money the brothers at Roche Abbey had given him, he was glad to go inside as the cold came down with evening. Frost already lay on the cobblestones and pavements of the city as the rain clouds moved away after sunset, and the stars shone clear.

Discovering that the fare on offer at the inn meant breaking his Lenten fast, John asked if they would be willing to serve him bread and apples, which he carried to a low seat by the fireside. Watching the flames, the falls of ash and glow of embers, drinking ale, and eating good bread and sweet, yellow, wrinkled apples from the store, John felt contentment expand in his soul until well-being warmed him through and through. "Home tomorrow!" his spirit exulted.

After only a little while, a man approached him, respectful—almost deferential—in his bearing.

"God give you a good evening, Father."

John looked up and smiled a greeting, shifting along the bench to indicate there would be room for more than just himself at the fireside.

"I wondered what house you might be from," the man ventured, "if it is no liberty to ask. We—my wife and I—are traveling to Byland Abbey. We are taking my son, who is to try his vocation there."

His immense pride in his son was palpable. Even so, John was also sensible to the tinge of sorrow inherent in most vocations to monastic life. To accompany their son to the place where he would leave them forever, encouraging and blessing his choice, meant a sacrifice that went very deep.

Though this undercurrent of human joy and sorrow moved him, John's mind was still primarily occupied with his own journey. He felt vague surprise that anyone who didn't live on the doorstep of Byland should bother to travel there to join the community. Wasn't the north country bristling with Cistercian houses, sprouting everywhere and flourishing? But the sense of surprise barely registered, quickly overshadowed by a sojourner's calculations: if he could get a lift to Byland in the morning, he would have little more than five miles to walk home.

"I am a monk of St. Alcuin's," he responded courteously, "not far beyond Byland, nudging up a little farther into the moor. It is a Benedictine house, and I am on my way home tomorrow. Perhaps we may travel together, friend? How are you going?"

He learned that the family had both horses and pack mules and two house servants staying here with them in the inn. With immediate generosity the father of the family offered to share his horse with John. "My good lady can ride up with the lad, if it suits you to come with us." John accepted the offer gratefully, humbly appreciative of yet another traveling mercy.

"Of your courtesy, may we sit with you here, Father, until they call us to dine?"

John cheerfully assented, glad to meet his new friend's demure and gentle wife and eager, excited son.

"What obedience do you hold at St. Alcuin's, Father?" the young man inquired with the knowledgeable air of informed youth. An obedience, not a job.

"I'm between things just at the moment," John responded. "I have been our infirmarian this long while. That's not something that changes easily; the care of the sick doesn't take kindly to changes. After making a nuisance of myself on the farm and in the kitchen, the sacristy and scriptorium—all the usual places—they tried me there, and I took to infirmary work. I have done that the best part of thirty years. But our beloved abbot died a year or so ago, and the brothers have sent me away to Cambridge to be priested and formed in ministry to replace him. I'm on my way home."

"You're going to be the *abbot*?" The boy's eyes bulged in admiration and awe. John felt ill at ease with this.

"Somebody has to," he answered simply. "The care of the sick and the old is a good training ground for responsibility, I guess. You have to be patient, you have to be firm. But I cannot say whether I shall make a good abbot. Father Columba, who came before me, served our community well: he knew how to lead us and inspire us, find the best in us, keep us holding fast to the way of Christ. And can I do that? I do not know. They have put their trust in me. I hope I shall not fail. When you are in your new home quite nearby to us at Byland, my friend, will you sometimes pray for me?"

The lad's father nodded approvingly at this modesty, which

made John feel as though he had been putting on an act to look humble. He had not given much thought to the suffocating expectations that came with status; until now he had put his mind only to the responsibilities he would carry.

"There are bad abbots as well as good," he added, "fools with money, men intoxicated with power, those without the gift to hold a community together in harmony. Being an abbot is just the same as being a porter or a kitchener or a scribe; it's what you said—an obedience. I'm looking forward to going home, but the prospect of the burden I shall be taking on weighs heavy already."

To his exasperation, John realized that the more he said, the more admiration he drew—not only an *abbot*, but so *humble* withal! He wished now he'd told them he'd come into York on an errand to return some books to St. Mary's and had to be back the next day so they wouldn't be shorthanded in the kitchen. With a small, involuntary gesture of frustration, he put the conversation to one side.

"Have you come far?" he asked.

It turned out the boy's uncle was the prior at Byland— hence the choice of that house—and the three of them had come from Ossett, near Wakefield, journeying leisurely over the past two days.

"It has not been pleasant traveling," the man remarked. "The floods have forded the way in places, and it only stops raining to freeze. But they wanted my lad with them for Easter, so I thought this way he'd have a while to catch his breath when he gets there."

The family was called away then to a table to eat their supper, and John took his leave of them until morning, retiring to say Compline and glad to go to bed.

THE

NINTH DAY

*T*hey woke to a morning of no rain. The sun rose in a pageant of glory, and John's heart sang. The whole party of them took the opportunity to hear Mass at the minster, gazing in awe at the pinnacled glory of its pale stone and marveling over the jewel colors of glass in the wonderful windows.

So John traveled in ease up to Coxwold on the good matron's jennet, while she rode behind her son on the sturdy palfrey, which would stay with him as a gift to the abbey when his parents returned home.

They parted outside the doors of the abbey with much affectionate well-wishing and promises to pray for one another in their new ventures. Then John took up his bag and wrapped his cloak about him, glad to stretch his legs the last few miles.

Intermittently the day darkened with cloud and the wind blew light showers of sleet across the landscape. But the farther John trudged up into the hills, the brighter and clearer the day became, until he walked in sunshine. It felt like an omen, a blessing: except that was not how John understood the ways of the divine. God, he thought, was steady. God was for the depth of night as well as the morning, for the downpour as well as the sunbeams.

"Brother John! Hey! Brother John!"

He looked around for the source of the voice and saw, standing high on the boulders scattered on the borders of the beck as it tumbled between the trees, a young woman whom after a moment's thought he recognized as Brother Damien's sister Hannah. She had her goats around her, one or two of them with kids running alongside and playing wild jumping games on the streamside rocks. Two years back Brother Damien had fallen seriously ill with a quinsy that had gone to his chest and prostrated him completely. John's devoted care had contributed considerably to pulling him through alive, winning the dearest gratitude of his family who loved him very much. In preparation for John's departure, Father Chad had sent Brother Damien into the infirmary as an assistant for Brother Michael. John had already taught him the rudiments of caring for the sick before he left for Cambridge.

Standing on the steep-rising track that wound upward to the moor, John lifted his hand to his eyes to shade them against the sunburst, slipping his bag to the ground and waving his other hand to Hannah in greeting as she came scrambling down the hillside.

"God give thee good day, Brother John!" she exclaimed delightedly as she reached him. "Eh, but they'll be overjoyed to see thee home!"

And before he thought quickly enough to forestall it, she folded him in a joyous embrace. It lasted but a moment, and he detached himself instantly, laughing. "Bless you, Hannah; yes, it's grand to be back here at last!" Somewhere unacknowledged at any conscious level slipped the recognition that it was quite nice actually to be enveloped entirely in soft female flesh, but he did not even look at that. John knew what his choices and promises were, and they mattered more to him than anyone or anything in the world. He directed attention away from the human encounter, gesturing toward Hannah's small flock climbing among the trees. "I see there are twins among the young ones; good increase this year, it looks from here. All healthy?"

Then after a few more pleasantries, he lifted his pack to his shoulder again and left her with a blessing as he set off on his way.

"Give my love to my brother!" she called after him, and he turned and waved to her. "Aye, I will!" He continued up the track.

✠   ✠   ✠

"Where should we put him to sleep? Should he go back in his old cell or straight into the abbot's lodging?"

"Well, we aren't going to hang about with it, are we? I thought we were going to receive him straightaway. So mightn't he just as well sleep in here right from the start?"

"What does Father Chad say? Has anyone asked him?"

"He's gone yonder to Holy Cross to say Mass for the sisters. But didn't Brother Boniface go into John's cell anyway? Father Chad has it in mind to receive John at once, to give him a few weeks to prepare for the Easter Triduum and all the visitors; so I think he will give his blessing to the notion of John sleeping here. Besides, it's only a bed, isn't it? There's no status to the place you lay your head."

Brother Tom and Father Francis stood in the abbot's lodge making the final preparations for John's return. Francis had brought a bag of powdered herbs to sprinkle on the floor, and Tom had decided to light the fire, because the table he had polished two days ago already showed signs of damp.

The door opened to allow a brief excited appearance by Brother Thaddeus—"Hey! John's back! Kitchen!"—who instantly vanished again.

Father Francis and Brother Tom concluded their mission, but with greater speed and application. They gave one quick glance around to see that all looked fair and presentable before departing purposefully across the cloister and thence to the kitchens.

They found John seated at the great scrubbed worktable, and Brother Cormac setting before him a large steaming bowl of something approximating a stew and a hearty lump of unleavened bread. A slight frown of perplexity momentarily clouded John's face as he sniffed the stew. He thought he'd start with the bread.

He looked up laughing at the eager arrival of Brother Tom and Father Francis. "God love you; it's so *good* to have you back! Brother Michael almost killed all the old men without your herbal wisdom to advise, and the whole place is at sixes and sevens, crying out for someone to take hold of the helm. We've got the abbot's lodge all ready for you!"

"We lit the fire—"

"—and spread sweet herbs—"

"—and we think Father Chad gives his blessing to your moving in right away. What kept you so long? Did you run out of money? Were the roads bad?"

"Did you travel safe? Did you find good lodging?"

Chewing on his bread and listening with amusement to the barrage of questions, John felt glad to his heart's core to be back home. As Tom fetched a stool and sat down opposite him, elbows on the table, chin on his hands, eyes shining with anticipation of hearing about John's journey, John cautiously tried a spoonful of the stew.

"By all that's holy, Cormac—what *is* this?"

Brother Cormac looked a little put out. "I can't quite say, not really," he replied, a touch defensively. "I thought everyone would like a bit of a change. We've had beans and squashes and lentils every day for a while now. So I started as usual with some onions and lots of garlic, then some leeks and the squashes that had started to rot. But everyone was sick of beans, so I put in barley and oatmeal instead, with as many herbs as I could find. Do you not like it?"

"This is left from the midday meal? You gave everyone this?

And they didn't complain? No? I *love* this community! Brother Cormac, you are a one-off. No, no, don't take it away. I'm hungry. Let me taste it again. No, it's delicious, I give you my word! But can I have a drink as well?

"And tell me now, who have you in the infirmary? Has Father Aelred made it through? No? I'm so sorry. God rest him. And Brother Cyprian? Really? He's still alive? That man is amazing! The strength of him! What of Brother Denis and Father Gerald?"

John slept that night in the abbot's lodge, with Father Chad's blessing. Before Compline and the Great Silence of the night, he asked Brother Tom, "After tomorrow, when I am abbot, will you be my esquire, as you were for Father Peregrine? I'm pleased to be back, but I'm more scared than I can tell you. Will you help me? Is that all right? I know you love the outdoors and the farm, but you understand about the abbacy so well."

"Brother—sorry, Father, I am honored. By God's grace, may I serve you well."

In the morning the community would receive him as their abbot in church after first Mass and before Chapter. Tired though he was, John slept not a wink. Sometimes he prayed, and sometimes he lay still, wide-eyed in the silent dark. He was glad when the bell rang for Matins, and in the morning for Lauds.

THE
TENTH DAY

*F*ather Chad knelt and kissed the holy altar, then turned back toward the community, his hands raised in blessing:

"*Dominus vobiscum.*"

The brethren responded, "*Et cum spirito tuo.*"

"*Ite, missa est.*"

"*Deo gratias.*"

And then it was time.

John rose from his place and walked down the aisle to the western door of the abbey church, where he took off his sandals.

He stood and waited. Father Chad had yet to remove his vestments from celebrating Mass and lay away the stole and alb with due care. Father Bernard, these days the sacristan, moved unobtrusively about the sanctuary, making all tidy on the altar, putting away the vessels and the cloths. He set the candles back in place and took the vessels back into the sacristy, reverencing the presence of Christ in the reserve sacrament before he turned away from the sanctuary.

The brothers waited in silence, and John waited, standing barefoot in the shadows at the end of the church.

At last Father Chad stood before the altar and signaled to the community to rise. While he remained at the altar, the brothers processed down in a double line to where John stood waiting, too full of the solemnity of this moment to take it in or connect with whatever he might feel. Flanking the aisle the brothers made way for John to pass barefoot through their midst as he trod humbly up the nave. He knelt to pray, as was the custom, on the stone step at the entrance to the choir. In that moment of prayer John felt suddenly completely overcome. Something like panic descended upon him. "Help me, help me, help me," he cried out in the silence of his soul. "Let me not fail thee, let me not fail my brothers. Oh, God, help me, for all I am is John."

Aware of Father Chad having left the altar and standing before him, John bowed low and kissed the ground before the prior, who then raised him to his feet and led him to the abbot's stall. Placing the ring upon John's right hand, Father Chad, acting as the commissary of the bishop, said, "Receive thou this seal of the faith; and may thou ever keep unsullied the troth thou hast pledged to the beloved spouse of God, his holy church. God give thee grace to continue faithful in thy calling to this household of Christ, and remain his good and faithful servant unto thy life's end."

"Amen," whispered John, his eyes blinded with tears. "Amen. Amen."

Father Chad then gave the pastoral staff into his care. Kneeling before his new abbot, Chad kissed the heavy ring he had placed upon his hand. Rising to his feet again, he looked John in the eye and smiled. He embraced him. And one by one every brother of the house filed by, kneeling to kiss the ring, rising to embrace the man chosen as their leader. In the eyes of every one of them, John read trust, warmth, affection, and encouragement.

When each of them had welcomed him, John sat down in the abbot's stall, dazed with emotion and overwhelmed by the solemnity of the task to which he found himself called.

He was brought back to the present moment by Brother Michael, who had worked alongside him in the infirmary for so long, now kneeling at his feet, fastening on his sandals, giving his knee a friendly pat, and whispering under his breath, "You'll be all right."

Abbot John felt dearly grateful that the Chapter following this institution would still be conducted by the prior. Not until the following morning did the responsibility pass to him.

THE
ELEVENTH DAY

$\mathcal{R}$eading the chapter of the Rule of St. Benedict set for this day, in his own preparations, John had wondered what anybody could possibly find to say about it. While he accepted that it was entirely appropriate for each of the brothers to sleep by himself in a single bed and have the intelligence to go to that bed without his knife still attached to his belt, he doubted whether the matter needed any further elaboration. He knew he could express some sympathy regarding the hard discipline of rising for the night office and then so early in the morning in the dark months of winter and could bring some humor to his encouragement that they persevere. But there seemed little meat for serious sermonizing. John resigned himself to accepting that this, his first abbot's Chapter, would be uneventful, forgettable, and essentially inconsequential. There was no special business, no news, no proposals of change. He had no notice of anybody needing to confess serious sin and be distressingly chastised. No contentious issue had arisen. The morning promised to be undemanding—even dull.

But presiding at the Eucharist for this first time in his own community moved John more deeply than he had ever imagined. It felt like a connection—an extension—to his work as an infirmarian: finding a way in to the deepest needs of human life; bringing to the vulnerability of his brothers the thing that could make them whole, the Christ-Communion. He thought that whatever might lie ahead in the road he had taken, no setback or challenge could devalue this unparalleled pearl of great price.

He took his place in the chapter house feeling purified, blessed, and at peace.

Father Peter read the chapter, and Abbot John added his bland commentary on the virtues of diligence and determination, which he managed to spin out to a respectable minimum length.

Then the door to the chapter house opened, and Brother Martin unobtrusively slipped in. As porter he did not normally attend Chapter unless somebody relieved him, the requirements of hospitality including somebody to welcome strangers at the gate.

He stood respectfully, waiting as John wound up his humdrum observations, but it became obvious he wished to catch his new abbot's eye because he had something to say.

"Welcome, Brother Martin. Is something amiss?"

"I ask your pardon, Father. I hope I have not come in untimely, but I thought this would be a matter of interest for the community."

"Go on." Brother Martin did not look upset or afraid. John wondered what warranted the departure from routine.

"We have a visitor, Father, not distressed, though dirty and disheveled. He has ridden hard and far and is asking to speak to you—to speak to you right now. He says he is the prior of St. Dunstan's, the Augustinian house near Chesterfield."

Simultaneously Brother Tom and Father John sat bolt upright and said, "What?!"

Amused by this coincidence of response, John glanced toward Tom and was startled to see his reaction.

Tom rose to his feet, visibly shaking. "He can't come here! He can't! We can't have him here!" Taken aback, John stared at Tom in astonishment, but then lifted his hand to command peace. "Just a moment, brother. Sit down. Just for a moment. Thank you. We shall hear you, but let's get this straight."

As if his abbot had never spoken, Tom remained on his feet, his eyes still fixed on Brother Martin, to whom John also had turned his attention.

"Are you sure this is who you have in the guest house? I thought nigh on all of the community of St. Dunstan's had perished!"

"Perished?" Father Chad's voice quavered in shocked distress. "They are dead? At St. Dunstan's? What? All the community?"

John felt a twinge of irritation as he turned to his prior. "Yes, Father Chad! Oh, but forgive me: their house was engulfed by a great fire less than a month ago. I thought you'd have had word before; and I confess it slipped my mind. The time since I returned has been so very full of events, and I own I have allowed other matters to recede. I did know for certain that not every man of them died though, for I met a brother of that house in Chesterfield after the fire. But most lost their lives, and something else besides was badly amiss. I'm not sure what, but I think there was more trouble than the fire only."

"So most of them are dead?" Tom cut in abruptly.

"I believe that to be true, Brother Thomas," John replied, noticing as he turned back to speak to him that Tom had ignored his request to resume his seat.

"Well, thank God for that."

John froze, appalled.

"What did you say? Did I hear you right?"

The slight moving and murmuring that had started among the community on hearing the news stopped instantly at the outrage in their abbot's voice.

John's attention fixed undividedly upon Brother Tom, who stood his ground, his expression hardening into something wooden, mulish, though he shifted his stance very slightly under John's unswerving gaze. "I was once in that house with Father Peregrine," he said defiantly. "I met their prior. He is a beast. Nay, I would not serve such injustice upon beasts. He is a demon. A cruel, ruthless man. He has no heart. His soul is rotten." Tom's eyes, as dull as lead as he spoke the words, held John's gaze stubbornly. "I would not admit him to this house for all he had to offer."

Listening to him, John took warning. He knew Tom well. There were times when it was beyond anybody's power to dissuade him. Whatever this was about, he had no intention of creating a confrontation in so public a setting. He broke the deadlock of their gaze by turning his head a little aside. "Brother Thomas, I hear you," he said more gently. "Of your goodness, will you please sit down?"

But Tom persisted, his voice hard with urgency. "Are you going to let him in?"

Theodore leaned forward slightly in the stall adjacent to Brother Tom's. He spoke so low that his voice barely carried at all, just loud enough for Tom to hear him. "Tom, please. This is John's first Chapter. Settle it after." And he stretched his hand out and gently touched the fingers of Tom's hand. "Tom! Please."

Unnerved by Tom's extreme reaction, Brother Martin looked anxiously for direction to his abbot. "Father John, have I done right in leaving this man by himself in the lodge? Is he safe to be at large here if what Brother Thomas tells us is true?"

"Safe?" Tom's answer flashed like quick fire. "Nothing would be safe with that man! If you told me he raped the milk-maid and stole the candlesticks and thought he'd take the chalice from the altar while he was here, it would hardly surprise me! He—"

"*Brother Thomas!* Now hold your peace this instant, and *sit down!*" John's voice suddenly thundered. "Sit down! Now! *Now,* my brother!"

It got through. Slowly, reluctantly, Tom resumed his seat.

"Father—" Chad rose to his feet. "May I speak? I know the man too. He is *not* somebody to trust, and he showed poor Father Columba the most shocking discourtesy when we visited in his house. I don't like to have to say it, but he was really nasty!"

Low murmurs of consternation ran throughout the community. Two men broke into speech simultaneously, and John raised his hand to silence them.

"Hush. Brothers, listen. Let me say my piece now. Thanks, Father Chad. Brother Thomas, I have heard you, and I will speak further with you, but do not interrupt me now. I wish to hear everything you have to tell me about this man, and we shall find a wise way forward when we have considered all. But for now let me bring you the news that I see did not reach you.

"St. Dunstan's Priory has been burned, razed entirely. I passed it on my travels and saw it—nothing left but a smoking, blackened shell standing like broken teeth in the rain. The tale told me had it that the fire came at night, when the brothers were abed. They died in the fire, it was said. From what I heard, I think it is true that nobody came to their aid, for the folk who lived close by did not love them—and with good reason, so said the man who unfolded the tale. There were even questions, I understand, about how the fire may have started.

"But when I stayed briefly in Chesterfield, near the market I met a man begging, clothed in the Augustinian tunic. His hands were burned and scraped. He was dirty and hungry. I had little substance left and little time to spare, only enough to give care to his wounds and leave him with a morsel of food to line his belly. It seemed that the reputation of his house had closed the heart of every man and woman against him. I had no time to draw forth his story, but I was troubled by what I saw. He did not say his name, but he thanked me with courtesy. And he said he had known others of this house—our house—whom he remembered with respect.

"Now, until I have met with our guest come today and heard what he has to say and got the measure of him, I cannot judge what I think we should do. I have heard enough to warn me that something was terribly wrong at St. Dunstan's, and I am willing to hear—privately, not here—what anyone has to tell me about that community.

"But before I hear anything further, and before I even set eyes upon our guest, this I do know, and I know it for sure: whoever he is and whatever he has done, he is neither a beast nor a demon but a man; and I think he is probably in trouble and seeking our help.

"How we receive him must be determined not by what *he* is but by what *we* are. We are here neither to judge nor punish, but to hold fast to the Gospel of Christ, which admonishes us to show hospitality with gentleness and generosity.

"I doubt there is need to go hurrying back to the porter's lodge in terror of calamity, Brother Martin, but you have permission to return there in peace to fulfill the needs of hospitality. And, brother, be kind to this man. Never mind what you have heard of him here. When we are done here, I think I must seek counsel of Brother Thomas. Not before then will I come to you, so our visitor must wait for me, of his courtesy, for now. Meanwhile, please offer the man something to eat and drink."

"Father, he has a horse. What do you want me to do about the horse?"

John stilled his hand's involuntary gesture of exasperation and spoke with an effort of forbearance to the now thoroughly nervous porter. "Perhaps give it some hay and a bucket of water, brother? And tie it up, so it doesn't run away? The horse can wait with the man this little while, I feel sure."

John waited until Brother Martin had closed the door behind his flustered departure. Then he spoke to the community again.

"My brothers, it seems wise to give this matter some attention, for it has brought unease among us, I think. This is the moment we would normally confess to one another our sins and speak of any day-to-day things needing our attention. But may I ask you, unless your sins have been serious and the other matters are pressing, please can they wait?"

He stopped, looking around the gathering of brothers. Nobody spoke.

"Thank you. Then, brothers, let's turn to the tasks of the day. Brother Thomas, of your charity will you step into my lodging, so we may seek counsel together how best to receive our guest before I go and meet him?"

Brother Tom walked along the cloister beside his new abbot, both observing claustral silence. John stepped aside courteously to allow Tom to precede him into the abbot's lodging, indicating as he followed him that they should be seated in the two chairs that stood near to the unlit fire. He was careful to give no sign of antagonism, but neither did he intend to let this go.

Once they were seated together, John asked softly into the silence between them, "Brother, what were you thinking of?"

Tom shifted restlessly. "Oh, I know! It's not how I'm supposed to feel and not what I was meant to say. But you weren't there, in that godforsaken hellhole. You didn't see what that villainous slick of scum worked upon Father Peregrine."

John recoiled at the force of Tom's words.

"Nay, but truly! He taunted and tormented him without pity. He made a mock of his lameness and his twisted hands. He lost no passing chance to belittle him and humiliate him. It broke my heart to see. It just broke my heart!"

John listened, frowning. "But why did he do that? What would it profit him? Did you discover?"

"Yes!" A dry bark of humorless laughter escaped Brother Tom. "I did indeed! He'd set in place a debate—spared no expense, invited every head of every house of religion for miles about, so he said—to decide whether justice or mercy be the heart of the nature of God. I found out after, his racket was that they should be brought to agree upon *justice*. 'Twas all about nothing but the fishing rights of the river that passes through their land—nay, truly! Sometimes folks poached the fish, and the evil slime wanted everything that crawls or swims or flies upon his land for his own table, nothing shared. He wanted them to say God prefers justice over mercy, so he might use it to lever the bishop into backing his greed."

Tom paused then, the intensity and ire of his expression relaxing into the beginnings of a smile. "But he didn't get his way. Father Peregrine stayed the course, and he spoke for God's mercy. You know how it was with him: even the hardest thing to do, he could make you believe in it, make you want to do it. He made them believe in mercy. And vote for it too."

His face softened as he remembered, and John sat quietly, allowing Tom to lose himself in the memory a little while. But not for too long.

"All of them except you?" John asked him then.

"Eh?"

"They all believed in mercy and voted for it except you?"

"Nay, I was held fast in the prison for my misdemeanors: I dunked the prior's vile, sneering visage in his gravy and parsley sauce."

John blinked. "I'm sorry—you did *what*?"

Tom shrugged. "I could take no more of it, his cruel persecution. Said to him that humiliating a man was nothing—could be done just like this, and I dunked his face in his dinner. He was not pleased."

"No. I imagine not. What did Father Abbot say?"

Tom grinned. "He would not let them beat me; they wanted to have me flogged. He made me beg the foul wretch's pardon, but he stood up for me stoutly. He said I had righted a few wrongs."

John nodded thoughtfully, trying to make sense of what he was hearing. Tom's impetuosity he knew of old, but he also knew Father Peregrine's obsession for courtesy and decorum. The injury must have been grave indeed for him to wink at such outrageous misconduct.

"So they had you in their prison. You will be in this one too, if you talk as wild as you did in Chapter today. But when I said he had the vote of every man for mercy except you, I didn't mean then, I meant now. The living reality of mercy is in the doing, not in the debate. Father Peregrine made you believe in mercy, when he spoke of it, you say. What happened? Have you forgotten what he said?"

Tom took a while to reply to that. When he did so, his voice was low but charged with passion. "I have not forgotten. I think never a word he said to me have I forgotten. He forged my soul as surely as a blacksmith twists and beats iron into something of purpose. But how would a rancid codpiece like this Augustinian know what to do with mercy? Mercy and he have never been in the same place in the whole of his life!"

"Well," persisted John quietly, "if we want to be faithful to what we learned from Peregrine, might we not choose the opportunity to change that?"

And Tom became suddenly still. "You have trapped me," he said.

John shook his head. "Not I. But sometimes Christ stands in front of us and asks, 'Did you really mean this?' For now, all I am asking of you, Tom, is that you will behave yourself a bit more seemly when you speak before the whole community, that you will hold back from spreading fear and alarm and prejudice about this man, and that you will allow me the space I need to see what may be done. Will you do that? Brother?"

John watched the struggle that followed his words, but in the end Tom nodded slowly.

"Aye. Yes, I will. Father, I will. Forgive me my haste in

Chapter. It was your first time, and I did nothing to make it easy. Forgive me that."

John smiled, feeling immensely relieved. "Mayhap all we shall need is to give him a bath and a good feed and a bed for the night and send him on his way, wherever he's bound. One step at a time. Let's wait and see. So now, let me see this malefactor firsthand. I am very intrigued."

"No," Tom shook his head, his face serious. "Don't underestimate him. He is sheer poison, John—sorry, Father John. You'll feel dirty just looking at him."

"Enough! I believe you. Oh—Tom, what's his name? I have so much to learn. I've been so wrapped up in the work of the infirmary all these years, I never paid much attention to what went on beyond our own walls."

"De Bulmer. His name is William de Bulmer."

"Then if you have no more to tell me, I must go to him." John stood up and Tom with him, for it would not do for a brother to stay at his ease when his abbot stood.

"But one more thing: Brother Thomas, what you said in Chapter, 'Thank God that the brothers of St. Dunstan's all died in the fire,' that cannot pass uncorrected. You must confess your sin in saying it in tomorrow's Chapter. No, truly, my brother; you must. Without fail you must promise me to do this."

Tom nodded, his expression heavy. "I know; aye, I know. But—"

"Thank you! Until later then, my friend. I will come back to you with news of what I find. God bless you, Tom."

✠   ✠   ✠

Much later on, John was profoundly glad that the first sight he had of this man was not his face but his demeanor. He thought things might have gone differently if it had been the other way about.

He entered the porter's lodge quietly, as any monk should, and found his visitor alone, seated on a bench before the fire, his back to the door.

When a man is in pain, he holds himself tense, instinctively splinting his body against further hurt. And Abbot John, standing in the doorway taking in what he saw, knew he was looking at a man in pain.

"Ah! Father John!" Brother Martin arrived from the kitchen, carrying in one hand a basket of bread and apples and in the other a can of broth, still cold because Cormac had only just started the kitchen fire, but ready to heat on the fire already lit in the porter's lodge.

The visitor turned around at these words, and his eyes met John's. John swallowed. Intelligent but not benign, cynical, appraising, missing nothing—the man's eyes seemed to look past all pretenses and see right into him, streaking past every virtue, all status, every achievement, to the soft places of uncertainty and vulnerability. John felt that in one sardonic, dispassionate glance the man had searched him and got the measure of him. He told himself that it could not be so, but there his reasoning failed entirely to convince his viscera.

The man was dressed in the Augustinian habit, but it was filthy and torn. His left sleeve was ripped, exposing the arm, also torn. Both in the fabric and the revealed flesh, John saw the marks of burns, and all soiled with smeared smudges of smoke and mud besides.

The man's face was gray with smoke dirt, and his clothes hung in the flattened folds of wool more wet than dry over many days. But in his eyes John saw neither self-pity nor defeat: just a cool, steady arrogance, weighing him up.

John thought back over Brother Tom's warnings. He did not like what he was looking at.

The time of mutual appraisal seemed to be extending beyond convention. A certain wry amusement stole into the

Augustinian's eyes, and John realized his own face must be betraying his misgivings, which he had not intended. For this he felt ashamed. Eighteen years in the infirmary should have left him able to trust his face to reveal no dislike or disgust, no negative emotion at all. He had schooled himself to a neutral benevolence for interacting with men in trouble: this one saw right through him.

"Abbot John?" Prior William rose stiffly to his feet. "I am sorry to take up your time. This is the last place I would come. I realize I cannot be welcome, but I must beg your help."

"You have come a long way, Father. What was it that brought you to us?"

The man's lips twisted in a bitter smile. "Desperation. Nothing else. You have heard what befell us?"

"I know there was a fire. I traveled by that way. I saw the ruins of the priory, met one of the brothers in Chesterfield."

Prior William's eyebrows rose in cool inquiry. "Did you so? What was his name?"

John felt himself blushing, ashamed to confess that he had never thought to ascertain the man's identity.

"I am mortified to admit, I did not ask. Time was very pressing. He had wounds that needed my help, and he was hungry. I did what I could, and I left him there. I'm sorry. It sounds very inadequate now."

William's eyes continued to hold John's in impassive appraisal for a moment, then he looked away, nodding in acceptance.

"You clearly do not know how exceptional was what you did. Maybe you did not hear how the fire started: six of our servants, plotting together. They fired the night stairs and the day stairs; they tied up our porter in the gatehouse and set him alight along with the building. The smell of burning awoke me, and though they had been in my lodging and set it thoroughly ablaze, there is a little door that goes out toward the river. I was not unscathed, you can see for yourself, but I had a way out. I ran to the stables and took a horse. Later they fired the stables and the farm as well. I fled for my life."

"Did you not try to raise the alarm?"

The man shrugged. "To what avail? Folk were gathered, watching. From what I saw and heard, they regarded it as entertainment. We have done well for ourselves at St. Dunstan's, Abbot John; we have prospered. Those without the imagination and strength to achieve the same often resent success."

John took this in. He found himself at the same time shocked by the barbaric horror of what had been done and unnerved by the aloof composure of his bedraggled guest.

Brother Martin, having heated up the broth, thought he would take advantage of this lapse into silence to invite their visitor to move to the table and eat. Martin crossed the room and laid a kindly hand upon the man's shoulder before John had a chance to stop him. William winced, gasping involuntarily as Brother Martin's hand descended in benevolence on his burned arm. Appalled and distressed at what he had done, Martin backed off, apologizing wretchedly. The prior did not even look at him. But John, watching William shrewdly, saw not stiff disdain but the tension of agony. He turned to his porter, giving the Augustinian a moment to recover.

"Don't fret, Martin; it was an accident. Thank you for getting everything ready." He turned back to Prior William. "Eat something now, my good lord, and then come with me. I will do what I can to comfort those hurts. And every place that is burned must be washed as well as salved, or the wounds will go bad. Eat and I will do what I can to help you, and then you can rest."

John himself took the prior across to the infirmary. He knew Brother Michael had every skill necessary, but he sought the place of intimacy that healing work leads to, so that he could find a way to better understand this strange man's soul.

Michael brought the salves and linen bandaging John had wished he'd had in Chesterfield. With careful attention, the abbot washed the wound free of grit and grime as his visitor sat motionless, stripped of his clothing, wrapped in nothing but a linen towel to preserve his dignity. His skin had been burnt away in a sizable patch on his shoulder, and soil had adhered despite the oozing of serum from raw flesh. The man had been many days on the road, and dirt and scabs mingled together in half-healed skin. John went as gently as he could as he cleaned it back, sensible of the man's rigid stillness, aware of his frown of distress and his lips drawn back from his teeth in a grimace of pain. The Augustinian did not even breathe as he bore the worst of it.

"Are you hurt anywhere else?" John asked gently when he felt satisfied the wound was quite clean. "Let's have a look at you."

There were other hurts. It seemed Prior William's escape from the house had not been without event. He had been seen, set upon, kicked, and beaten and had run for his life to the stables. Both his knees had been abraded raw and his body bruised. John realized that the discoloration of his face came from fading bruises as well as dirt and smoke. Turning over the man's hands in his own, he saw savage abrasions on their palms, evidently where he had fallen in the terror and darkness of his flight. In every case the wounds had scabbed over, but there were sore and oozing places still, and everything had been soiled with mud and smoke. Without comment John washed and salved and bandaged, working quietly over every painful site, feeling the man's bony body relax a little under the firm gentleness of his touch once the sore places had been cleaned and anointed.

As he worked he noted old scars too, faded and silver, multiple scars, on William's back and the back of his legs. Evidently he had been beaten severely and often, at some early stage in his life. An overzealous novice master? John wondered but thought such a question might be intrusive, unwelcome.

"You have healing hands," William remarked unexpectedly, not as a compliment, but with the detachment of simple observation.

John smiled. "Thank you. There—you'll do, I think. Nothing here will take too long to heal. I'll warrant it hurts bad as it is now, and it's going to be sore for a while, but it's superficial, really. If others died, you came off light. Is there anything I haven't seen? You've not passed blood in your water or coughed up blood? No? Then I think a few days more will see most of this mending, and in a couple of weeks what's left will be fading too. We must keep that big burn clean—that is the only thing to watch."

Brother Michael brought clean undergarments and a habit that seemed roughly the right size. "These used to be Father Peregrine's—Father Columba's—who used to be our abbot; you'll feel distinguished decked out in these!" he remarked cheerfully to their guest and was shocked by the completely unexpected response his words produced.

With the instinctive, terrified recoil of a man who has disturbed a deadly snake, their visitor resisted Michael's attempt to put the habit over his head. He sat shuddering, his breathing labored as Michael drew back; then he began to shake his head in repeated, emphatic denial.

"I will not wear his clothes! Even if you have nothing else, I will not wear his clothes! Get them away from me!"

Brother Michael's mouth dropped open in astonishment. "Er . . . well . . . I'm not sure what else we have. I can take a look," he offered.

"Thank you, brother. Leave us a moment, if you will; leave the clothing here," John interposed. After a moment's bewildered pause, Michael withdrew gladly, careful to close the door softly but fully.

John sat down on the stool beside the bed where his naked visitor trembled and glared.

"Well now," he said, "what's this about?"

"I shall not suffer this!" his guest hissed in vehement reiteration.

John looked down at his folded hands and waited a few moments. When he raised his head again, the defiant glare and tense horror seemed unabated.

"My hands," said John, "learned their gentleness from Father Peregrine. This house learned what mercy it knows from Father Peregrine. From Christ himself as well, surely, but it was Abbot Peregrine who showed us and taught us. Now you have come here for healing and for mercy: he has already wrapped you in his mantle, by your own free choice. Whatever habit we give you, you will be dressing in his clothes, for this was his family, and (under God) he was our father. I should not have had you down as a superstitious man; more rational, I should have guessed.

"You are welcome here. You are welcome to eat our food, to sleep in our bed, to our stabling for your horse. You are welcome to whatever healing arts I have, and to my time. I will listen to you, and I will defend you against the animosity I think you know you will have provoked in this house already. That's the good news. The bad news, Prior William, is that nobody here gets to be picky. You take our hospitality as it is or you can try somewhere else. Your own clothes not only are impressively foul, but Brother Michael will have put them to soak in a tub out back by now. Do you want to get dressed or not? If you do, I will help you put this on, for those sore arms won't thank their owner for further hurt."

However imperious, and however furious, a naked man is at a disadvantage.

✠ ✠ ✠

Once the prior was dressed, John said, "Come with me then to our guest house and get some rest."

As they walked across the grounds of the abbey, John asked, "Where will you go from here? This is far from home for you. Bolton Abbey is an Augustinian house: might you go to them? Or go back down to Darley? Or Kirkham, though I hear they're badly in debt and struggling to keep going at all."

His inquiry met with silence. The men walked on together. Eventually William spoke. "This is the nub of it, Abbot John. You cannot imagine this house would be my first port of call. You will know—you must surely know—there was little love lost between your Abbot Columba and myself. We were not friends; we were adversaries. As an adversary, I admit it, he was stronger than I, but I gave him a good fight, and that fight has not won me admiration. The result of it has been, I have begged refuge at nigh on every community between here and Nottingham: none of them would open their doors to me, not one would offer me shelter or refuge."

The prior stopped and turned the disconcerting gaze of his pale eyes upon John. "With every house I tried, with every rejection, I knew—knew without doubting—that Abbot Columba would have taken me in. So in the end I came. There was nowhere else to go. I am here, even clothed in his habit, begging your mercy. I shall have nowhere else to go tomorrow . . . or the next day either."

As they walked on in silence, John digested this appallingly unwelcome information. He knew that the longer the silence continued, the more evident his aversion to the proposition must become. But Prior William said no more, giving him space to consider. In the inner sanctum of his soul, John prayed desperately for wisdom, for the right response, the words to say that would keep the community safe without rejecting outright this plea for sanctuary. Finally he knew what he must say, though he guessed his brothers would not receive his decision with enthusiasm.

He stopped and confronted the prior. "Look," he said, "let's not beat about the bush. You are not loved elsewhere. Neither are you loved here. From what I'm told, you used our Abbot Columba most cruelly. It has not been forgotten. The same choices and disposition that won you no friends in Nottinghamshire have won you no friends on the north York moors either, nor in any other place between there and here. If we even think about opening our doors to you, you could not live here as you have always lived before; you would have to change. That's one thing. The other thing is this: I am the abbot of this community, not its despot. Such an invitation would have to come from the brothers themselves, or it would tear the household apart.

"I think you have certainly taken good measure of me in this last hour, but I dare to presume I have seen something of who you are as well. I can see immediately that you have the power to wreak total havoc in this place, unless you are understood and welcomed as the man you really are, by the whole community.

"So I invite you to rest well today and tonight, eat and sleep, and allow your wounds to begin healing well. Then in the morning you must come to Chapter and make your request of the community. For you cannot possibly come here as one of them if that relies on me standing in between you and the brothers. That's all I can offer."

Prior William inclined his head in acceptance. "You are generous," he said without emotion. "And I may be all you fear and more; I hope I am. It is my strength. But I shall honor your generosity. I shall not forget."

With deepest relief to be rid of him for the while, John turned the Augustinian over to the guest master and moved on to the other duties that crammed his day. When evening came, weary beyond measure, he opted for the new luxury of eating alone in the abbot's lodging. But he released Brother

Thomas from waiting at his table, as he had no other guests to entertain and felt he'd seen quite enough of Prior William for one day.

Solitude restored his equilibrium and gave him a chance to pray, urgently, for wisdom.

THE
TWELFTH DAY

*I*n his childhood Abbot John had made pets of some of the cats that ran loose on his father's land. He remembered the inevitable sequence of events every time he introduced a new kitten to the family of cats already admitted to the cottage. Spitting and snarling and walking backward on stiff legs, their tails erect, with every hair standing on end, the resident cats had greeted the newcomer with undisguised, full-on loathing.

Not many things could have prompted a comparison in John's mind between Prior William and a kitten. But something in Tom's face when he saw their new guest accompany Abbot John into Chapter reminded the abbot of the detestation and appalled revulsion of the resident cats. It occurred to him, too late, that it might have been intelligent to put aside his weariness of the night before and take the opportunity to prepare his esquire for this.

Father Chad read the chapter from the Rule, a short direction on how to deal with the arrogant and the grumblers: warn them quietly first; publicly rebuke them if that fails; beat them as a last resort.

John had little prepared to say about this, but thought it timely enough. He reminded his community of their commitment to humility and obedience.

He turned then to the confession of faults and the business of the day. First the novices had opportunity to confess, and

Brother Boniface knelt to ask forgiveness for offending against holy poverty by losing his shoe in the river—easily done, crossing by the stepping stones in the floods of early spring. John blessed and absolved him and encouraged him to be more careful in the future, and then the novices rose and departed before professed brothers confessed their sins.

Not until Brother Thomas stood, made his way to the open space in the center of the room, and knelt did Abbot John remember with sinking heart the promise he had exacted. He saw nothing in Tom's face to reassure him, but he hoped Tom would have the forbearance to express himself in general terms. Forlorn hope.

"I humbly confess my lack of charity and my unforgiving spirit in saying yesterday morning in Chapter that I wish every one of the house of St. Dunstan's had perished in the fire: and I ask forgiveness of God and of you, my father and my brothers."

Abbot John looked at his kneeling esquire, whose lowered eyes and composed face betrayed no emotion now. "You confrontational, provocative wretch!" was all he wanted to say. For a moment he couldn't speak at all. Against his will he found his eyes compelled to seek Prior William's face. John saw a glimmer of humor below the veneer of indifference, which he felt was the best he could have hoped for—not hatred, at least. But he did not know what to say.

"Brother," eventually the words came low and unhappy, "God forgives you, of course God forgives you, and so do I—but you have let our house down this day."

The words found their mark. When Brother Tom was a novice, in this circumstance he would have felt ashamed to look his abbot in the eye. In those days he had longed for approval; easily abashed, he had wanted so much to get things right. Now, so many years later, he got slowly to his feet, recognizing the hollowness of this petty victory, and he made himself look steadily at the disappointment so clear in

John's face. He had confessed his sin; it seemed ridiculous to kneel and say sorry again, though he did think of doing so. Turning from Abbot John, Brother Tom looked at the hated Augustinian, wondering momentarily if he should cross the room to him and make his apology. But the moment passed; he realized he should have got it right the first time. As Tom returned to take his place in the chapter house, John sat looking down at his folded hands.

All this, Prior William watched.

"Prior William de Bulmer, of the Augustinian priory of St. Dunstan, has come seeking refuge with us," John addressed the community then. "I have told him, in view of what he asks, the decision must rest with all the brethren, not only me. So I have invited him here to make his request. Then you can ask him what questions you will and make the observations you feel right. Prior William, here is your chance to say what you wish. Please speak."

John's voice sounded flat and tired. Father Theodore's eyes rested on him thoughtfully, until his attention was drawn, along with the others, toward Prior William, who now stood before them.

"I am not accustomed to begging."

John listened with his eyes closed to William's light, smooth voice as he began to speak. Keeping companionship with men facing pain and death had carefully tuned John's ability to listen. He detected, under the voice used to mockery and derision, the familiar note of fear, but he doubted it would be easy for others to identify.

"From Nottingham to here I have sought refuge from hatred and violence. I have found no such refuge. This is the last place in the world I would have come. Your Abbot Columba and I were not friends. It is because of the enmity that was between us that others turned me away. I do not conjecture this; I was told it. In the end every door was closed, and I had nowhere else to go.

My house is burned and my brothers, for the most part, with it. My roads lead to nowhere, it would seem. The way has run out under my feet. It sticks in my craw, but I must ask you for refuge, in the name of Christ."

As the Augustinian stopped speaking, John waited, lest there should be more. But Prior William stood loosely erect, the pale fire in his unnerving eyes directed straight ahead, looking at nobody in particular.

"My brothers?" John invited their participation. The silence in the room felt uneasy.

"Er—how long were you hoping to stay with us, Father William?" inquired Father Chad at last, visibly unsettled as William's intimidating gaze came to rest on his face.

"It is as I say. So far as I know, I have nowhere else to turn." The words sounded unemotional, as though the man took no interest in his plight but merely stated a fact.

"You mean . . . you actually want to come and *live* here?" In response to this query from Father Francis, the Augustinian nodded slowly, as to a slightly simple child.

Silence welled up and flooded the room. Nobody moved, and nobody spoke. John waited. Prior William shrugged and sat down.

"Well, if no one else is going to say it, I will." Brother Tom stood then, looking neither at his abbot nor at the supplicant, but fixedly at the ground. "I have been in your house and have seen how you ran it; and mighty glad I was to come home, I tell you straight. In all my life I have never beheld such mean-spirited, pointed cruelty. You say you and Abbot Columba were enemies, but that doesn't tell the story, does it? He heartily loathed you, 'tis true—but why? You taunted him and mocked him, held him up to ridicule, made his disability into your opportunity—and all as no more than grist to the mill of the purposes of your own greed. 'Tis a shame you find yourself friendless and homeless, but I don't know how you could have failed to see it coming. You got yourself into it—right then; you can get yourself out of it. Can you stay here? No."

Tom sat down, still looking at the ground. Nobody else spoke. The silence swelled until it was deafening.

Finally John made a decision. "One voice is not enough. We cannot simply turn this man away. His body is covered in wounds. He has fled from those who would have had his life. He has traveled far. There may be a satisfactory solution to be found: we have lands and houses beyond the abbey walls, and no doubt we could employ the services of a shrewd man who can read and write. Let it be for now. Today and tomorrow you are free to come to me privately if you would be heard. Tomorrow I will seek your counsel again in Chapter—not with our guest present, only the professed brothers of this house. The day after that he will join us here again, and we will come to a mind. But don't just think, my brothers, pray as well. When we take counsel again in Chapter, the direction we take should be following the footsteps of Jesus. What would our Lord have us do?"

THE
THIRTEENTH DAY

*P*rime began in darkness and ended as the morning sky was flooded with light, just before sunrise. Abbot John left the chapel as soon as reverence permitted, to watch the sun birthed in vermilion resplendence on the eastern horizon. The moment never lost its magic for him. As he stood looking across the valley, it felt as though his soul expanded and took wing, flying out and exulting to find completion in union with glory.

He took note on a less exalted level of the flaming splendor of the sky, accepting that the price to pay would probably be rain by midmorning. By the time the bell rang for Sext, the clouds had massed and the rain pelted down as if it had been thrown from the sky by the bucket load.

"Dear Lord! Stone the crows! Will this *never* stop?" Brother Michael peered out of the infirmary, where every available corner seemed to be festooned with dripping washing. With all the brothers, he longed for the sunshine, the easing of bodily tension, and the joy of the light. At the end of a long hard winter, spirits plummeted; the fast of Lent sent everybody into endurance mode, withdrawn and inclined to despair or irascibility, according to temperament.

This time of year when the brothers gathered in Chapter, the room reeked faintly of damp wool; though it meant his feet were cold all the time, Michael had given up wearing socks, because his feet got wet every time he made the dash from infirmary to cloister.

In the novitiate, the damp could be relatively, if not completely, kept at bay. The fire sulked because yesterday's wood had been used up and today's was not dry enough—but at least the day stairs connected almost directly between novitiate and cloister, so everyone except the novices working in the farm and garden and infirmary kept close to the main buildings and could hope to stay reasonably dry.

"Theo? Is this a good moment?"

Father Francis appeared in the door of the novitiate during the quiet afternoon time when the young men followed their studies privately in solitude. Theodore sat by the fire, its light augmenting the candle backed by a burnished plate of copper. He was reading Aelred of Rievaulx's treatise *On Spiritual Friendship* in preparation for the lessons of the following day. The light was dim. Theo had chosen the fireside over the place under the window for reasons of light rather than warmth, though he felt grateful for the comfort of the fire. The gloom of the day made it hard to read anywhere, but as he had copied and bound the book himself, the script had the ease of familiarity.

"A good moment to talk? I have time to talk. Come in, my friend. Pull one of those stools up to the fire and thaw out for a while."

Francis crossed the room to him and sat on the stones of the hearth, holding his hands appreciatively toward the glowing embers.

"So," he said after a while, looking into the fire, "what *would* our Lord have done?"

"With Prior William? Is that not obvious to you?" A small frown of perplexity creased Theodore's brow. "Jesus made Judas his treasurer and Peter his right-hand man, yet we do not suppose Christ to have been stupid or myopic in assessing human nature."

Francis sighed and frowned as he turned the matter over in his mind. "The thing is . . ." he began, before losing himself in his deliberations. "Well . . ." He glanced at Theo. "The thing is, if you have Jesus right there with you, it makes a difference, doesn't it? I mean, if Jesus gives the money bag to Judas and the weighty leadership of the church to Peter, that's an inspirational act of trust: if *we* do it, it's more like institutional suicide."

Theo met his gaze calmly. "What d' you mean 'if you have Jesus there with you'? Of course we have Jesus here. That's why *we're* here, isn't it? Isn't that the entire point of the Ascension? And the Resurrection. Isn't it the heart of the teaching of the Christian faith?"

"Ye-es . . . " Francis grimaced, dubious.

"Francis, wake up! If someone arrives on our doorstep wounded and destitute and rejected by absolutely everyone, and we say, 'Oooh no; sorry, you upset us long ago!' well, what does that make us? We might as well pack up and go back to farming and silversmithing and things that made some positive contribution to the human community!"

"M-m-m. When you put it like that . . . But when you look past that first instinctive and admirable response of the heart, I think you come to what Tom was saying. I think he means it's like a flock of sheep getting a polite knock on the door of the sheepfold late one night, only to find a wolf standing outside shivering in the cold wind, asking pitifully to be allowed to come in and find shelter from the weather. The sheep say, 'Yes! Yes! We are gentle creatures, and surely there is room in here for one more.' And they have no idea of the carnage there will be before morning."

He looked questioningly at Theo, who nodded thoughtfully, transferring his gaze to the fire.

"Oh, yes. I did understand what Tom meant, and I don't doubt his assessment of the possible consequences. You only have to look at Prior William—that cynical eye, that proud bearing—to see we've been presented with incarnate disaster. Even so, suppose we turn him away, what have I left to teach these novices? Where is the beauty of the Gospel without the risk of its grace? It's like amending the Gospel story to remove the crucifixion, in case it gives the children bad dreams."

"Simply vote for him to stay with us then, you think?"

"Yes to the 'vote,' but not to the 'simply.' This community and the life we share is something precious, and it's kept that way by the boundaries put in place in our Rule. I think we should allow him to stay, but on the same basis as a novice— and I don't mean I want him in the novitiate. I wouldn't have him in here for all the king's silver! He should be admitted, but on condition he conducts himself the same as anyone else. If he wants mercy for himself, he has to contribute to the gentle spirit of the house that fosters mercy. Only foot soldiers here. No one gets to ride; we all slog along the same."

Francis thought about this.

"So you think we should admit him like a novice, but actually, if it comes to it, you don't want him anywhere near the novitiate? Is that consistent?"

Theo nodded. "Certainly! We have to protect our novices; they're in formation, but *we* aren't. I know we carry on learning the whole of our lives, but there comes a point surely when we're meant to have grasped the basic tenets of the Gospel and at least learned to drive it after a fashion as far as the end of the road. But why are you asking *me* about this? Have you talked to John?"

"No." Francis took a twig from the basket of kindling and held it in the heat of the embers, lost in thought as he watched it glow and spurt flame, twisting it in his fingers. "John looked weary and harassed when we went through it again in Chapter today, and he sounded low. He has all the preparations for Holy Week and Easter to attend to. He is taking time in the infirmary to tend to our unexpected visitor's burns and scrapes. If I take my soul-searching to him, I don't doubt he will listen, but I think he might appreciate being left an hour or two to himself. So . . . " Father Francis shook loose from the despondency that had settled about him. ". . . you will be voting for him to stay?"

"Assuredly," said Theo.

"Brother Tom will be disappointed," commented Francis, tossing the charred remnant of his consumed twig into the fire.

"Tom?" Theo shook his head, his expression somber. "He should know better than this. That's all I will say."

✚ ✚ ✚

Brother Thomas felt the Augustinian's eyes upon him as he brought the bowls and drinking vessels to the table.

Abbot John and Prior William sat before the fire, while Tom fetched a jug of water, spoons and napkins, and a bowl of apples. He busied himself with his tasks and did not look across to the fireside.

"Brother Thomas—" Eventually his abbot compelled his attention. Tom stood back from the table and turned to face them. "You have met Prior William de Bulmer of St. Dunstan's— before today."

"Aye. I have," replied Brother Tom.

"I doubt if I should have forgotten him," observed the prior in a casual drawl, "but from what I have seen so far, he seems little changed."

Brother Thomas inclined his head in brusque acknowledgment of this. "I hope that may be so, my lord prior. Will I get the supper, Father?"

Abbot John sighed, seeing no good purpose to be served by prolonging the conversation. He indicated to Tom that he should continue his errands.

So Brother Thomas brought to his abbot's table the food prepared for supper: bread and lentils cooked with garlic, onions, and herbs. The iron pot of lentils had unfortunately hung too long and too low over too hot a fire—and burnt. Cormac had tried to be careful in ladling it out, but crunchy black bits had still infiltrated here and there, adding a carbonized flavor to everything.

"The food is set ready for you, Father," Brother Tom said in an even, neutral tone, and John brought his guest to the table.

William regarded the dish Tom set before him with an expressionless face as Abbot John gave thanks. Then both men lifted their spoons and toyed a little with the mess of pulses.

John felt the force of Brother Tom's presence behind his left shoulder, a steady seepage of glowering disapproval that bore so heavily upon him, he could think of nothing to say and find no desire to eat whatever. Sensing William's exact discernment of the oppressive dynamic, John struggled to come up with some kind pleasantry, some affable civility that would afford a diplomatic pathway through the evening. Nothing came to mind. He wished he had invited one of the other brothers to eat with them, but reflected that the atmosphere might have simply intensified if he had.

"You have only just been inducted as abbot?"

John felt irritated with himself for feeling so cut down to size by the smooth urbanity of his guest's tone. He put down his spoon. He thought he could not eat another mouthful of anything. "Yes," he said. "Does it show that badly?"

Silence greeted his question, and he made himself meet his guest's disquieting gaze.

"You seem entirely in command of yourself and your situation," William replied simply. But something in the calm self-possession of his regard made John feel unreasonably flustered. He thought he could detect a glint of derision that made him feel very small and foolish.

"You find me ridiculous?" he asked in reply.

William's eyebrows rose. "No," he responded. John thought if he hadn't before, he probably did now.

"Well, I'm doing my best," he mumbled, feeling mortified that his words sounded petulant and defensive.

William did not immediately answer him. Then he laid his napkin upon the table and looked John in the eye with unruffled evaluation.

"You look very tired, Father John. I think it might help if I leave you. You have many burdens of responsibility, and nothing new is ever easy. The evening may sit lighter upon you alone."

With these words, he got gracefully to his feet, offered John the courtesy of a small bow, and quietly left the abbot's table and his house with no backward glance. John had never before felt such a deep and depressing sense of inadequacy.

He sat where he was a moment longer before glancing around briefly at Brother Tom. "Thank you for your help. I . . . thank you, brother."

Brother Thomas said nothing, and John left the table, tossing aside his napkin. He went into his chamber, where he sat curled up on his bed, hunched in the angle of the wall against which it stood, his knees drawn up to his chin, completely demoralized.

Tom took the remains of the supper across from the abbot's lodging, finding Brother Cormac setting all in readiness for the next day. Cormac had stacked the bowls, and the cooking pots stood orderly on their shelves. Tomorrow's dried beans had been set to soak in water from the well, and he was sweeping the floor.

He threw a glance in Tom's direction, then looked again, his attention caught. "They didn't care for their supper then? That's not like John, to waste good food."

"I agree: it is not. Perhaps it was not the food but the company he was keeping that blighted his appetite."

"He dined with our Augustinian guest?"

"Well, he entertained him in his house. You can see for yourself it would be an exaggeration to say either of them dined. Neither did their conversation sparkle."

"Perhaps he finds our fare here not to his taste. I remember you saying his house was accustomed to luxury. Obviously our humble fare disgusts him."

Tom grimaced dismissively. "If what's served here is half as poisonous as he is, we shall probably all be dead by Holy Week."

THE
FOURTEENTH DAY

The ripple of robed men who have the art of walking peacefully is a very distinctive sound. Prior William listened to that river of quietness flowing by and around him as the Benedictine community of St. Alcuin gathered in the chapter house once first Mass had been said. Stilling the instinct for self-advertisement is a discipline learned early in monastic life. With neither hurry nor delay, without exchange of glances or demeanor that makes a point, the brothers convened as unaffectedly as leaves accumulate in the corner of a yard.

Father Theodore came to the lectern, reading to the assembled community the chapter in the Rule about excommunication for serious faults: "None of the brethren may associate with him in companionship or conversation. He is to be left alone . . . nor may he or the food that is given him receive a blessing from anyone who passes by."

Theo's voice sounded bleak in the silent assembly as he read the chill words. In taking the monastic way, much is sacrificed. In choosing to live in community, the little mannerisms and idiosyncrasies of others can chafe the soul raw at times along the journey. Yet the pledge to stay the course, to lift one another up, to stop short of condemnation, having the spaciousness of soul to understand, creates a living tissue of durable hope and faith. Monks do not aspire to own much, but they have Christ and they have each other—at once the cross and the crown of the monastic way. To be excommunicated—put out of the community in disgrace, sent to sit and eat alone and unblessed—is punishment indeed.

Theodore closed the book, his face sober, and returned to his seat.

"Holiness," said Abbot John, "has to do with belonging. When they brought the sick to Jesus, he would say, 'Be thou whole.' When people are sick, or lost in sin, their being fragments and disperses. That is what happens ultimately in death; when somebody dies, he is lost to us, he goes beyond the horizon of our sight. Sickness and sin bear the image of death. When death arises in a community, be it physical or spiritual death, we lose one another, we are torn away from each other. A community is well when it tends toward wholeness. Where men turn away from one another, turn their backs in indifference, the community sickens; death steals in among all the interactions there.

"This is why in this chapter Father Benedict describes excommunication as being handed over to death: not because we cut the man's throat or run a sword through his heart, but we may as well do so. To be rejected, cast out—it is so very, very painful. It is the hardest thing to do to somebody or, for that matter, to endure. It is never done lightly, for we wither—we lose ourselves—when we are left alone or when we condemn others to be left alone."

He stopped speaking. The mood in the chapter house intensified into heaviness. Father John invited the novices to make confession of sin, but none of them moved or spoke, so he dismissed them. They left with careful decorum, their hands folded, their gaze humbly lowered. Brother Cassian, the last through the door, shut it carefully behind them, with no more than the tiniest click of the latch.

Once outside the closed door, Brother Cedd whispered low to Brother Felix, "What is it? What's the matter with them? It feels as though something terrible's going on!" Brother Felix shook his head in perplexity. He felt the same, but the world of the professed brothers was to a great extent closed to the novitiate.

In the chapter house Abbot John invited the confessions of the community. They sat like men under enchantment: motionless, nobody glancing up. So John moved on.

"My brothers, today we come to a mind regarding Prior William of St. Dunstan's. Very few of you have spoken with me in these last two days. Is there any man who wishes to speak now?"

The community sat rooted in the same tense hush. John nodded. This did not bode well. He turned to Prior William, saying formally, "What do you ask of this house, my brother?"

William looked at him. It crossed John's mind that in all his life he had known only one other man whose gaze could examine him with such dispassionate candor, going straight past all pretension to the living soul. He wondered if it was as much their similarity as their differences that had caused them to hate one another so much.

"Is it worth my asking?" said William then.

For one split second the sorrow and compassion in John's face made a living bridge between them, but the moment passed so quickly, John thought he had probably imagined it. "I hope so," he replied. The Augustinian nodded, rose to his feet, and came to kneel in the center of the room.

"I humbly beg," he said—as he had been schooled—in his even, light tones, "that for the love of God you will admit me as a brother of this house, so that I may learn to love and follow Christ according to the most holy Rule of St. Benedict, to do penance, amend my ways, and serve Christ faithfully here until death."

"I ask of you, my brothers, will you admit him? Will those in favor please raise their hands?"

John looked slowly around the chapter house, as did also Prior William. Father Theodore raised his hand, then Father Francis, and finally Father James. John waited, but there was nobody else.

"And those against?"

This time the air stirred slightly as every other man in the community raised his hand. John had kept the possibility of a casting vote, but it was irrelevant here. He sat stunned, the pity in his eyes reaching out to the kneeling man.

"Brother, I am so sorry. I am just so sorry," he said.

His face as closed and withdrawn as the moor on a winter morning, Prior William got to his feet and gazed cool and aloof at Abbot John.

"What will you have me do?" His words fell austere in the silence.

This time John took no counsel. It was his right as abbot to direct everything in every aspect of life in the community. To force men against the way their feet wanted to go was rarely wise, but he had to soften the judgment.

"Stay with us as our guest, my brother, until your body has properly healed, another week or so maybe. I will inquire if we can find you some lodging—some place you will be safe and can find employment. This abbey has many friends. I will see what can be done."

William nodded. "I think," his dry, ironic voice responded, "this one place is the single eye of my particular storm. But, my lord abbot, I honor you for having been willing to help me."

THE
FIFTEENTH DAY

*H*ow could you vote for him to stay? After what he did to Father Peregrine! How could you possibly want him here—a dirty crook on the make?"

Father Francis detested confrontations, and in some unrealistic crevice of his soul he had held out a hope that he might be able to evade this one, but it seemed that would not be the case.

He knew it would have been more intelligent to avoid the warming room for a while, but the lure of the fire had proved stronger than his judgment, and he had chosen the comfort of this place, where the brothers gathered to relax at the end of the day, over the bleak seclusion of his cell.

"What were you thinking of? How could you agree to let that scum come and live with us here? That is such a betrayal!"

Francis could see that Brother Tom was not disposed to let this go. He glanced quickly at Tom's flushed, indignant face and averted his eyes again.

"Tom, don't stand so close to me—and please stop shouting at me."

"I'm not shouting. This is a normal tone of voice. Does anyone else think I'm shouting? If you think this is shouting, you should hear Brother Stephen calling the cows in!"

"You *are* shouting." It was not like Brother Germanus to take on Brother Tom, and he looked distinctly nervous. Father

Francis shot him a grateful sideways glance but felt it unwise to escalate this into a matter of taking sides. Brother Thomas looked in astonishment at Germanus's temerity. Who was he anyway?

"You aren't shouting in your voice, but your soul is shouting," Germanus persisted obstinately. "It's downright deafening, what's blaring out of the whole of you."

"Is that better?" asked Tom belligerently, making an exaggerated effort at speaking more quietly.

"Not much," muttered Brother Germanus, and Tom glared at him, then turned his attention back to Father Francis.

"So . . . what have you got to say for yourself then?"

A short while later, as he took the stairs two at a time to take refuge in the privacy of his cell, Francis wished he'd thought to point out that he was not answerable to Tom in his choices and decisions. But at that moment he had simply felt cornered and could think of nothing to do but blurt out his only truth: the actual reason he had voted for William to be allowed to stay.

"All my life I've had a dread of being left out and abandoned—of being rejected and turned away," he said. "I came home from that to Christ: I found my security. I found the way out of fear into peace. That has never faded or gone sour, never run out. My trust is in Christ, anchored firmly in him. He stabilizes me, so that I am not afraid.

"When I looked at William in the chapter house, I could see he was afraid, and I knew why. What kind of man would I be, if, knowing the blind terror of it and having been lifted out of that terror into peace, I shrugged and turned my back—let him slide into what I was rescued from?"

"Amen," said Brother Germanus softly. Brother Tom, who had been listening keenly to what Francis had to say and looking fractionally less pugnacious as he heard it, now had his wrath rekindled.

"'Amen'? What are *you* saying amen about? You didn't vote for him to stay!"

"No," Germanus admitted after an uncomfortable pause under Tom's indignant glare. "I didn't, because he sounds like bad news for any community. I thought it'd be like inviting a fox into the hen coop. I still think so. But I admire what Father Francis just said. That's why I said *amen*."

Tom snorted dismissively. "Anyway, you hardly knew Father Peregrine. I don't suppose he means that much to you. But Francis should have cared about his memory—should have shown some loyalty! He was good enough to Francis—doesn't he deserve someone to stand up for his memory and speak for him still? Or is he just forgotten? Doesn't he mean anything anymore? Eh? Doesn't he?"

Father Francis, very pale, his lips set in a thin, straight line, said quietly, "Excuse me." Walking with light, deliberate tread, he left the room.

As the bell began to ring for Compline, Father Francis emerged from his cell, and in the near darkness he almost tripped over Brother Tom, who was sitting on the top step of the stairs.

"What . . . are you not satisfied with berating me and insulting me? Are you trying to kill me as well?"

"I think I owe you an apology," said Brother Tom penitently as they walked down the stairs together. The two of them had perfected the art of arguing in an undertone years ago. No conversation was permitted in the cloister, but they paused at the foot of the stairs.

"I should think you do!" Francis spoke very low, but this did nothing to disguise his vehemence.

"What can I say to put it right?"

"I cannot imagine, but it had better be good!" Francis broke off; after a moment of evident turmoil he continued in a different tone. "That was *so* unfair, Tom!" His voice shook as he added, "I *did* love him. I would *never* have betrayed him."

The bell continued to ring. Looking carefully at Father Francis as the lights of the bright moon and the cloister lanterns glinted in reflection on his face, Brother Tom realized the words he had spoken earlier had cut very deep.

"I am so sorry," he said soberly. "Please, please forgive me."

As he knelt to kiss the ground and beg his brother's pardon, which was honestly and instantly given, Brother Tom wondered how other people managed—ordinary people outside the monastery walls who tried to muddle along without this discipline of humble contrition to heal the wounds made by human carelessness.

THE
SIXTEENTH DAY

*B*rother Thomas might have restored his relationship with Father Francis, but it was beyond him to forgive his abbot. He found it incomprehensible that someone who had nursed Peregrine back to health after the terrible beating that left him disabled in the first place and made the slow, terrible journey through infirmity and despair with him at the end could contemplate with equanimity welcoming into the community someone who had taunted and tormented him.

He could hardly bring himself to look at Father John and found he had nothing to say to him at all. Brother Thomas was sincere in his vocation and obedience: he carried out his responsibilities as abbot's esquire punctiliously in every respect—waiting at John's table, keeping his house, and seeing to his wants. Every day he was at his side—silent, sullen, and morose as he faithfully served him.

Tom sat in the choir stall next to Theodore's, and he had always liked that. Even in their turbulent, difficult novitiate days when almost nothing had seemed restful, Tom had appreciated the sense of Theo's gentle spirit and liked to sit beside him.

On this day as he came into chapel for the afternoon office, despite the jangling disquiet William's arrival had set in motion in his soul, Tom felt the quiet power of the life he loved: the peaceful movement of his brothers to their allotted places, gathering for the familiar rhythm of prayer, the heart-beat of their life. This community—the sanity of its chosen way, simple and humble and honest, centered on the beautiful Gospel—meant everything to Tom. Resolve hardened in his heart until it became like a stone: he would not have all this shattered for one sneering, pitiless bully who was short of an easy berth.

Tom took his place beside Theodore, taking in as he did so the sense of rest in being near him, marveling as he often did at the journey and the soul work represented in the spiritual equilibrium Theo had finally found.

As they sang the responses and chanted psalms, Tom reflected on the curious effect of influence. He felt sure his entire experience of community had been different because he sat next to Theodore in chapel. And he thought it would take a very different direction if it fell out that he had to spend the rest of his life sitting next to William de Bulmer. He felt profoundly thankful that the brethren had grasped the imperative of getting rid of the man, but he wished his abbot had not gone sentimental at the last moment and given him leave to stay on, even for a week. Anything could happen in a week.

When the community had united in the Pater Noster, and the office was done, Theodore moved his hand in a slight gesture for Tom to wait as the rest of the brothers went about the business of the afternoon. When they were alone, Theodore turned toward him. Speaking very softly in this holy place of silence, he said, "I want to talk to you about William."

"Fair enough, but we can't talk here," Tom hedged.

"Yes, here," Theo insisted in the same quiet voice. "I want you to look at the cross."

The huge, life-sized crucifix that hung above them had been Father Peregrine's mainstay in every time of anguish. Tom loved it for that as well as for the Christ who hung and suffered there. But he accepted this invitation warily. He would have to see where Theo was going with this. He was not open to any manipulative persuasion.

"When you look at William"—Theo went straight to the point; the chapel was not a place for general conversation—"can you not see, or at least look for, that Christ in him?"

"Look for, certainly. See? No," Tom replied shortly.

Theodore tried again. "Not the example of Christ's love and goodness necessarily. Look for a different way in. Can you not see Christ's rejection, the stones and loneliness of his wilderness, the ugliness of his cross?"

"Plenty of ugliness," Tom conceded. He turned toward Theodore, impassioned by this thought. "Yes, when I look at William I trace the Gospel story. I see Judas who embraced his brother with a kiss and then turned him over to torture. I see cynics who gathered to watch and mocked his suffering. I see the thorns and rocks and sand of the wilderness, where it's useless for farming because, try as you might, nothing grows. I see the snake in the garden and the treacherous voice of the tempter in the desert. Is that what you meant?"

Theodore sighed. "No. What you say is true," he went on. "When you say it, I can see those things too. But where's the faith and hope in that? Tom, every front has a back, and the bigger the front, the bigger the back. Like St. Paul. He was never going to be a pale primrose shrinking silently under the hedge, was he? It was a matter of getting him going in the right direction. That's what repentance is, just turning around, setting off as before but going the right way this time. And it will be so with this man, because that's simply how human beings are. We've all had a good look at the truly obnoxious side of him. Now if we can turn him around and set him off in the other direction, we'll have a chance to see the other side of him. And it will be there. There will be goodness in him somewhere."

"Well, good luck to those who have to look for it," Tom replied. "I'm only thankful it won't be us."

Shaking his head, Theodore tried one more time. "Don't look at William, Tom. Look at the cross, look at Christ. Set the passion of Christ between yourself and what you see. Have you no pity for him at all?"

Tom sat in silence, considering these words, saying finally, "If I saw him reduced as he reduced others, I think I might be open to thinking again. If I saw his back flayed as Christ's was flayed—because, unlike Christ, that's what he deserves—I might even feel a little bit sorry for him. But I tell you what: I still wouldn't want him here, spreading his evil influence through this community."

"He *is* here," said Theodore. "He *is* influencing this community—just listen to yourself!"

He reached out a hand and gently patted Tom's fist clenched on his thigh. Then Theodore got to his feet and walked with slow quietness out of the chapel.

✠ ✠ ✠

John stood in the pottery watching Brother Thaddeus at work. He wanted to understand how every bit of the monastery functioned, and he had rarely ventured into the pottery.

"We have a little bit of blue clay here, down by the river, but the red clay is mostly carted in from the vale, which comes expensive because it's heavy," Thaddeus explained. "We spread it outside in the yard first, to open it up. The sun and the frost, the wind—clay has a hard time, Father! And that's before it goes into the fire!"

He took a big handful of clay from the wooden drying box and inspected it. "We let it dry right out, so we can put it through a sieve—make sure it's fine enough and get out the impurities. It's all theology, is making pots! Then it goes into hot water, and we squidge it around, check for lumps and squodge them out. You get your hands dirty, being a potter! We leave it to stew after that, through the dark hours. We come back to see how it's getting on in the morning. Then we put it through a finer sieve while it's still runny. Then we hang it out to dry in linen bags or a box like this one. After that comes the kneading and wedging. Like this." Thaddeus looked up at his abbot with a cheerful grin as he picked up the lump of clay and pummeled it, kneaded it, thumped it around on the slab.

"This is what the Old Testament says God does to us. You have to do all this to purify it and get the air out of it—turn it into something useful instead of just a lump of mud. Then you wedge it—cut it in two and slap it down hard on the slab—and knead it again. If you want to get anywhere with clay, you have to put it through every kind of hell!"

John leaned against the door frame, his arms folded, observing thoughtfully.

"All that you just said—I know what that feels like," he said.

THE
SEVENTEENTH DAY

$\mathcal{T}$he abbot was finding it extremely difficult to work. After Chapter his cellarer Brother Ambrose had handed him a letter sent by one Ralph Dalingbridge offering St. Alcuin's the opportunity to rent a parcel of land that he owned. The agreement he proposed seemed very complicated, but undoubtedly the offer was tempting. The land in question abutted the reaches of the farm that came down south of the moor, so it offered some very useful extra grazing in a gentler and more sheltered location. It also included some unspecified buildings, and a good-sized brook ran through it, all of which added to its value.

The rent required seemed a low figure, but the accompanying conditions ran into a detail of complexity that John found quite bewildering. Tied into the rental agreement John found a stipulation that in the event of Ralph Dalingbridge's demise, a pension for his widow should be provided, this being a sum matching half the amount of the original rent to keep her supplied in clothing, ale, and bread from the abbey's kitchens to be supplied every day (*Has she ever eaten here?* John wondered) as well as three mutton carcasses and two hundred salt herrings every year, along with two wagonloads of wood, the same of straw, a bushel each of beans and oatmeal (ready milled), half an ambra of salt, and a pound of pepper. In cramped letters at the end of the page came an addendum: a pair of felted boots every Yule and a pair of unfelted boots on May Day.

As the abbot worked through this inventory, noting in passing that should Goodwife Alice Dalingbridge predecease her husband the lands would pass to the abbey without her widower receiving anything, he began to wonder if Ralph Dalingbridge had received diagnosis of a terminal illness. This began to look like a corody by another name and not the simple offer of subtenure it had first purported to be.

Brother Ambrose had said he needed a decision on this so that he could respond to Ralph Dalingbridge when he visited them at Easter. St. Alcuin's had first refusal, but others had expressed interest in the land. Abbot John could not see how he might begin to guess at the wisdom of this plan without conferring with Brother Stephen about the needs of the farm, but he wished his cellarer had been able to offer him some kind of guidance, as he had not yet found the time to explore the financial condition of the community himself.

Normally he would have sought an opinion from Brother Thomas, but at the present time he felt reluctant to ask him anything. As John sat at his table perusing this letter among so many others, Brother Thomas was cleaning the abbot's lodging in loud silence.

It is hard to rebuke a brother for silence. Monks are supposed to keep silence. Rules are a convenient refuge at times. Brother Tom's interpretation of silence could for the most part be summarized as "try not to rattle on too much." This was now the fourth day that his rendering of silence had escalated to being brusque if answering direct questions and being mute otherwise. Evidently he took his abbot's wish to take pity on their Augustinian interloper as a personal affront of some magnitude. He had refused to speak to Father John since Tuesday's Chapter meeting when John had extended William's permission to remain beyond the voting.

Tom swept the hearth and took out the ashes. He brought the firewood and laid the fire. He swept the floor and strewed the herbs. He remade the bed that John had already made. He brought some hot sage tea, which he placed with irreproachable care within his abbot's reach, not meeting his eyes but responding to his "thank you, Tom" with a polite nod. Then he let himself out without a word and shut the door behind him.

Miserably, John tried to persevere with his duties of administration. He looked down at the documents awaiting his attention, without the slightest hope of bringing his mind into focus. "I don't know what to do," he whispered. "Heaven help me, I just don't know what to do."

He sat and thought a few minutes longer, then got to his feet. He left the pile of work waiting for him, then went out into the cloister and up the day stairs to the novitiate. Pausing to listen outside the door, he heard no sounds of conversation from within, so he let himself in quietly.

On the hearth the embers remaining from the modest fire of the morning still gave out a little warmth. Theodore sat on the hearthstone, leaning against the chimney breast, alone.

John felt as though a great heavy bundle slipped from his shoulders the moment he entered that room. Theodore had nothing in his hands—no book, no rosary—he was engaged in no particular task, just sitting. As John opened the door, Theo looked up, his face calm and kind, interested. "Good morrow, my abbot. Come on in. You have chosen a moment of peace. Were you looking for me?"

"Oh, God reward you, Theo. You do me good! How on earth do you stay so serene? The novitiate was *never* like this in Father Matthew's day. He found cause for alarm and reproof in every mortal thing. What time we novices were not on our knees confessing some trifling blunder we spent sobbing in the solitude of our cells!"

Theodore laughed. "True enough. God rest him. Bring a stool over, sit you down. You sound upset."

John sat on the hearthstone on the other side of the fire and leaned like Theo on the wall of the chimney.

"How do you do it then? How do you stay so serene? I should be doing the same, but all my feathers are ruffled, and I feel so out of sorts I can't think straight."

"Ah, but the obedience of novice master doesn't compare to the responsibility you bear. Mine's a joyous task and not hard to do, most of the time. Serene? If you say so. I often feel frantic enough. And when I do, I stop to get my breath and remind myself to put into practice something Father Peregrine taught me when I was a novice myself."

"Oh, yes?" John looked at him, intrigued.

"He said that when things were going wrong, it might help to take a careful look and ask, what's missing in this situation? Then, when the picture cleared and I could see what was missing, my service to Christ would be to bring it and put it there myself. I thought it over—what he said—and it seemed to me that in our novitiate we were taught well and disciplined well, but kindness and understanding were missing. At the time I was too caught up in my own daily nightmare to be spacious enough in my soul for generosity. I was just surviving, and only just. But later on, by God's grace, I got a second chance when Father Peregrine put the novitiate into my care. And I have done my best, in my service to Christ, to maintain the standard of teaching and discipline, but also to bring what was missing, understanding and kindness, and put them there myself.

"Sorry, this is getting a bit long-winded! What I'm coming to is the word you used: *serene*. Because it seems to me now that this community has lost its peace. And I believe that peace is not merely a precious thing—it's also absolutely basic. When pilgrims come to touch the hem of Christ's robe, when folk come seeking sanctuary and comfort and good counsel, or even as we interact with each other day by day in all the little things, everything begins to destabilize if we are not rooted in peace.

Even without speaking to a man, even without looking at him as you pass him in the cloister, you can feel whether his soul is at peace. It's in his walk, in the way he carries himself, in the way he sets his feet, in the way he wears his robe, in the way he's breathing—everything.

"We have taken a wrong turn and lost our peace; and now everywhere I go I find a man in a mood: scowling and touchy and on the defensive. Critical of their brothers, men start to be on edge and afraid of attracting criticism themselves. So . . . in my service of Christ I am trying my best to bring back what we have lost from our community, the thing that heals *us* as we offer it to others for *their* healing: peace. And if I look serene to you, that's an encouragement. I've been putting quite a bit of effort in that direction."

As Theo fell silent, John did not reply but sat absorbing these thoughts.

"Peace in oneself, peace between brothers, peace in the whole community," added Theo.

"Yes," said John. "What's concerning me most right now is Brother Thomas, who will not speak to me, or even meet my eyes, and has left peace so far behind he's lost sight of it, I think. And William. He looks like a hunted creature who has come to a wall and turned to face his attackers. There is no peace in either man. And I think the hardest thing to do will be to bring Tom to the place where the two of them can possibly live in peace together in community. Perhaps that hardly needs saying. But Brother Thomas will surely need to move first, from his present position of entrenched resentment."

Tracing random finger patterns in the ashes, Theo found a small twig. He picked it up and looked at it absently, turning it slowly.

"For all of us here," John said, "there is a tension that has developed now, between what we are planning to do to William and what we are called to be. Wherever you get a tension of that nature, there will be resentment. It's inevitable. We hate the people we fear, and we hate the people we victimize. The people we fear threaten our security, obviously, and the people we victimize threaten our good opinion of ourselves. The problem comes when we are acting in self-interest against our own conscience. We are created to choose what is good. So when we choose what is shabby and unworthy, we have to twist it about until our reasoning has been satisfied that we could do no other thing—it was essential, important for the upholding of discipline, necessary for the well-being of others, and all that claptrap.

"William? We listened to what Brother Thomas said, and we didn't hear the right thing. What we should have heard was grief and loyalty, old hurt and resentment—things that needed to be comforted and forgiven. Instead we hooked into the outrage and resentment and made it our own. It got into us like a tapeworm and fed on whatever we put into it since. We saw William, and he looked the part, with his silver hair and sallow face, pale eyes: he's the very countenance of winter. And that lazy, mocking look in his eyes—what's behind it? What does it mean? We don't understand, so we assume the worst. Anyway, now we've decided to throw him out, we have to cling onto every shred of evidence that supports our decision, so we can carry on avoiding admitting that basically it's cruel. We can't keep feeling good about ourselves unless we create a very strong framework to hold up this construct of our own making that there's nothing good in the man. How could we possibly know that without giving him a chance? I am deeply ashamed of being part of this."

✠   ✠   ✠

Brother Thomas came out of the reredorter as William approached its doorway. He stepped aside to accommodate

Tom's passage through the entrance. Tom stopped and stared at him.

"Why are you here?" His tone was formal and cold. "What's wrong with the garderobes in the west range? Those are for the use of guests. Our reredorter is for the community."

THE
EİGHTEENTH DAY

William trod silently along the cloister in the quietness of the morning when the brothers were occupied about their various tasks. He stopped and looked through the arches into the cloister garth, where purple and yellow crocuses bloomed among the clumps of jonquils, diminutive wild daffodils. In this sheltered space the flowers escaped the wind and did well. Native to the hard northern winters, they grew undeterred among the jewel-green moss. A small tree, its branches still winter-bare, stood patiently waiting for the spring. Hellebores bloomed here, purple and white and pale green. Informal, verdant, artless, the little square of life at the heart of the abbey lay inviting and full of hope. William lingered for a long time, his gaze ravenous for the safety of this harbor of life.

He walked up the day stairs and stood listening to the sounds of the morning. From behind the closed door of the novitiate came the trace of conversation, then the chanting of a psalm. Their master of novices in there, he had seen, had voted for him to be allowed to stay. He remembered his face, the man who had first raised his hand in Chapter. Later he had asked Father John, "Who is that?"

"Father Theodore," John had told him, "our novice master."

"Well, God bless you, Father Theodore," whispered William's silence now as he stood outside the closed door of the novitiate, catching the faint music of the chant.

The door to the scriptorium stood ajar, and he heard the familiar sounds of scratching, scraping, pounding: not heavy-weight sounds, but those belonging to goose quills on parchment, the grinding and mixing of inks, the scratching back of the evidence of errors, the scrape of a stool as a scribe got up from his bench, the shuffle and flow of sandals and robes as he crossed the room.

Then William walked along the galleried passages that ran above the cloister and around the garth, where the brothers slept in their cells. One door stood half-open, and William stopped at the doorway and stood looking inside. He did not know whose room it was. He saw a bed, a prie-dieu, a crucifix hanging from a nail in the wall, and a nightstand where the occupant of the cell had left a beaker of water which concealed the lowly item called simply "cell furniture." The room was sparsely and plainly equipped.

William turned and walked down the night stairs to the cloister again.

He stepped into the warming room. At this time of day only a low fire of embers lived still on the hearth. The scent of wood-smoke comforted the air. William went quietly past the abbot's lodge and walked across to the kitchens. He stood in silence at the corner of the building, listening and watching. Cormac's lean figure, sinewy and quick, erupted out of the kitchen door and crossed the cobbled yard to the well. William heard the clatter of the pail and the splash of water, the rattle and creak of the handle turning to draw up the pail. A robin perched bright-eyed on the uppermost twigs of the bay and uttered a careless thread of song.

That morning, as he did most days, William walked quietly around the whole abbey—the farmyard . . . the infirmary . . . the orchard . . . the frater . . . the library . . . the pottery . . . the reredorter . . . the chapter house . . . the checker . . . the stables . . . the kitchen garden—he walked and looked and listened hungrily, wistfully. He neither admitted to himself nor hid from himself the ache he felt to belong here; he just allowed it to be. He did not want to leave.

As he stood in the chapel, he put his hand on the pillar beside him, feeling the texture of the honey-colored stone. His gaze traveled up to where the stone curved and fanned out into the roof. He traced with his fingertips the polished wood of the stalls. "Please," he began, but the whispered prayer died on his lips. William no longer felt sure he had a right to pray. Though he sang the psalms and joined in the responses with the others, he judged it likely that the private longings of his heart might be disqualified. It was better to ignore them until they would be still. But he thought that walking out of these gates forever would be the hardest thing to do.

THE
NINETEENTH DAY

On this day sleet fell, riding wildly on a cruel wind. Every man shivered, so cold to the bone that he could hardly get to sleep at night. The abbey crouched like an animal under a lowering sky. Even at midday the light got up to nothing better than a sullen dusk. In the robing room Father James couldn't see to cut the cloth. Black against black just blurred into darkness. He left his task unfinished and went through to the scriptorium, where the desks under the windows were all taken, so he had asked permission to light a candle to be able to do work of any sort. Monastic silence, the cheerful quiet of a light heart, the eyes of the soul fixed steadily on Christ, somewhere lost its footing and slipped into a speechless despair, hanging on, waiting out this interminable winter. Easter light had come to feel like a forlorn hope that would never be realized—the season of the mausoleum.

Gusts of wind blew back the fire in the kitchen chimney, and the men worked in a room full of smoke. The bread didn't cook through to the middle, and most of the brothers endured bellyache through most of the silent afternoon.

THE
TWENTIETH DAY

Abbot John had thought it a necessary kindness to invite Prior William to share his supper in the abbot's lodging the night before he should leave the abbey. It seemed the only kindness he felt willing to accept. He turned down John's offer to find him lodging and employment among their tenants.

"And what will you tell them," William asked him, "when they inquire why I am not following the more obvious course of staying here?"

John, unhappy, had no answer for this. William waved it aside in an impatient gesture of dismissal. "Fret not. I shall discover a way of dealing with it. I can find my own solution. Let it be. In the morning I will make my way. But I thank you for your company tonight."

Brother Thomas, serving at their table, William ignored as if Tom had simply not been present. Brother Tom, in his turn, looked as friendly and welcoming as frostbite. Though alone with either man Abbot John was able to connect with honesty and authenticity (in the moment when he could get past Brother Tom's frozen withdrawal and catch him off guard), here with both of them together the air crackled with tension, and he could think of nothing more, now, to say.

"I fell into conversation with your kitchen brother while I was looking at your vegetable garden today," remarked Prior William idly. "I passed some comment—a mere pleasantry of some description—about the privations of Lent; said I couldn't wait to get my teeth into a fat wood pigeon again, for preference braised in wine and cream. Extraordinary reaction. I'd like to see it again. For a moment, looking at him, I could have sworn his eyes developed actual spikes. He does not share my taste at table, it would seem. Still, 'tis fair enough no doubt, for I do not share his."

As the prior spoke, Brother Thomas took the covers from the dishes Cormac had sent and placed them, without a word, on the table before the two men. John thanked him and blessed their meal; then for a moment both men regarded their supper thoughtfully.

"Has your kitchen brother been the cook in this abbey long, Father Abbot?"

John contemplated the supper that Brother Tom had set before him. Soggy and unappetizing, it faithfully fulfilled the monastic dietary requirements of Lent, but no other culinary criteria. Resignedly, he picked up his spoon: there seemed to be no need for a knife.

"Sixteen years," he said.

Prior William's eyebrows lifted. "Sixteen years?"

In silence the men made cautious forays into their repast. Prior William chewed thoughtfully.

"A little less mud in the leeks and a little more salt in the millet would have gone a long way," he murmured reflectively.

Abbot John did not reply. He felt suddenly embarrassed by the simplicity of his house. The decisions had never been made on pragmatic grounds, to enhance smooth management or increase comfort and prosperity, but always for the spiritual formation of the brothers. Brother Cormac had been sent to work in the kitchen initially because he detested Brother Andrew the cook (this feeling was mutual), and he had been left there because he had grown to love the old kitchener, with his blunt speech and vinegary temperament. Cormac handled the relationship well. Then, when Brother Andrew died, Brother Cormac grieved deeply, bereft of the adversary who had become so dear a friend. So he had been left where he was, because running the kitchen helped him heal. And there he had stayed.

John struggled to break his bread, which resisted him. "It's Lent," he said quietly, finding it hard to see anything to smile at in this situation. "There is no fruit yet but the apples in the store. Brother Cormac has only grains and what has lasted through the frost or was stored in the clamp. Without leaven, without butter and milk, it is not easy."

Humor glinted in Prior William's eyes. "Lent? Bread, stones, bread—assuredly Christ had a point. But the creature keeps its reverence for the Creator. This bread would not seek to lead the Savior Christ astray. It would reveal to him this little patch of mold here; and he would know at once, 'Ah! Bread!'"

"You're just a patronizing, contemptuous, spiteful, smug, sarcastic toad, aren't you? You just can't help it, can you?" Unable to restrain himself any longer, Tom spoke not so much with aggression as with a kind of wondering indignation.

Looking up sharply to reprimand his ill-disciplined esquire, John noted that Prior William was neither disturbed nor offended by these words; his eyes rested on Tom with an amusement that bordered on affection. William did not reply. He left that to the abbot.

John drew breath to reprimand Brother Tom and then hesitated, caught in a quandary. Such discourtesy could not go unchecked, but Tom had expressed John's own feelings absolutely. Tom stood, his face stubbornly set, waiting resentfully for his abbot's scolding. William watched in ironic detachment to see what Abbot John would say.

John felt the pressure of their expectations so tight about him that he hardly knew which way to turn. Suddenly he knew he'd had enough.

"What am I to say?" he demanded of them, exasperated. "What?"

He looked at neither of them, but stared down at the table, until he obtained sufficient command over himself to speak with restraint and without shouting.

"Brother Thomas, you have expressed my sentiments exactly, but how can I condone it? Father William, you look to me to keep order in my house but spare nothing to try and provoke him!"

He closed his eyes, his jaw clamped tight, his body slightly rocking. Then without warning his fist pounded the table, and he shouted at them both, "I am so *sick* of arbitrating in this entrenched antagonism! What can I do to make anything work? Of what use is the status of abbot where it is not respected? *I* cannot make peace between you! You came into monastic life—*both of you*—not to be chastised by me but to discipline *yourselves*! William, you are a guest in this house and a guest at my table. Behave like a guest then, with gentleness and consideration; stop wearing us all away with this wearisome point-scoring and fencing and feinting. Thomas, you are a brother of this house, and you ought to know better; you have been in the life—is it eighteen years or seventeen? If in *all this time* you have not managed to get a grip on some basic forbearance and humility, what has been the purpose of all our efforts and your own?"

He stopped, trembling. "Ah, for God's sake you weary me, both of you, you really do! I dread it when I see the both of you enter the room. And now here am I, left feeling wretched because I have stepped into the shoes of a man who would have handled this so much better than I. What would he have done? I don't know! What am I to do? I don't know! Sort yourselves out. I'm going to Compline."

Without a glance at either of them, John pushed back his chair with grating violence, leaving his supper and his lodging behind with swift and angry steps. But he had been in monastic life for twenty-eight years, so he did not slam the door.

William likewise got to his feet, but with unabashed composure. He calmly placed his napkin alongside his unfinished meal and left with soft and even tread. He did not glance at Brother Thomas or speak to him.

Tom stood in obstinate silence, like a carving of stone, until William had gone, then set about the mundane chores of clearing the table from supper. He scraped together the uneaten food and stacked the vessels moodily. He hadn't felt this bad in a long time. Everything—even John—seemed to be completely falling apart.

THE
TWENTY-FIRST DAY

The wind and weather turned. Bright and fair, the day dawned. Small white clouds scattered the glorious azure of the sky in a world flooded with sunlight. With the lifting of the gloom came the sense of a new season of hope. Life seemed more possible.

Steam rose in the morning sunbeams, from the sodden hurdles of the wood yard fence. Brother Conradus, chopping logs into kindling for the guest house, the warming room, the abbot's lodging, the novitiate, and the kitchen, paused to lift his face to the sun and to watch two wrens flirting among the bare flowering twigs of the winter honeysuckle.

Brother Cormac stood at the kitchen door crumbling bread and throwing it down for the fat wood pigeons that hung around hopefully most of the time. He flung a few crumbs farther beyond, toward the place under the wood stack against the kitchen wall where he had two or three times seen a small gray mouse vanishing into a gap between the logs. Brushing the last remains of bread crumbs from his hands, he went down into the kitchen garden in search of the coarse, hardy parsley that had weathered the frosts, and some sprigs of rosemary, maybe a handful of bay, and chervil, the Lenten herb that Brother Paulinus had sown in the shelter of the wall and mulched with straw to keep it going through the winter frosts.

Walking slowly out of the infirmary into the sunshine, leaning on Brother Michael's arm, Brother Gerald shuffled to the wooden seats among the physic garden herbs. Michael settled him comfortably on a sheepskin, tucking a blanket securely around his knees and feet. Frost still lay on the ground in the shadows, and Michael would not let his charges suffer from the cold.

Up on the hill, the lambing had got well under way now; half the ewes were delivered, and every day brought more births. Brother Thomas walked up the track toward the farm, carrying a pot he had just fetched from the kitchen, containing apple and root peelings to feed to the pigs. Brother John had suggested he make himself useful by helping Brother Stephen on the farm, since an experienced pair of hands would surely be welcome with the sheep, and only two pilgrims on the road to Lastingham were passing through the abbey—no one who required the special hospitality of the abbot's table.

Tom thought that if things had been different, his abbot probably would have invited the visitors to dine with him. It would have served as a useful rehearsal for the many occasions to come when he must play host to the church's aristocracy and the world's. Brother Tom had an idea that he was bound for the farm this day not for the good of the lambs, but because Abbot John had no wish to see him, had no wish to see anyone. Mulling over the dissensions of the past few days as he climbed the track, Tom's mind focused on Prior William in a resentment bordering on hatred. The wonder of the lambing, the joy of spring returning, the excitement of John's homecoming, the hope and energy of having the abbacy filled after all this time— everything had been scattered and besmirched and upstaged by this selfish Augustinian's arrival. Tom wondered bitterly why it should be that out of all the men who had died in St. Dunstan's fire, this one loathsome troublemaker should have survived. At least after today he would be gone.

Then as he reached the top of the track, Tom stopped. He

paused by the field gate and tried to purge his heart of this sour trickle of complaint. He made himself listen to the drumming of the woodpecker and the robin's song, made himself look at the hazel catkins swinging in the breeze on the slender twigs, but he could find no joy in any of it.

The milk cows, two with calves, had been turned out to graze already, and Tom thought he would find Brother Stephen in the byre with the ewes whose lambing signs had begun. As he came level with the farm buildings, he noticed with irritation that the barn door stood ajar. He stopped and listened. The noises of daily routine are always familiar. Tom could identify and place the rattle of a feed pail, the sliding of a bolt, the shuffling and grunt of a man hefting a shock of hay, the hard squirting of milk against the side of a wooden pail. The time of day and the familiarity of every tool and building on the farm allowed him to recognize each smallest sound, even when its source lay out of sight. But he couldn't place the sounds he heard now, emanating from the barn: a scrape, a creak . . . a silence . . . a scuffling and the creaking of a beam . . . the crash of something wooden overturned on the stone floor. Puzzled to hear anything on the farm not instantly identifiable, Tom stepped nearer the barn and paused to listen again. Something . . . he could hear something . . . as indefinite as a disturbance of the air, then a choking cough. Deciding it was probably Stephen fetching hay for the sheep, which would account for the door standing open, he turned toward the pigs' orchard with his pot of scraps; then he hesitated. In his experience, faint rustling sounds he could not quite place usually came from animals where they had no business to be. He thought he'd better check the barn.

As Tom pushed the great door open and looked in, it was as though the turning world suddenly stopped dead. The earthenware pot he was carrying dropped from his arms and smashed to pieces on the flagstones of the barn floor at his feet. Unable to move for a moment, he cried, "Oh, Lord Jesus! No!" He turned and bellowed "Stephen!" at the top of his lungs across the farmyard before diving into the barn toward the writhing, jackknifing body of the monk suspended from the crossbeam by a rope around his neck.

Tom looked about him wildly for something to stand on. He saw the stool kicked aside in the hay, grabbed it, and climbed up beside the hanging man, seizing his body in his arms to take the weight from the rope. The running noose had tightened, and the man continued to cough and choke, his face cyanosed, his breath sticking and gagging in his throat. "*STEPHEN!*" Tom roared again, and this time Brother Stephen appeared in the sunlit doorway, having heard Tom calling so urgently for his aid.

After an instant of frozen horror, Brother Stephen moved fast. "The milk cart—get the milk cart!" panted Tom, with forty-five seconds' thinking time advantage. Brother Stephen ran for the handcart used for barrowing the milk and fetched the stone used to keep the door open when the hay was being brought in. He blocked the wheel and cautiously climbed upon the cart, holding onto Tom's clothing as the deck of the two-wheeled cart swung and tipped. Balancing perilously, holding with one hand to Tom's habit, Stephen pulled his knife from his belt. He grabbed the rope, released his hold on Tom's clothing, and transferred that hand also to the rope, freeing the hand that held the knife to begin sawing frantically.

The moment the last strands gave proved spectacular. The body of the choking monk dropped fully into Tom's arms, knocking him completely off balance as the cart also tipped. Stephen tried to keep his footing but fell. All three of them, crashing amid the cart and the stool, collapsed in a tumbled heap on the stone floor of the barn. Stephen's knife fell from his hand and clattered to rest at a distance. Both men hastened to straighten their brother's body and loosen the rope about his neck, which mercifully proved not too difficult to do. Still gagging and coughing, still with the rope loose about his neck, the man gasped and groaned, rolled over on the hay-strewn floor, and began to vomit. Tom knelt beside him, holding him up in his arms lest he choke again.

"I'll go and fetch Brother John," said Stephen, almost incoherent, scrambling to his feet and limping crazily for the door, leaving Tom clasping the man snatched from death, as if he dared not let him go. Stephen's running feet beat away, into silence, down the stony track. Bright sunbeams streamed from the cold, clear morning through the open door. The brightness seemed surreal as Brother Tom knelt there, trying to process what he felt.

"William de Bulmer," he whispered, bringing his brow to rest on the prostrated Augustinian's shoulder, suddenly dizzy and cold and shaking as the adrenaline ebbed away, "you are nothing but trouble."

THE
TWENTY-SECOND DAY

*D*irectly he had broken his fast, before Terce and Chapter Mass, the day found Abbot John in the infirmary, checking William's progress for himself.

William ran his tongue across lips cracked and dry and reached for his beaker of water, from which he took a cautious sip, swallowing with evident difficulty.

"At the moment," he said in response to Abbot John's inquiry, his voice hoarse and low, "I cannot tell the end of pain from the beginning of myself. Every part of me on every level hurts. I have become a burnt bruise."

Abbot John listened for but could not find the distinctive color of self-pity in the Augustinian's voice. Unemotional, William spoke as one merely stating the facts.

The prior looked at the abbot, his pale eyes offering a sardonic challenge. "What will you do with me now?"

John shook his head. "The whole community is wondering the same thing, my brother."

"Brother Thomas—" His throat rasping dry, William began to cough, which evidently hurt. Swearing softly under his breath, he reached for the water again. John saw that his hand trembled slightly. William took two or three sips of water, swallowing painfully. Then, grimacing his impatience, he set down the beaker again. "Brother Thomas runs true to form, does he not? The maximum disturbance, the maximum inconvenience, and no solutions offered whatsoever."

He shot John a baleful glance. "I have enough water left in this pot to throw at you if you dare to tell me I should be grateful."

John smiled. "Once only," he said, "has this infirmary had the care of a man as difficult in temperament and as impossible to nurse as I see you are planning to be, and you are wearing his clothes. I thank God I am not the infirmarian now. Brother Michael has to be back to wheedling and soothing again, I see."

A flash of fire like the glint in an opal flickered in the eyes that watched Abbot John. "Do not mock me," he muttered vehemently, but the words ended in a spasm of coughing. "Ow . . . ow . . . ow . . . " he groaned softly when it subsided and sat with his head bent, recovering himself for a moment before reaching again for the water. "Please, go away."

John nodded. "Gladly, my lord prior. First, though, let me look you over and see what fresh hurts you have achieved and how well the ones I have bandaged already are faring. What was it you said about the maximum disturbance and the maximum inconvenience? Let me help you off with those clothes. Eh! By our lady, you *have* added a few bruises. When they cut you down, I suppose. I have a good salve here. Are you warm enough? Yes? Good. Nobody else in this abbey is; wind's blowing strong from the east for all the sun is shining. Michael must be feeling sorry for you, to have lit this fire in here. Can I take a look at your knees now? Forgive me, I did see you wince then. I'll do my best to be gentle."

"You are gentle," commented the dry, hoarse voice dispassionately.

John checked every scabbed-over burn and scrape and new bruise. He touched the fingers of his left hand to William's chin, tipping back the prior's head a little, tracing the fingertips of his right hand along the leather-brown ligature scar that circled his throat. Cautiously, watching for reaction, he palpated the larynx, estimating how little pressure evoked a response of pain. Then, satisfied that all was progressing as it should, he helped William on with his clothes and from long years of habit began to sort and tidy the salves and cloths Michael had brought and the dirty dressings.

"Would you like to see Brother Thomas?" he asked as he gathered up the soiled bandages.

Prior William looked at him wonderingly. "See Brother Thomas? As in, ever in my life again? Assuredly I would not. And I tell you this . . . " He leaned forward possessed of a sudden intensity. ". . . lest anybody should be asking himself, I did not want to see him yesterday either!"

Their eyes met. John shook his head. "There's little wonder—is there?—that you and Peregrine had such a war! What can two flints do but strike sparks? You have no wish to see Brother Thomas? That will be a relief to him then, as you can imagine, I'm sure. But tell me this: I had been thinking it would serve the purposes of Christ to plead your case with my community, to see if their hearts might not be softened by your obvious despair. And Brother Thomas is part of this community now and, God willing, for the rest of his life. What am I to do? Do you still want to stay with us, if they will have you?"

William reached for his water, steadied his grip, and took a few sips, swallowing each one painfully. John set down the dressings again and seated himself opposite on the stool. In the distance he could hear them ringing the bell for Terce. William heard it too; he looked up, nodding and glancing in the direction of the chapel. John didn't move. William took another sip of his water, and the beaker was drained.

"'*Domine, ad quem ibimus*?' I have nowhere to go but here."

John considered him thoughtfully.

"You know, that can't be true. We can find another way forward, of that I have no doubt. To enter a community as a last resort, a kind of permanent bolt-hole, is not a healthy beginning. Over time it couldn't work. It would imply a separation in your heart: 'I'm here only because I have to be, and if I didn't, you'd better believe I'd be anyplace else.' How can I ask the brothers here to support that? If you want to stay with us—if it's what you are choosing, not what is forced upon you, if you open your heart to us—then I will ask them again. And if you want to stay with us, that means living with Brother Thomas. The only currency Christ trades in is love. You have to learn to love him; that's the deal."

Abbot John had a sense of consciously standing his ground every time the calm evaluation of those eyes sifted his soul.

The hoarse voice rasped softly in reply, "And Brother Thomas? Does he also have to learn to love me?"

John sighed. "Yes, he does. I fear he *does*. But when I hotfooted it up to the farm yesterday morning and found him kneeling on the barn floor holding you in his arms lest you lose your life choking on your own vomit, I thought he had made quite a good start in that direction. Did not you?"

Prior William lowered his gaze and did not reply.

The door opened, and Brother Michael entered peaceably. "Father John, they will be waiting for you in chapel. Your routines have to be different now, my abbot. No—leave those things to me. That's right; off you go. Thank you for what you've done. My heart was sore that you and I should not work alongside anymore, and it's been grand to have you back, but now get you gone; they will be thinking you don't know how to let go of your old obedience. They've been ringing the bell long enough, my father—go on now; you will be needed."

He squeezed John's arm gently and gave him a little push in the direction of the door. "Never fear, this cantankerous rascal will be comfortable in my care, and I shall make him smile one day, if it's the last thing I do!"

As John went through the door and along the passage, he

heard Michael saying, "Oh, have you finished your water? Let me get you some more. We can try if you can manage a little broth at midday. We will soon have you right again; there's nothing amiss with you we cannot mend."

Detained as he often was by the necessities of the infirmary, Brother Michael had not been in Chapter on the day Prior William begged for admittance. Abbot John wondered how Michael would have voted if he had been there.

Along with the brothers gathered for Chapter after the morrow Mass had been said, John listened to the steady, peaceful tones of Brother Germanus reading the portion of the Rule for the day, outlining in the clearest terms the essential importance of each brother's abstaining from the inimical vice of aspiring to own private property. Something of the fire and passion that had made Benedict of Nursia the man he was came through in his insistence that not even a monk's own body or his own will might remain at his own discretion and disposal, for all had been in humility surrendered. The reading ceased, and John allowed the thoughts it stimulated to expand into the shared silence for a while.

The community heard the confessions of the brethren, and the novices left them. Brother Robert tried his best with the latch but had to take two goes at it. The second time the iron upon iron was noisy in closing, and he followed his brothers up to the novitiate feeling irritated and disappointed with himself. "Mother of God! That chapter house door latch!" he whispered to Brother Felix as they took their seats on the novitiate benches. "The doors up here are no trouble, but that latch is so *heavy*, it doesn't balance right; trying to shut that in silence is the hardest thing to do!"

In the chapter house the professed brothers had listened to the rattle of the latch in the silence, well understanding the effort and failure it represented. Memories of their early days at St. Alcuin's passed through their minds as they waited for their abbot to speak: tears of despair sometimes, adjustment, personal turmoil, the humiliation that comes before the longed-for self-acceptance of humility, confusion and the sense of the task being impossible, wrestling to find the way into this life that promised so much and cost so much and needed such equilibrium to achieve. The memories of their own years of formation remained vivid. Soul change always does. But eventually Abbot John broke the remembering silence.

"Brothers, I have to tell you that though yesterday William de Bulmer was due to leave this house, he has not yet done so because yesterday morning he tried to take his own life." Even in a community that values silence, news spreads with astonishing rapidity; but John knew from the sudden frozen stillness, the cessation of all movement that followed these words, that what he had told them was by no means common knowledge.

With a sense of weariness that was by this time becoming a habitual state of mind, he wondered what struggle lay ahead now. Would their hearts be softened at the plight of a desperate man? Hardened at the shocking, sinful action of a man who flouted the laws of God? Or just steadfastly indifferent to William's condition and protective of community stability?

"He attempted to hang himself in the hay barn up on the farm. By the mercy of God, Brother Thomas came by at that precise moment. His and Brother Stephen's prompt and practical action not only saved William's life but averted the danger of lasting physical damage. Even so, his condition needs care now. We are keeping him in the infirmary for the present time.

"My brothers, I don't know at all what you are thinking—no two minds react exactly alike, I suppose. But in these days that follow, as we work to restore his health, I lay it upon you that you must pray for him—and for us as we think what to do. And when you pray, have in your mind also the question, 'If this was me—if I were William—what would I be hoping for, what would I be longing for, and what would I need?'"

Some common daily concerns occupied their attention after this. Brother Ambrose had a provisions list for the abbot to approve, and Brother Dominic had a list of guests who had sent notice that they would need a bed in the guest house. Father Gilbert needed permission to take the singers among the novices out of their lessons to practice the unfamiliar chants of the Holy Week music. Brother Stephen reported on the progress of the lambing: no losses, God be thanked.

John was conscious that though he made himself listen carefully and respond appropriately, his thoughts were always tugging in the direction of the infirmary. He wondered if in truth, especially when someone was in trouble, that was where his heart would always really be.

But for now so much clamored for his attention. He said yes to Father Gilbert when Father Theodore nodded his assent; he congratulated Brother Stephen, received Giles's lists, and promised Brother Ambrose he would come over to the checker directly after Chapter.

THE
TWENTY-THIRD DAY

Abbot John sat on the edge of the bed observing the shivering, sweating man with thoughtful care. During the night when the community had gathered for the office, Brother Michael crossed the dark-shadowed choir to the abbot's stall, whispering to him that William had developed a chest cough and a fever. "He seems low, debilitated. His breathing is bad, and he's coughing up some splendid muck."

"Keep him warm; don't let the fire go out in his room," Father John had responded quietly. "Wrap a hot stone in a cloth, and put it at the small of his back when you settle him down to sleep. Make him a tisane of thyme and yarrow, and sweeten it with the elderberry cordial. Crush a clove of garlic, some ginger root, and cinnamon. Give it to him in a spoonful of honey. Have a care that he's not delirious and that he's sitting up properly when you give it. Don't rush him; if he's having any trouble at all swallowing, let him take it in tiny amounts, but do make him have it. If he argues, fetch me from my bed."

Brother Michael had faithfully and accurately carried out these instructions. His patient seemed too weak and indifferent to argue; he merely did as he was told.

In the morning Abbot John came straight from Chapter to the infirmary. He laid his hand on the head of the feverish man, whose body shuddered in shaking chills, huddled under his blankets.

"William . . . we will do all we can for you, but we cannot do your part. You must have hope or you will sink further into this."

Brother Michael stood watching with sober countenance. "Is it because of the strangling from the rope?"

Abbot John nodded. "Yes. He will have breathed in something that should have been swallowed. But he hung there hardly any time, and Tom was holding him up well when I arrived. I think this will pass. It's only . . . he has suffered too much. He cannot see a way forward. Life is sustained by hope, in all of us."

"His body bears many scars, you know," Michael commented. "I know," said John, "I have seen."

John stroked the prone man's head slowly, tenderly. "William, lay hold upon Christ," he said gently. "Christ is your hope, and he will hold you up and rescue you. I will pray for you, but you have to hang on with all your strength."

The abbot straightened up. "I'm going to have to go. Father Gilbert is coming to me this morning with the details for the Tenebrae devotions and the music for Easter Day. I'll be keeping him waiting. Take care of him, Michael. Send for me if you get out of your depth. This man did not come here to die; he came to learn how to live. We mustn't lose him now. Hold him fast in your prayers."

THE
TWENTY-FOURTH DAY

*M*idnight. The abbey lay lapped in the deep silence of the night. High in a sky clear of cloud, the last sliver of a waning moon described a slender curve of light. Mars glowed red, and Venus outshone every other star in clarity and beauty. The henhouses and dovecotes had been shut tight against the hungry fox that nosed around empty feed bowls and climbed up onto the compost pile in search of scraps of bread.

Cold closed like iron bands around the earth, and frost tinged every blade of grass, every twig and premature blossom. Up on the hill the sheep slept packed together in their byre, their noses tucked in to breathe air warmed by each other's fleece, the lambs snuggled close against their mothers.

In the chapel the perpetual light glowed ruby in the sanctuary, but all was still. Moonlight stole through the windows, gleaming here and there upon the polished wood of the stalls, the outline of carved saints, the silver of candlesticks, and the intricacies of the altars. The smell of mingled incense and beeswax permeated the air. Even in the emptiness of the night, the church felt like a living place, alert and curious, watching and waiting, like a dog that sleeps with one ear cocked and one eye vigilant, attuned even in sleep to every incipient movement and mind-set of the master.

The frater lay quiet, inhabited only by moonbeams; the kitchens likewise, only ashes faintly stirred as the last embers died away. The cloisters stood spacious in the fullness of silence. An owl flew across the cloister garth, sweeping up the hill toward the barns. In the dorter, brothers who had shivered and found it hard to fall asleep by now lay lost in oblivion. The night was short: at half-past two the nocturn bell would call them out of sleep to stumble drowsy into the first office of the day, but for now slumber claimed them entirely. Alone in his lodging, Abbot John slept rolled into his blankets, burrowed down among their thick woolen folds against the cold.

In the infirmary, where the small lights of stubby candles comforted men in their second childhood and kept fear at bay, Brother Michael, methodical and capable, finished the rounds of the night, checking that all was well. He brought a lantern and sat a little while at Brother Cyprian's bedside, seeing that the old man was sinking low. He watched the light rise and fall of Cyprian's breath, concluding that though the time was not far off, it was not here yet.

Then he came to the small room where William lay limp and exhausted, carried on tides of fever to the shores at the far edge of life. Michael set the lantern down on the table and added two split birch logs to the low-burning fire on the hearth. Leaning over the bed, Michael felt the burning heat of William's brow and noted the light, racing pulse. Drawing up a stool to the bedside, he observed the spasms that intermittently racked William's body. Occasionally a dry cough took hold of him, and his face contorted momentarily in pain; but the coughing now was weak and ineffectual. He had no strength left. Brother Michael could see that, even by the light of one candle lantern.

He thought it increasingly unlikely that William would pull through this; and he had come to keep watch through those deep hours of the night, the time in whose boundless depths so many souls had slipped away.

He judged that William lay beyond hearing him and probably would never recover. This brought its own freedom and intimacy, and Brother Michael began to talk to the almost extinguished soul half in and half out of the inert body on the bed.

"Where are you, William?" he asked softly. "What dark paths are you walking? I think you are in the valley of shadows. The Shepherd is with you, wherever you are. He will find you and bring you home.

"Where are you going, my brother? Which way are you turned? Are you walking out on the trail that leads where we cannot follow, or are you searching for the way back to us here? Or are you just lost and out of hope, out of answers?

"Can you hear me, my poor brother, in your fever and your terror? If you can, I have something to say to you. May you be robed in Christ's grace. May his love be a cloak about you and his peace be the robe of your true self. May you touch and know his healing, find for sure his forgiveness, wherever you are, and whatever happens now. Find thy lamb, O Jesu, good Shepherd, in thy love, and free him of the thorns that bind and cling.

"What happened to you, William? How did you come to lose yourself and lose hold of Christ? How did you fall out of the security of human community and find yourself left so alone? Listen, my brother, listen—I am here with you. I'm here now. You are not alone anymore. You will be safe here. We will not turn you away. We will not abandon you. Never, never, never. Come back, William. Please come back. There is a place for you here; see, we are not complete without you. Don't go home just yet; please stay with us for a while."

Brother Michael had no idea if any of this was true: his words arose not from his reasoning but from the instinct of his compassion. He sat beside the sick man, talking quietly on in this vein all through the deepest hours of the night. At about half-past three in the morning, as the lantern's candle flame failed in a vague wraith of smoke, Michael finally fell asleep, his head resting on his arms on the bed where William lay:

their body warmth and the light of their souls fused in the same space—William's ebbing and guttering, Michael's shining with the steady peace of faith.

Brother Damian came into the little room in the morning and found Michael still sleeping there. Leaning closer, wondering for a moment if William had actually died, he saw and recognized the pallor and profuse sweat and the restful sleep that follow the crisis. Turning to Brother Benedict who had come in with him, he said in a low voice, "Go and tell Abbot John that all is well here. This man will live. Go now; he will be anxious to know." Then, "Brother Michael," he said, laying his hand on the infirmarian's shoulder and giving it a gentle shake, "Brother Michael, it's past daybreak. I think he's going to be all right."

THE
TWENTY-FIFTH DAY

On this day, when the bare, dark trees stood disconsolately in the ice-cold fog, Brother Michael, who could only be bothered to eat his soup and bread because he felt guilty at his own ingratitude, wished someone had mentioned to him in the novitiate that the severest task wouldn't be the extreme simplicity, the abstention from sex, or humbly submitting to the will of another. Trying to carry on looking cheerful when he was numb with weariness would be the hardest thing to do.

His abbot caught up with him on the way out of the frater and told him to go to bed.

THE
TWENTY-SIXTH DAY

The door to William's small room opened. He looked up, anticipating Brother Michael or Brother Benedict, but the novice master stood in the doorway. This being Sunday, the lessons were a little shorter, and the hours of solitary personal study longer than usual. That gave him a chance to slip across to the infirmary.

"God give you good morrow, my friend. Can I come in?"

William nodded. "Aye, do." He looked weak and tired, and his breathing came alarmingly high and shallow.

"I shall not stay long. I know how ill you have been. May I sit down a minute?"

William waved his hand in shaky indication of the low wooden stool. "You are more than welcome," he said faintly. Then he started to cough, the pain of it clear in his face. Mucus rattled loudly in his chest, and he grabbed his handkerchief from among the folds of the rumpled sheet, pressing it to his mouth to catch and conceal the sputum. "Oh, God," he said wearily as the coughing subsided and he closed his eyes and lay back exhausted on the pillows stacked behind him, "please forgive me."

Making the effort to open his eyes, he looked at Theodore's smiling face. "You find this funny?" he asked with bleak incredulity.

"No! I'm sorry. Truly I'm sorry. It just struck me as incongruous and unexpected that you'd managed to get everyone hopping mad at you and seemingly made enemies of the whole of England—and now you're begging my forgiveness for coughing! But I didn't mean to belittle what you're going through." Theodore did his best to sound penitent, but the residual twinkle in his eye did not escape William's detection. He nodded, allowing his eyes to close again, his face relaxing a little in a softening gleam of humor. "Well, thank you for coming. And also for—" He began to cough again, the spasm of it racking his body and leaving him gasping for breath as he sat trembling, the sodden handkerchief clamped to his mouth.

Theodore got up from the stool, took out his own handkerchief, and gently exchanged it for William's. "I'll ask Michael to boil this," he said, "and I'll leave you in peace. I just wanted you to know you are not forgotten."

William nodded. "God reward you," he managed before he started coughing again.

THE
TWENTY-SEVENTH DAY

*B*rother Germanus had scrubbed all the way around the cloister, the day stairs, the night stairs, and the floor of the frater. He felt virtuous, and his hands were nearly numb with cold. The water in the pail was filthy. His abbot stopped briefly to commiserate with him as he passed him in the cloister, on his way to the chapel to quieten his mind and steady his soul with half an hour's prayer on his own before the end of the morning, which had been unusually hectic. Brother Cyprian lay dying in the infirmary where William was making strides toward a good recovery. John wanted peace and space to pray for Cyprian in these last days as his soul drifted loose from its moorings, but his own lodging rarely afforded more than ten minutes between interruptions; besides which, tranquil contemplation had been seriously undermined on this day by housework.

Father Chad held the responsibility for ensuring that the abbey offered a presentable and hospitable environment for the influx of guests at the end of Lent, and his program of works for the spring cleaning of the entire house had now embarked.

Cautiously and with deep reluctance, Brother Clement had permitted a delegation of novices to tidy the scriptorium cupboard, containing ingredients for inks, and rationalize his rolls and piles of parchments and fine vellum. But he became agitated when they wanted to dust the ledges and sweep the floor.

"No, brothers, no! Three of us are working on a book of hours this morning, two of us painting and one of us gilding the capitals. We cannot have the air full of dust while we're painting or people flapping cloths and feather dusters about while we're working with loose gold. The *slightest* draft lifts the gold. You must leave us alone! Please! Just leave us alone! Father Chad knows *nothing* about manuscript illumination; it is a fine work. This is not a cowshed to be scrubbed down after milking! Just go away!"

Prior Chad seemed a little affronted when his team dejectedly reported the rebuff. But Brother Felix, Brother Cassian, and Brother Cedd had their rags and brooms put to good use in the guest house, while Brother Placidus and Brother Robert went to the lady chapel with instructions to brush down the stonework and polish the intricately carved wooden screens and rails and ceremonial chairs.

They worked in industrious silence for a while, Brother Robert rubbing in the fragrant polish mixed by the herbalist Brother Walafrid from the beeswax Brother Mark had harvested, while Brother Placidus brushed the cobwebs and dust from the stonework, swept the floor, and buffed polished surfaces with a dry cloth once he'd given the wax time to soak in and dry.

Brother Robert finished first. He sat on the stone-flagged floor, his back against the carved wooden screen dividing the lady chapel in the south transept from the choir. Idly twirling the dirty cloth stiff with beeswax, he stared thoughtfully at the statue of Our Lady of Sorrows, who occupied a niche of discreet retirement here in the side chapel.

A voluptuous if doleful image, the Madonna gazed stricken at the doomed infant perched on her forearm, a broken flower that assumed the shape of a cross clutched tellingly in his plump fist. Her robe had been carved with great artistry to represent much graceful draping of full folds of cloth, yards of it, except her dress seemed a little scanty around the bosom. Abbot Peregrine had never been enthusiastic about this effigy. But as she had been presented at great expense (though with no prior consultation) by the abbey's devout and very wealthy benefactress Lady Agnes d'Ebassier, he had deemed it prudent to keep his reservations to himself—or at least restricted to a modest expression of irritation with senior brethren he trusted. Father Peregrine had as wholehearted a reverence for our Lady as any of the faithful; he just felt it sensible to ensure she was adequately covered before she ventured into residence in a monastery.

Sometimes thoughts merely pass through a man's head without mishap, but sometimes they fall out of his mouth on the way through. It was the latter case with Brother Robert as he aimlessly wondered aloud, "D' you think Abbot John ever kissed a woman?"

Brother Placidus, arrested in his burnishing of a particularly ornate poppyhead at the entrance to the priest's stall, followed the line of Robert's gaze as it casually took in the form of Our Lady of Sorrows. "If he did," he volunteered, "I'll wager you whatever you like the damsel would have looked a tad more chipper than that!"

"Mmm. Maybe . . ." Brother Robert was drifting into a mood of thoughtful conjecture. "But Father John looks grim enough himself most of the time. Maybe he could fancy a more lachrymose kind of a lass. She has charm in her way. 'Twould be a question of stone calling to stone. They would like each other. But anyway, I didn't mean her in particular. I meant any woman. I mean, can you imagine—"

Brother Robert's unguarded rambling froze suddenly as the quiet voice of his abbot interrupted the development of his line of thought, from the choir side of the dividing wooden screen. "Brother, you have no permission for conversation in the chapel. I regret my devotion to Our Lady of Sorrows has not been as zealous as you suppose. I am sorry to disappoint you. If your work here is finished, it may be that Father Chad can find you something else to do."

Scrambling to his feet, Brother Robert did not even lift his face to look in the direction of that voice from the choir but left the building with all possible speed. He left Brother Placidus polishing feverishly, accomplishing in ten minutes what he had planned to stretch out to a comfortable half an hour.

☩   ☩   ☩

"Theodore," said Abbot John as his novice master stepped into the abbot's lodge during the afternoon to return the breviary he had borrowed, "do I look grim to you? Most of the time, I mean? Tell me truly."

Theo put down the breviary as he considered this question, which John felt disconcerted to see he did not immediately dismiss.

"You have authority about you," he said thoughtfully, "and authority sometimes has to look grim. I remember vividly that you achieved a workable level of submission in Father Peregrine in the infirmary on one or two occasions. That was in my mind when I proposed your name for abbot. I couldn't see that any of the rest of us had that level of authority and assurance about us. And since you've been back here—yes, most days I guess you *have* looked fairly grim. But then I think so should I or any man in your shoes. It's hardly been an easy beginning. Why d' you ask? What's been said to you?"

"Not *to* me." John smiled. "About me. Theo, you need to know this because these young men were badly out of order." He recounted to his novice master the conversation he had overheard in the chapel.

"It's not what they said; it's that they were spending time in idle speculation and gossip at all—especially in the chapel, where they were not keeping silence as they should have been. And come to that, they were not discussing their abbot with the greatest respect, nor yet the holy statue in the chapel! But grim . . . I hadn't realized . . . "

Theodore regarded him with sympathy. Then, with an inquiring lift of the eyebrows, he asked, "Well? Did you? Ever?"

"What? Oh—kiss a woman? Yes, indeed. Did not you?"

"No," Theo said simply. "And I often wondered . . . especially since I've been the novice master, because there are areas of experience that most of them have, and I do not."

"Surely. But that will be true in every case. I have kissed a woman, but I've never forged an iron hook or a door latch, which you spent your boyhood doing before you came to us here."

"Yes, but . . . well, if you wanted to, you could go to the forge and ask the smith to teach you that skill tomorrow." Theo looked at the incredulous expression this remark brought to his abbot's face and added hastily, "Not in practical terms, I mean. I'm not suggesting you sit here wondering how to pass the afternoon, but it would not be forbidden you. I was only wondering . . . John, what was it like?"

John laughed, taken aback by the frank question. But Theodore waited for an answer.

"Theo, I don't—"

"John, tell me. Please. Who else can I ask?"

John nodded. "It is a renunciation," he said quietly. "Well then . . . sensual . . . pleasurable . . . No. No, that's not it. Those are the words of a monk who'd prefer to belittle and forget it. It was intimate . . . and beautiful. Something you could lose yourself in like music. Like two birds taking flight together, right up into the blue. Something that took up your whole being, a movement of the soul. It satisfied something very primal. Theo, I'm not talking about a peck on the cheek, you understand? And . . ." He stirred, restlessly. ". . . it was intensely arousing . . . I have work to do, and I'm not going to talk to you about this anymore!" He laughed, half-embarrassed.

Theodore didn't laugh or even smile. "Thank you, John. I shall remember that. I'm glad you have that memory as part of who you are. Nobody could become entirely grim while his heart still holds the memory of a kiss. I think that was part of what was the matter with Father Matthew. He let the tender, open softness in him dry up and shrivel away. It makes celibacy easier, I suppose, but still, I'd rather not do that if I can help it. As long as I live, I want to be completely a human being. If that means that longings ache and hunger sometimes, well, so be it. It's the path I've chosen, and I'm glad I did. I wouldn't change it. But I sometimes wonder."

A knock at the door, though very timid, jarred the space of trust that had opened between the two men. Nevertheless it did not close like a flower or shiver into dust; it lingered on.

"Excuse me," said John as he got up to respond to the interruption. Again the knock. "All right, I'm coming!" he said under his breath: "Glory! Do they think I spend my time standing just inside the door waiting ready to open it?"

Theo grinned. "Now you look grim," he said as his abbot put his hand to the latch, and that made John laugh.

On his doorstep stood Brother Robert, visibly shaking; he went completely white when he glimpsed his novice master within. "Father, I came to apologize," he said.

THE
TWENTY-EiGHTH DAY

*J*ohn!"

He struggled up out of the waves of sleep at the sound of his name. "John!"

"What is it?"

He sat up then, completely alert. Brother Michael stood at his bedside in the dark room, carrying a lantern.

"I'm so sorry to trouble you."

"What is it?" John asked again.

"Brother Cyprian won't see the morning, I think. Now is the time to anoint him for his passing. I've had the oil ready and the bread and wine for the viaticum, but I didn't want to disturb you unless I felt sure."

Abbot John was already out of bed and fumbling on his belt over his night habit, feeling with his feet for his sandals, before Michael finished speaking.

He shook his head as Brother Michael murmured again, "I'm so sorry, John; you've been so very tired."

In the dense mist of four o'clock, the lantern barely sufficed to light their way, but they walked light-foot through the wet air of the night, across from the cloister to the infirmary.

In the little, square chamber where Brother Cyprian lay dying, John made his checks for himself and affirmed Brother Michael's conclusions.

Michael hung the lantern on the iron bracket. The small

radiance of the night-light already stood duty for a sacristy lamp among the holy things Michael had gathered ready on a fair linen cloth.

"It is consecrated," he said. "'Tis our reserve sacrament. I judged the time short, maybe."

Abbot John nodded. He picked up the stole from the table, kissed it, and put it on. The time looked short indeed. He dipped his hand in the holy water and sprinkled it on Cyprian's head: "*Asperges me Domine . . . Miserere me Deus.*" He dipped the bread in the wine and placed it in the slack mouth. "*Accipe, frater, Viaticum Corporis Domini nostri Jesu Christi, qui te custodiat ab hoste maligno, et perducat in vitam aeternam. Amen.*"

He dipped his thumb in the sacred oil and slowly marked the sign of the cross on Cyprian's waxy brow. "*Per istam sanctam unctionem indulgeat tibi Dominus quidquid deliquisti.*"

A trickle of golden oil ran sideways into the gray bristles of Cyprian's eyebrow. John had no time even to take the scrap of linen laid ready and wipe the trickle away. With a thin, indeterminate, extended expiration, the breath of life departed from Cyprian's body. He was gone.

"*Proficiscere, anima Christiana, de hoc mundo.*" Abbot John sent the son of his house forth on the great voyage beyond all sight and knowing, beyond every horizon to his eternal home, asking Christ to pilot him safely over—his welcome, his guide, and the wind in the sail of his going.

The two men stood in silence at their brother's side, John gently stroking the aged head.

"Thank you, John," said Michael quietly. "That would have meant a lot to him. I can do the rest. Go back to your bed. It'll be a while yet before the morning."

THE
TWENTY-NINTH DAY

The sun shone joyously now, and the rains of so wet a winter seemed to have finally ceased. Several clear days brought sweet relief to the spirit as the year turned toward the light and the days slowly lengthened. But the wind still blew very cold.

Abbot John and Brother Michael stood in conversation among the herb beds of the infirmary garden, leaning on the wall that enclosed the place where the old men sat out in the sun in the afternoons. After ascertaining that all was in place for moving Brother Cyprian's body to the chapel, John had gone briefly to see for himself the good progress reported in William's condition. He paused to talk this over with Michael before turning his mind to the mountain of tasks awaiting him.

Michael, eating a wrinkled yellow apple from the store ("Mmm! These are nice!"), listened to John's assessment of their charge's state of health.

"You have cared for him so well, as ever. It was grand to see him sitting up and managing a whole bowl of broth and reassuring to hear that cough and see all that rubbish being expelled from inside him. He told me that you'd shown him the breathing exercises, and I see you'd lit the oil vaporizer to keep the air from drying out. I think you had lavender and pine in there, didn't you? Perfect. And the chimney in that room *never* smokes, whichever way the wind blows, which helps. I have nothing to add to what you have in place already. You've done us proud. He'll be coughing for some days yet, and very tired and weak for some time still after that. It'll take a while for his flesh and skin to heal up completely too, but it's all clean, no poison, nothing gone bad. My concern for him now is all that we cannot touch and see. What can we do for his soul? As far as I can judge, he had lost his hold on most of what is good and true a long time ago, and what's left that could have been redeemed is all seared and terrified and shuttered away now. He's so tense and watchful, keeps us so much at arm's length. What can we do?"

Michael considered this as he nibbled the last bits of his apple and threw the core into the bed of herbs.

"Well, he needs to relax, be less on guard. He needs to learn to trust us."

"That's clear enough, but I don't see how we can coax him into trusting us at the same time as planning to throw him out as soon as he's halfway healed."

"True. Will you be asking the brothers again if he can stay?"

"I shall indeed. Oh, Michael, how *could* we turn him away? How could we? But I dare not force it upon them. I can only appeal to their compassion. The hardest thing is having the power to overrule but not using it, accepting that not everyone sees things my way—I have to respect that."

Michael nodded, seeing the force of this. "People are never lovable when they are tense and scared," he commented. "Their faces go hard and pinched; their eyes look like something boiled. Unhappy people get mean and suspicious, always looking out for what others might be doing to them, never at peace. Happy people look soft and quiet, gentle, at ease in the world and with themselves, even when they have ailments and troubles to bear. I can't help thinking, if we could help this poor soul to calm down, relax, trust you and me even if no one else, then he might look less grim and dangerous. He needs to laugh."

"Laugh? I can't imagine William laughing. I've seen the occasional wry smile twist his face out of place, but I can't visualize him laughing whatsoever!"

A sudden resolve seemed to enter Michael's body. "I guess you will want the community to come to a mind on this matter," he said, "but even if they won't have him, he will be able to stay with us until Easter, won't he? To recover properly and get strong again, and so we can find him a safe place to go?"

"Yes," said John thoughtfully, considering this, picturing William and his present state of health. "*Yes*," he repeated with finality.

"Then," Michael replied, "I'll wager you ten Hail Marys and a pot of Brother Walafrid's really good muscle rub I can make him laugh before Easter."

THE
THIRTIETH DAY

*B*rother Conradus hesitated. He lifted his hand to knock at the door of the abbot's lodging, then paused. He felt suddenly very shy. Though he'd had plenty of opportunity to observe and listen to his new abbot in Chapter and at the office, this would be the first time he had been summoned to discuss his own progress in the novitiate. What he had seen so far of Abbot John gave him the impression of a serious, even rather forbidding man: tired, preoccupied, and not especially cheerful. They had borne Brother Cyprian's body to the burial ground on this day at first light; and Brother Conradus had observed the dark weariness and sadness of his abbot's composed, quiet face as he spoke the prayers and they laid the worn-out old body in the cold earth, beside Father Aelred who had died last summer. John looked bleak.

Conradus had not been eager in his anticipation of their meeting. But he began to feel foolish and conspicuous standing in the cloister just outside the door of the abbot's lodging. So he gathered his courage and knocked. After a moment the heavy oak door opened, and Abbot John welcomed him in with a smile. Brother Conradus did not think he had seen Abbot John smile before. He felt both intrigued and encouraged by the warmth and kindness he saw in his abbot's face.

John invited him to sit by the fire, for which Conradus felt very grateful. The east wind outside blew so bitter it got past every layer of wool, got into his ears like shafts of ice, and smote painfully against his face when he walked across from the wood yard. Appreciatively, he turned toward the friendly glow on the hearth.

Abbot John had been briefed for this conversation by his novice master. "Brother Conradus has his heart in the right place, but he does not find the life easy," Theodore had said. "He feels it a privilege to be here, but finds the complexity of daily life and liturgy very bewildering. We need to help him find an area where he can really excel, to give him confidence. Shame and failure do not make a man humble; they make him depressed and inclined to fumble everything. The key to this will be finding something—anything—that Brother Conradus is actually good at."

John considered the young man sitting nervously in the unaccustomed grandeur of a chair. The novitiate had only benches and stools, and the same was true of the home he had come from. Only the nobility had chairs; too much craftsmanship went into them for the purses of common folk, and the man who owned the land owned the trees. Even apart from the chair, finding himself alone in the company of the abbot felt intimidating. Brother Conradus looked subdued and somewhat overwhelmed.

"Are you . . ." John thought it might be unfair to ask this question, but felt the need to establish some honesty and reality between them. ". . . are you afraid of me?" He wondered anxiously if all the novices thought of him as grim.

Brother Conradus looked at him in blank terror now. He had no idea what the correct answer to this question was supposed to be.

"That wasn't a trick," said John hastily. "I meant . . . really."

"Yes!" gasped Brother Conradus. This frightened reply put the abbot in mind of a day in his boyhood when his mother had asked him to move the pile of firewood seasoning in the yard into the shelter of the woodshed, nearly empty as summer approached. As the pile diminished, John had become aware of an anxious sound, a little whimpered grunt of terror occasionally repeated. He had continued his task, but going carefully, eventually revealing a young rabbit that had taken shelter there and now lay immobilized with fear. It didn't move until he bent to stroke it, and then it fled. The novice's scared affirmative quite vividly recalled to the abbot's mind that rabbit's whimper of fear. John wished being the abbot didn't do this to people. He thought that if he could only induce Conradus to see his humanity instead of his status, the young monk might breathe easier in his company.

"Well, I am only John," he said. "My father was a soldier, and he died before I knew him. I grew up being the man of the house. I have a younger sister but no brothers. They depended on me quite a lot for strength and protection, though my mother would never admit it. Leaving them when I chose to come here was the hardest thing I ever had to do. And possibly selfish too. My mother is a wise woman. She taught me and my sister to read—but secretly, because she knows more than folk feel easy with in a woman. People need wise women, but they do not always like them. And she knows the healing arts. Before I came here, she taught me all that she had learned, and besides that, for a summer an itinerant surgeon lodged with us in exchange for letting me help him and glean all I could from him. After I came here, they eventually sent me to work in the infirmary. I read the books by Abbess Hildegard in the library—we have them both, *Liber Simplicis Medicinae* and *Liber Compositae Medicinae*. And we have Avicenna's *Canon of Medicine* too, which is worth its weight in gold—it has almost everything in it. You might have seen them; or . . . not."

It was sometimes hard for John to remember that others did not share his enthusiasm for finding out what ailed people and making them well again. And it did not escape his notice that the young man, who had begun to look interested as John diverted his attention away from himself, looked now thoroughly alarmed again. Clearly he had not been filling what free time he had delving eagerly into the deliberations of Avicenna and Abbess Hildegard.

Abbot John persisted, "So I am nothing special—only John, and my hands love to heal. It rejoices my heart to help a man sit up in bed and drink a little broth when only two days before death had him already dragged half out of this world. I am abbot because somebody has to be. Perhaps you will be the abbot in your turn one day. In the meantime please, brother, will you do two things for me?"

John felt relieved to see Brother Conradus looking intrigued again.

"The first thing is, will you hold me in your prayers and, when you pray for me, remember I am only John who loves to heal people? In this present obedience I am often out of my depth, so often weary and confused, and always ill at ease among the high and mighty. When we meet, yes, you call me father and abbot, as I call you brother. But when you pray for me, pray for John."

Brother Conradus had visibly relaxed as he listened to this and looked at his abbot with an entirely different light in his eyes. "What was the second thing?" he asked, more confident now.

"The second thing is, just as you did not know me, so I do not know you. What have you learned from your family and the years before you came here? What sets your soul afire and rejoices your heart?"

Something of the light died in Brother Conradus's eyes, and he hung his head as his face flushed.

John waited a moment, but the young man did not speak. "Brother, I'm so sorry," said John. "Have I—did I—what's wrong?"

His own discomfiture proved the key to restoring the novice's courage. He looked up again and smiled shyly at his abbot. *Only John who loves to heal people*, he reminded himself silently.

"The things I enjoy doing are not as worthwhile as yours," he said humbly. "Reading is difficult for me. I can read, but it goes slowly and hard. The Latin and the Greek are too complicated. I try and then forget what I have learned before even the next lesson. I can copy in the scriptorium without difficulty, but I do not enjoy the work. The infirmary work makes me feel really, really queasy, and I know nothing of farming. I am not powerfully built, and the heavier work is tiring, though three months in the wood yard is building up some strength. I like the garden though—the kitchen garden."

He stopped, and John felt the lad's gaze weighing him up. Eventually he seemed to come to a decision: this abbot, who was only John and who loves to heal people, could be trusted.

"In my family, what people liked best was eating——please don't laugh," he said hastily, and John didn't laugh. "We never had much money, so we couldn't really go anywhere or buy anything much, but we did have to eat. We had a bit of land, from money that my grandfather gave my mother when she married my father. And we had our own cow and kept a pig—and hens, of course. We had an orchard, and my dad grew the best vegetables of anyone around. So we put our hard work into that, and we always had such delicious food to eat. It was something to look forward to every day—coming home for supper."

Conradus paused again, unsure of himself, then made up his mind and continued in a rush, like someone confessing a terrible secret. "But for me, the thing that really set my soul afire, as you said—and I'm sorry, this is going to sound so trivial, so shallow—I'm sorry, Father, to be so frivolous, but it's true!"

"What is?" asked John, bewildered.

"The thing I like best is making cakes and pastries. See, my grandfather—this is how he got his money, it was a gift from the king who appreciated what he could do—my grandfather was the head pastry cook for King Edward. Not *our* king obviously, I mean Edward the First. And he had taught our mother how to make all the dainty things they eat at court. Well, of course she couldn't work in the kitchen of a noble house because of being only a woman and because she had us at home to look after anyway. But she cooked for us, and—like your mother—she taught us what she knew. And that's what I love doing. And I'm sorry. In Lent and all, it seems even more frivolous. There's no call for such dainties here."

He glanced shamefacedly at his abbot who was sitting quite still, his lips parted in wonder, his eyes aglow.

"No call for your gifting here? Oh, mother of God," said John, "there is!"

Brother Conradus looked at him in disbelief. "But . . ." He frowned, puzzled. "But the food here is so . . . well, it's. . . . The food here is . . . er . . . plain. Because this is a holy place. And cakes and pastries are very worldly, Father."

John began to laugh. "The cooking isn't plain, it's atrocious—and it's kind of you to attribute it to holiness, but maybe you don't know us as well as in time you will! We haven't contrived a special spiritual cuisine on purpose, brother! That's just the best that Brother Cormac can do—amazing though that may sound to you. And none of the rest of us has anything better to offer. Where have you been working? In the wood yard and the scriptorium? You tell Father Theodore from me, you are to go directly—*directly*, mind—to the kitchen—today and onward. Tell Brother Cormac I sent you and that I want you to make the bread and the pies. This Sunday for Jesu's sake let's have a break from all the gray stodge and roots and greens; 'tis permitted for the Sabbath, even in Lent. Make us some honey cakes, my brother—make us anything you like. Tell Brother

Cormac—no, wait, I'll go there right now and tell him myself to expect you. Oh—was there—is there—are there other things you need to talk to me about?"

Brother Conradus was smiling. He looked like a different being from the timid, dejected boy who had knocked on the door. "Even in Lent you can make some delicious things to eat, Father. It's not hard to do—you don't have to be clever or anything, like you do to care for sick people or paint illuminations or write a sermon. You just have to understand food. I can make us some almond milk while we are fasting from the milk of the cow. And there is a sort of cream you can make from oats. There's a thing I can make like crispy pancakes, but you don't need milk or butter. You can do it from just beans and flour and oil, then the oat cream and honey. And a crumble—oh, and I know how to make a really good sourdough, Father. With some dates in it, cooked quick in small rolls and eaten hot, it can be delicious. And," he added confidingly, "once Lent is past, my mother has the recipe for the cake that the Lady Giacoma di Settesoli used to make for Father Francis of Assisi: the very same one that he specially asked for, the last thing before he died. I carry that recipe with me in my head, for I am bound not to write it down. When we have all the eggs at Easter, instead of boiling them, I can make that, and with the yolks a rich cheese custard. And then there is this apple and raisin cheesecake that mother used to make . . . "

Father John wiped his hand across his mouth. "*Jesu Domine Christe!* Have mercy, son, you'll set me dribbling! Go back to your lessons. I'll speak to Brother Cormac. From this hour hence, your work is in the kitchen, where you belong."

THE
THIRTY-FIRST DAY

*D*ominus vobiscum.*"

"*Et cum spiritu tuo.*"

"*Benedicamus Domino.*"

"*Deo gratias.*"

"*Fidelium animæ per misericordiam Dei requiescant in pace.*"

"Amen."

"*Pater noster, qui es in cælis, sanctificetur nomen tuum. Adveniat regnum tuum. Fiat voluntas tua, sicut in cælo et in terra. Panem nostrum quotidianum da nobis hodie. Et dimítte nobis debita nostra, sicut et nos dimíttimus debitoribus nostris. Et ne nos inducas in tentationem: sed líbera nos a malo. Amen.*"

As the community filtered quietly out of the chapel to take up the afternoon's work, Brother Thomas did not move from his stall. When Theodore rose to go, Tom reached out a hand to detain him. "Please," he mouthed as Theo raised his eyebrows inquiringly.

Theodore sat down again. Eventually they were alone in the friendly peace of the chapel, with its vague aroma of incense and beeswax and stone.

"Can I talk to you?"

"Must it be here? No? Shall we go up to the novitiate?"

They kept the silence of the cloister as they walked from the chapel and up the novitiate stairs. They found Brother Felix collating the Easter music the young men had practiced in the morning and Brother Boniface replenishing spent supplies of firewood.

"God reward you. Thank you so much," said Theodore pleasantly. "It's still bitter cold; I do appreciate the fire. Thank you so much. I'll see you at Vespers."

Brother Tom reflected that this was possibly the most diplomatic form of "go away" he'd ever heard. The young men hurried to complete their tasks as Tom and Theo each pulled a stool close to the fire, and the novices unobtrusively left the room, closing the door behind them without a sound.

"Theo, have you been making them *practice* closing doors quietly?" Tom asked with a grin.

"Yes. Why not?" the novice master replied. "I wish you'd practiced when you were their age. Now what's amiss?"

"It's William. Oh. You don't look surprised."

Theodore didn't answer. He swiveled on his stool and bent toward the fire, holding his hands to the warmth. Tom, like most men, told his troubles more easily away from another man's direct gaze. Theodore occasionally had cause to reflect that if he had one pastoral resource that he valued above all others, it would probably be the fire. He remembered from his own novitiate days Abbot Peregrine making exactly that use of his fire, though Theo hadn't realized it at the time. Later he had stumbled upon the technique through his own observations. "Tell me," said Theo then, when Tom still didn't speak.

"I hate the way I feel about him, Theo." Tom blurted out his distress. "And I hate myself for feeling as I do. When he first came here—well, you know; you heard what I had to say—all I knew was that I hated him. But it made everything different, did something to me, seeing him choking and throttling, hanging from that rope. *Sancta Maria*, it scared the life out of me! And of course I had to save him. How could I not? I didn't even think about it. After that I stopped hating him, just suddenly—snap! Stopped.

"But I'm left with this awful bitter residue, this kind of toxic sludge. It still rankles so badly: what he did to Father Peregrine, how he made him suffer on purpose like that. And I don't know what to do with it—that resentment, I mean, and the sore it's left inside me. I can see well enough what Christ is asking of me: to get over it, basically. I'm meant to let go of what's gone by and move on.

"But I need him to see that what he did was so *wrong* and that it mattered. And if he won't—then what? Where does that leave me? How can I be a monk when I feel like this? What can I do with all this old bitterness? I can't see how to turn it into something different. And inside a man, the living soul, it's like a cistern, a kind of closed reservoir with no outlet. What way is there for it to drain away? It just seems to stay in there, stewing and fermenting and not getting any less. How can I get rid of it? What am I to do?"

Theo waited, not speaking, watching the fall of ash and the red glow of the burning wood. But that seemed to be all Tom wanted to tell him.

"Haven't you talked this through with Father John?" asked Theo then.

"No," replied Tom miserably. "I've hardly spoken with him at all these past two weeks."

"Well," said Theo, "that's the first thing then, isn't it? You'd better sort that out. But that's something separate. When it comes to William, I think there are two things. The first is, sooner or later you'll have to talk to him. You need him to have to listen to you telling him what he did to you, as well as what he did to Father Peregrine. That's the main thing. Don't wait for a convenient moment or a chance meeting; ask Father John if you can use the parlor and make a time to talk it through honestly. It's not just your problem; it's his as well. But there's a second thing, and it's just as important.

"When you go to talk to him, you might be thinking that as

soon as he hears what you have to say, he'll be sorry, and it can all be sorted out quickly because he'll see your point of view. But it might not be that simple. Presumably he has a point of view of his own, and you may be as unaware of his point of view as he is of yours. Do you follow me? Everyone has a point of view. It's a matter of trying to stand where the other man is standing and seeing it how he sees it, and then it starts to make some sense. But since you do actually have a point of view of your own filling your lines of sight, grasping how someone else sees things is just the hardest thing to do. I mean, I suppose Father Matthew had a point of view when I was a novice and he was making the best job he knew of being my novice master. But I couldn't see his point of view then, and I still can't even now that he's dead and I'm a novice master myself. I am too entrenched in my own point of view; how we saw things stood too far apart. I will never understand. And it may be the same for you; even so, you'll have to try.

"You look a bit bewildered. All I'm saying is, you need to talk to him, but be prepared to listen as well. Then see how you go. See what changes. And, Tom, I want you to know: every day, through all of this—we see only too clearly how hard this is for you—John and Michael and I are praying for you especially."

THE
THIRTY-SECOND DAY

*O*n this first day of spring, the brothers moved to the summer pattern of hours. The longer days as the light returned brought hope of warmer times, but the wind still cut like a knife. Summer was no more than a dream carried in the heart's memory. They got up in the dark as usual and came out of Compline into silence in the dark. But the year was turning.

As they met for Chapter, they heard Benedict's wise counsel about the abbot's responsibility to see that the hours the brothers keep in their work and worship and mealtimes foster a quiet and peaceable household, giving no one cause for grumbling, and so promoting the salvation of their souls. John privately thought that those who were inclined to grumble would do so whatever he did for them; but he did not include that observation in his comments on the chapter.

As the novices left the chapter house, Abbot John reflected, as he watched them go, on what a contented and well-disciplined bunch this present crop seemed to be. He blessed the day Abbot Peregrine had appointed Father Theodore to watch over the novitiate. Brother Felix, the last out, closed the door with perfect silence behind them.

The abbot then heard his brothers' confessions of minor faults. Brother Damian resumed his seat, having been forgiven for needlessly breaking silence yesterday morning. Time to address the business of the day. On some subliminal level,

Abbot John registered an anxious tightening in his belly as he started to speak.

"Brothers, I must bring to you again the question of what we should do with Father William de Bulmer. After that awful day when he tried to take his life, we have cared for him, and we have seen him through the time of acute sickness that followed on—it was connected. He is much recovered now, but he has been knocked around, body and soul. He needs us still. I come to ask you again today: please, won't you give him a chance?"

"Did we not decide this already, Father? Surely the community has voted."

"Yes, Father Chad. We did vote. We did decide. But I think things are different now. The extent of his desolation has become apparent to us. It seems to me appropriate that we think again. I believe he needs our shelter. We are making progress. While he is with us, he is safe.

"Brothers, I intend to bring him one more time to Chapter, that he may ask your mercy and plead for admittance to our community. You know his story better than when first he came. When he begged admission before, there was almost no discussion, no wisdom offered. Can we do this properly this time? Will you put your minds to it now? We need to explore it carefully, mull it over, not just close our hearts to him and make an end of it—and of him, mayhap. Speak, brothers."

The short silence that followed these words was broken by the cultured and dignified voice of the precentor, who rose to speak. "Father, the events of the past days have surely served to underscore Brother Thomas's misgivings. To attempt to take one's life is a very grave sin. So we see already, just as we feared, having been with us only a matter of days, this man is already rushing recklessly into sin."

Others murmured quiet assent at Father Gilbert's words, but the bold challenge in his eye faltered as Abbot John met his gaze.

"I cannot find it in me," John answered his precentor, "when a man has been despised and rejected by everybody to blame him if he judges his life no longer worth the living. Could you bear it? Could I? When he speaks to me—to any of us—his manner is smooth and easy. He is a proud man. He refuses to admit or betray his emotions. That does not mean he does not feel. But, Father Gilbert, you are quite correct in what you say. It is a sin for a man to try to take his own life."

"Father John . . . " Brother Stephen got to his feet to address his abbot. ". . . I've been up on the farm and haven't had much to do with this man—apart from being there when Brother Thomas thankfully found him in the barn, of course. I've heard what's been said of him—which has not been much, in truth, and mainly by Brother Thomas. You'll understand me right, I hope: I am not wanting to play down anything, but Brother Thomas is not given to half measures. It may be that the man is more malleable to our ways than we have imagined. It seems only fair at least to do as someone told me Father Theodore thought in the first place and give him a trial. But I take Father Gilbert's point: what he did *is* sin—grave sin, not something to wink at—and what he did to our Abbot Peregrine was nothing funny furthermore. I do not see that we can simply say, 'That's all right, lad, come on in!' Our Rule lays down that we chastise a man for serious faults—you read it to us yourself just the other day, or Father Chad did or somebody. Give him his trial, let's be fair, but for what he's done he should be beaten—that is my view."

"Ah, Jesu mercy!" the abbot exploded in anguish. "He is battered and bruised and burned and half hung himself, and not ten days ago Michael sat up all night to pull him back from the brink of death as he burned up with fever. What more do you want? Beat him? For Jesu's sake, mercy! Does there never come a time when we simply forgive? Yes, of course he's done things wrong—serious things, dreadful things. As far as I can make out he's been an out-and-out scoundrel the whole of his adult life and probably his childhood too! There'll be no 'come in, little lamb' about this. We do it with our eyes open.

"But I tell you, brother, what you do to him, you do to yourself. That's the lesson of his life. What he did to our abbot has come around and settled on his own head. And now it's come back around to us. What is the Spirit saying, asking of us? Maybe let's sing that tune again and try to get it right this time. Punishment, beating, sin, old grudges—for God's sake, let them go! Just give him a chance. Please! *Please!*"

Brother Paulinus, old and bent from so many years of gardening, his face rosy and weathered, his eyes bright as a robin's, pulled himself to his feet. "Nay, my lord abbot, we cannot do this just to please thee. It is not good to pull men's heartstrings and pressure thy brothers into choosing the way tha wants to go. It's thy right as our superior to decide thy own way if that's what pleases thee. But I would not judge that wise. Tha's opened this to us all to think on: then tha must hear and respect what men say."

His abbot inclined his head in acceptance of this. "I am so sorry, brother. Yes. But is there no one except me to speak for this man?"

His arthritic hand gripping the wood of his stall, his knees creaking a little, Brother Paulinus slowly sat down.

Brother Michael then stood. "I have something I've been ashamed to say, because I maybe ought not to have done it. It's been weighing on my conscience ever since. I said it from my heart, and at the time I never doubted it. But hearing all this now, I have such a horrible sinking feeling."

"Well, spit it out then," murmured Brother Tom under his breath.

"Thanks, Tom. Yes, I will." Well used to listening for the whispers of the dying and the frail, Brother Michael did not miss much of what anyone said.

"Well, what happened was that I had William in my care in the infirmary, and he took a fever and trouble in his chest because of breathing in what should have been swallowed when he strung himself up in the barn. He was grievously ill, and I sat up with him all night when the crisis came. Sometimes— not always but sometimes—if we just keep talking to someone, it can hold their spirit here. Sometimes they go so far out of their bodies that they can't get back, and we lose them then; but if we can sit and talk to them, they sometimes stay to listen, and it turns them around toward earth and life and warmth instead of drifting out into death. When they are old or too ill for the body to be safe housing for the spirit anymore, we just wrap them in prayer and bless them on their way and let them go, as we did for Brother Cyprian; he was full of years, his life was complete. But we, Brother—sorry, Father—John and I— we judged William's time was not yet, and his way lay with us, and what Christ was doing in his life was not complete. So we saw it as our task in Christ's service to keep him here by every means we could. Br—Father John talked with him and spent time with him and tended to his wounds to show him without words what mercy is. I could as well have done those tasks myself, of course, and he—Father John—he didn't say what he was doing, but I know because I've done it myself. He was opening up the way of mercy to the man's imagination so that he would see the way and discover how to walk in it for himself. You have to show people, you see, if they can't do it naturally. Compassion, forbearance, gentleness—you have to show them. And much has been said here about our Abbot Peregrine and how cruelly this William treated him. But I nursed Peregrine day in and day out in the last months of his life, and I tell you, whatever William may have dished out to him, I'll wager he got thrown right back at him and plenty more to follow. I loved Abbot Peregrine, loved him with all my heart, but no one ever simply pushed him around."

"Michael . . ." As Brother Michael paused, a little breath-
less, not used to speaking his mind before such a large gathering, his abbot recalled his purpose to mind, saying gently,
"Michael, get to the point."

Brother Michael nodded. "Forgive me. I didn't mean to
be garrulous. The thing is, this all is the point. It's a complex
thing. It's not as simple as 'He's a sinner? Right then, let's throw
him away.' Is it? Anyhow, what I needed to explain is that I sat
up with him all that night, and I had to keep talking to him. I
don't know if you ever sat up and talked to someone the whole
night long, when you've been working all day already, with just
the firelight and a candle; but it takes you into a different kind
of place from the everyday. You don't talk out of your considered judgment and utter cheery platitudes or mundane patter,
because that won't bring them back. You have to latch on to the
holy Spirit of Christ and speak right out of the deepest place of
your own heart and soul, else they won't listen to you; the soul
will just slip out of the man.

"And what I'm coming to—brothers, I'm so sorry, I think
you might be angry with me for this—but what I said to him is
that he would be safe here, that we would not turn him away
or abandon him. Never. I told him we have a place for him here
because we are not complete without him. Now, he was burning
up with fever and shaking with chills, and he was as sick as it's
possible to be and still be alive. But I wouldn't like to say he
didn't hear me. When he tried to take his life up on the farm, he
really meant it. He saw no future and no hope, and he wanted
to get out. And when that failed, he fell into sickness. He's just
been trying to get out of his body because the earth is not a safe
place for him anymore. And he may be everything we fear and
more—though I doubt it, because everyone's more normal than
we tend to suppose, if we aren't afraid of them and treat them
gently—but I don't see how we can be part of hounding him
to death. Suicide is grave sin, you say, Father Gilbert? Well,

what's the first thing you think he will do if we throw him out of here? Except, if we do, I shall go with him."

Abbot John looked up sharply, startled at these last words. Brother Michael sat down, his face flushed and patchy from nerves and emotion. To work behind the scenes, quietly, was his chosen way. He had never spoken so much before the whole community or anywhere else.

"Go with him?" Father Chad spoke now. "Did you say that if we ask him to leave, you will actually leave our house to go with him, Brother Michael?"

Quickly, before Michael could reply, Father Theodore rose to his feet. "He did, Father, and might need to reconsider that if it came to it, but let's not get sidetracked."

"But surely," Father Chad persisted, "this is the kind of thing we feared! Brother Michael speaking of leaving us, the Rule with its guidance for chastising those who commit serious faults just set aside, the grave sin of suicide dismissed as understandable—this man is causing mayhem, and he's only been with us three weeks! What comes next? What kind of a Trojan horse will he turn out to be?"

"No kind of Trojan horse, Father Chad." It was the first time John could ever recall hearing Theodore sound thoroughly irritated. "The whole point of a Trojan horse is that you don't know what dangers it carries inside. If this man murdered us all in our beds, I doubt we should have underestimated him. And he is not randomly causing chaos in our community; we're managing that nicely for ourselves. What he's brought to the surface here was there already. We see things differently; we never needed to notice or explain that before now. Good. We know each other better now.

"The central problem, as I see it, is that our focus is wrong. If you don't focus on the right thing, when you let the arrow fly, you miss the mark. Your eyes always lead the way. Some of us are focusing on Father William and are badly misguided to do so. He is afraid, desperately afraid, and fear is catching. Fear is spreading like a fire among us. And, Tom, you have blessed no one by fanning the flames. If we look at his fear and at his sin, if we focus on the man, we shall miss our mark. He will end up dead—by his own hand or by the brutality of others—and we shall be the lesser for allowing that to happen. People know what happened between him and Abbot Peregrine. They will watch to see what we do. If we turn him out, he will be seen as fair game to be kicked to death. Do you not know how mobs think—if 'think' is the word?

· "Some of us are not focusing on Father William but on the community—the Rule, the system of discipline, how the abbot should conduct himself, our stability, our security, our equilibrium—identifying quite accurately that Father William's arrival has blown a hole through all of that. And note, my brothers, it has *already happened*. We are too late to speculate what effect it may have if we let this man join us. He has joined us, he's here, and he brought his chaos in with him. His own private storm has already joined us right inside our boat.

"But, if we intend to get this right, to hit the mark, we have only one hope: and that's not to focus on William, not to focus on ourselves, but to focus on our Lord. There's a storm—so what? What did Jesus do? He rebuked his friends who had so little faith, and he told the storm to be still. We are the friends. William carries the storm. Christ's peace is adequate to address the situation.

"There is a story Christ told, of a rogue tree that did not bear fruit. The only solution seemed to be to cut it down, throw it away as firewood. But the story offered another possibility: leave it in the ground for a year; feed it, water it, care for it, and if it still proves fruitless, *then* remove it.

"What do we know of what has gone into this man? As Brother Michael said, if you want people to understand and see the way of Christ, to have even a chance of walking in it, you have to model it for them. All right, he's an Augustinian friar; he should surely know the way already. Well, he does not. So why don't we show him? Let's give him a year—our twisty crab apple tree—and mulch in all the loving-kindness we normally keep only for each other. At the end of a year, if we really think he's a bad lot, then discreetly we can find him another place to be, by which time his own despair will have quietened and the mob will have forgotten him. That's my recommendation. Oh, and I should say, when I came to this house, my novice master, who liked to do everything by the book, God rest him, thought I was a total dead loss. I was wretched, I was unhappy, I was scared, and everything I touched seemed to break or turn to ashes. And I thank God that Father Peregrine saw fit to be gentle with me and to give me a chance."

Father Theodore sat down.

"Brother Thomas," said the abbot, looking very directly at Tom, "you have played a central part in this. Have you anything new to say to us today?"

Brother Tom looked at him thoughtfully, then rose to his feet. "Yes, but it's all in a muddle inside me. That's why I haven't spoken before. It's not thought through. I can only speak out of my heart now. My head's just a mess."

"Nothing new there then," murmured Cormac with a grin.

"I feel different now from the way I felt before. If I imagine watching him walk out of our gates, knowing that he might be set upon, that he would be alone or even string himself up from a tree in some quiet spot, I simply can't bear the thought of it now. Somehow life seems to be insisting that this is our problem, like when you bring an orphan lamb to a ewe whose babe has died. She'll want nothing to do with it, will kick it good and hard, not let it feed. So you skin the dead lamb and tie the fleece about the orphan's body. The ewe will still act suspicious, but with patience you can generally make it work, get through it, though it's sometimes a bit of a tussle.

"When I came through the door of that barn to see him dancing and swinging from the crossbeam, it turned me right over. I didn't say to myself, 'Thank God, there's one problem less.' I didn't even stop to think at all. When it actually came to it, I just grabbed him and held onto him for dear life, until Stephen could come and help get him down.

"But you know—I haven't said this to anyone—I think he must be wearing Father Peregrine's old habit. Because when I held him in my arms . . . "

Tom stopped, discomfited.

"Don't misunderstand me now. That habit was clean and all. But when Father Peregrine was sick, most days I had to lift him up into his chair or out of it again. And when he wept, which he did often enough, I would hold him in my arms to comfort him. Then when I put my arms around William de Bulmer to take his weight off the rope, well, he smelled the same. And it's been all muddled up in my head ever since. As though, like one lamb is the same as another lamb inasmuch as they all need to be fed and accepted or you haven't got a flock, so there's a sense somehow in which he *is* Father Peregrine, in needing to be taken care of, needing someone who will try to understand a bit.

"Now you know me, and I'm not a theologian, so you'll just have to overlook it if I've got this wrong; I may be speaking out of turn. But isn't the whole idea of the body of Christ that what you do to him you do to me and you do to yourself? Like there is no division in truth: no me and him but only us?

"He's a pesky nuisance and the wiliest beggar I ever had the misfortune to meet, this Augustinian. I'd never trust him behind me where I couldn't see, the Lord only knows what he might be cooking up. But I have to say, he does seem to have been sent to us. I little like to confess to it, but if I'm honest, I've changed my mind. I'm with Brother—sorry, Father—John now: this thing looks to me to have Christ's fingerprints all over it.

I'm only sorry it's taken me as long as it has to see. And if you're looking for someone to beat for the sin of trying to take his life, ask yourself who pushed him to it. Maybe you'd better beat me."

"Father!" Father Gilbert took the opportunity to wedge a word in. "We are past time for Terce."

"And we have heard what we need to hear," said Abbot John. "I know we already voted once, but on Tuesday I'm bringing him back to you again, to beg admittance. We have to sort this out once for all, before Easter is upon us and all our guests. Take thought and pray through Sunday and Monday. Try to put yourself in his shoes, Christ's awful wolf-lamb."

THE
THIRTY-THIRD DAY

What do you want me to say?"

Tom had acted on Father Theodore's recommendation and sought a private audience with William, with his abbot's permission, in the small parlor where conversation of greater length was permitted.

He had begun well, he thought, setting forth candidly but without undue antagonism the unhealed wound of bitterness and outrage that still festered in him toward William, from the grievous cruelty of his taunting and humiliation of Father Peregrine.

It had felt clean and good to speak frankly about this to William, not fighting him but talking honestly about this root of enmity. William, thin and haggard, his eyes shadowed and his face drawn, wrapped in a woolen shawl over his habit, listened impassively as Tom unfolded the old rancor that had lodged in his heart. And when the tale was done, Brother Thomas looked to William expectantly for a response. William returned his gaze thoughtfully, then allowed his eyes to wander to the small window where a twig tapped insistently in the wind. "What do you want me to say?" he asked then, his gaze returning to Tom's face.

Tom stared at him in exasperation.

"You just don't get it, do you? What would be the point of that? I could say, 'I want you to say, "sorry,"' and you could say,

'well then, sorry!' And we would be locked out even more completely from what's real and true. I don't know what I want you
to say. I don't want you to say anything in particular. It doesn't
matter what you say. But I want you to care. I want you to
grasp what you did to Father Peregrine and what a torture to
him his disability was. He was so proud, so private, as a man.
He found it so hard to bear the humiliation. That was a deep,
bloody wound you twisted your knife in, and I think that's why
you did it. It suited your advantage. And you didn't care. You
just wanted your own way, and I find that appalling. I don't give
a toss, frankly, what you say. But I do want you to care."

Silence filled the room—silence in every space and corner,
in the voiceless dust and the clarity of sunbeams slanting
strong through the little windows. Then Tom sat back and
looked at the Augustinian, shaking his head. "Oh! This is useless, isn't it?"

He rose to leave, but William gestured for him to wait. So
Tom waited, and the silence continued. *I've been here before*, he
thought.

"I am not certain . . ." The leaf-dry voice picked its way cautiously. ". . . what you are asking of me. I get the drift of your
words, and I perceive your passion very well. But I think you
cannot realize that I do not know what it is to care, in the sense
you mean it.

"I understand how to make a choice. And when I choose, I
do so with my head, not my heart; that seems the only intelligent course of action to me. I recognize that the choices I made
with Father Columba have not served me well—neither in the
gamble of the short term nor in the long-term consequences.
They misfired. Choices do sometimes."

The prior paused. Once, then a second time he drew wheez-
ing breath to speak but did not continue. He shook his head,
frowning. "This is more difficult."

Indignation rose like a tide of blood in Tom when he

heard William's cool assessment that what he had done to Father Peregrine had not served him well. He checked his first instinct—to walk out in disgust on this sterile specimen of humanity—and decided to give the interaction one more chance. He continued to wait.

"'That particular choice—to exclude Abbot Columba, if I could, from our conference—I have come to recognize as having been destructive." The soft, hoarse voice continued, deliberating. "I expected to hurt him. He came to fight me. Hurting people is what happens in a fight. Of course I hurt him. I imagine he anticipated that. It was his intention to do me damage in his turn if he could—and he certainly did."

"Aye, but he fought fair! He debated well," interjected Brother Tom.

The prior looked at him thoughtfully. He nodded.

"He did. Columba fought fair always, but that was the difficulty. He was more than my match, so if I wanted to win (which I did), what would have been the use of fighting fair? For me, I mean. I fought to win. He knew I would. He needn't have come."

"True. But he knew you would be working some weaselly rotten scheme—and so you were! The reason he fought you at all was because you were up to no good, levering your own advantage, manipulating."

William looked at Tom carefully, and Tom wished that lambent, calculating gaze would not always make him feel so uneasy.

"Columba? What did he know of my personal motives? From whom?"

"He—well, he . . ." When he stopped and thought about it, Tom acknowledged that William's motivations had not been known to them when he and Abbot Peregrine had made the journey to St. Dunstan's. Only after their epic battle had the underlying politics of the conference come to light. "No," he said slowly, "you're right, he didn't know. He just sensed that whatever you were planning, you'd be up to no good."

William inclined his head in acceptance. "That's how it was. Adversaries. So he sensed I had something planned and thought he would block it if he could—whatever it was. Is that a choice you admire?"

This cast a different light on past events, which Tom felt unwilling to acknowledge. "He was right though, wasn't he?" he insisted stoutly. "Fishing rights! You *were* up to no good!"

The prior looked at him in genuine puzzlement. "Brother Thomas, I was the prior of St. Dunstan's. Our river formed part of our resources, as yours does here. Any pilgarlic who wanted to scrounge a free meal would poach in our woods, our stream, our fields. We lost significant annual revenue to our unsolicited and unconsenting hospitality. I wanted to stop them. Why is that unreasonable?"

Tom shook his head in disbelief. "Unreasonable? I don't know. But it was wondrous mean. You were rich. They were poor. What were a few fish in the brook to you?"

"I was the prior. They were our fish." William shrugged. "I cannot see why you object. But Columba knew nothing of that. He came looking for trouble. He got it."

Tom felt his understanding of events beginning to blur. He sat thinking, trying to frame what he felt in his gut into some kind of articulate form.

"I think," he said eventually, "that we are talking about two different things. Let me confess outright that I hadn't seen your point of view whatsoever, and when you put it like that, yes, I guess it was your river, your fish, your priory. Father Peregrine must have known what he would stir up in sticking his nose in, though you did invite him! But what I'm trying to get through to you is that you don't seem to care! You didn't care about the poor derelicts who stole the occasional fish—you were comfortable; they were on the brink of starvation, some of them, I should imagine. You ground Father Peregrine into the dust with your harassment and bullying, and you didn't care. And that's what I can't stomach. How could you not care?"

After a moment's thought, William responded, "I do not care because I am not like you. I prefer accuracy and effectiveness to emotion. It's not that I have no emotions, but I set them aside. They are not useful, I find. You care, but as a result you are not very precise. You wax passionate about the destitution of those who 'stole the occasional fish.' But it was not occasional, and you may take my word for it, not all of them were destitute, which we should have been had we stood aside and watched while others helped themselves to our wealth. You cared beyond measure about the well-being of your Abbot Peregrine. You cared about him so much that it seems to have made you very blasé about his motives. I hesitate to say it, for it seems presumptuous, but you even seem to care about me. Had our places been reversed on the farm a fortnight ago, I should probably have found it expedient to let you swing. Why not?

"You cared about the fact that I came here, very much; you were emphatically furious. You wanted to throw me back to the wolves, and you candidly wished me dead: that's passion! But when you actually found me dying, you were swift to save me.

"I am not like any of that. You choose with your heart. I choose with my head. And there is no going back from our choices. We do not ever come to the same crossroads again, though some of them appear very similar.

"Brother Thomas, will this do for you? Your beloved abbot is dead; it is late now for me to say I knew how deep the knife went and ask his forgiveness. Even so, without asking, I am confident of his forgiveness; for I well know what he was and the tides that moved his soul. There walked another man who thought mainly with his heart, though he had a good head on his shoulders too.

"But this I can do—see, I have watched and learned the idiom of this house."

William had such force of personality that Tom had felt no need to deal with him especially gently in this encounter. But beholding him now, he recollected how ill he had been. William, clutching the shawl close about his thin chest, his sallow face lined and almost gray with the physical exhaustion of illness, moved slowly and stiffly from where he sat to kneel before Brother Thomas. Bending low, letting the comforting shawl go from his grasp, he placed his hands around Tom's sandaled feet. "I confess my fault to you, my passionate brother, of so many mistakes: hard-heartedness, willful ignorance, unfaithfulness in my call as Christ's disciple. I have allowed compassion to grow cold and die in my soul. I did not care, and I do not care, and I wish I did. I ask your mercy, passionate brother. If I am permitted to stay with this community, if there is time, I ask you to help me learn how to love. Please. Help me find my way in. I ask forgiveness, my brother, of God and of you."

Softly and lightly, slowly, deliberately he kissed Tom's feet.

Why do these things happen to me? Tom asked himself, incredulously. *I'll wager nobody ever did this to Father Chad!*

He leaned forward and, mindful of flesh still sore and bruised, carefully put his hands on William's shoulders and raised him up.

"You are forgiven," he said. "God forgives you. I forgive you. I realize I owe you an apology of my own. It must have been hard to arrive desperate and exhausted on our doorstep—with your flesh torn, turned away from every refuge—and be greeted by me saying I wish you'd died in the fire. I am so sorry I said that and for every other unkindness that followed to ram it home. And I'm so glad you seem to survive everything, and you're still here for me to say I'm sorry. Teach you to love? Certainly, if in exchange you'll be willing to teach me to think before I speak."

William got up from his kneeling position. "You have more faith in me than you should. I have seen you in action, and I know full well that what you have just asked me is impossible. Besides, the good brothers may have me on the road again after tomorrow. But I thank you for being willing to forgive me; and I thank you for saving my life."

THE
THIRTY-FOURTH DAY

I am afraid."

Abbot John sat quietly on the low infirmary stool, allowing William to speak. The conversation so far had not been easy. In preparation for the Chapter meeting in the morning, when the professed brothers would vote one more time, John wanted to discuss thoroughly with William the attitudes and presentation of himself that tended to prejudice the community against him.

"They see you as aloof and indifferent," he told him, laying the matter before him more frankly than sensitivity and kindness would normally permit, because this would be William's last chance. If he didn't get it right this time, John could no longer shelter him. So he said the things that diplomacy might prefer to skirt around.

"They see no emotion in you. It makes you appear cold, and cruel as well, because of what they know of your rough treatment of Father Peregrine. When they look at you, they see you so cool and withdrawn, and they read it as contempt. If it is not so, we need to help them understand."

William had listened to him without moving, his face giving no sign of how the words were received. John sighed. "It seems impossible to reach you," he said, the finality of defeat in his voice. William's eyes flickered in unreadable response, and he stirred restlessly, trying to frame the reply he needed to make. Until at last, "I am afraid," he said.

John waited. William glanced at him and looked away again, then said what he had to say in cool and level tones. "I am frightened of what must pass tomorrow morning—frightened to step into the center of that room again and feel men's souls shrink away from me, the space in which I stand growing bigger and bigger, so that I become smaller and smaller before their revulsion and their distaste. And I recognize this. I remember it. I know it very clearly for what it is. This is what I did to Columba, to isolate and crush him. I almost succeeded. I remember the look on his face. I remember his dismay, his humiliation, his vulnerability; I almost had him. And now the isolation has returned in its full malevolence and intends to crush me. I think it will, for I do not have the strength he had. I did this. I set this in motion. It is mine. I know that, but I cannot face it. I am afraid to kneel down alone tomorrow and bear their judgment. This is not a mask I wear. The face you see is just my face—it is only myself, and I am consumed by fear. They loathe me, as everyone does. They will cast me out. They will find me unacceptable. There will be no place for me, and where shall I go?"

The unadorned honesty of these words entered John's heart like a knife. He sometimes thought his instinct to protect anyone who struck him as struggling and defenseless might be overdeveloped, and he knew well enough that the best solutions are those we find ourselves. But he felt the familiar fierce flare of compassion as he looked at William, rigidly still, his face as composed as a carving of stone, and understood now what he was seeing.

"They may not reject you," he said quietly. "I have done what I can."

William glanced at him in quick acknowledgment of this. "I do not understand," he said then, "why people hate those who achieve what is generally admired. It puzzles me. You will find it, for sure, as abbot of this monastery. You will have to win wealth, win fights, secure power and safety: if you don't, you will be useless as an abbot. But how do they think these things are achieved? By meekness? By largesse? I consolidated our situation at St. Dunstan's—made us powerful and strong. That's what I was supposed to do. Yet it has brought no admiration; only resentment, even hatred. Now that I see the way I took was the wrong one, I am lost to know what would have been the right way. What *was* required of me? And without the triumph of a victory, the thrill of an achievement—getting ahead of the pack—where is the sense of purpose in life, the spur to do well?" He looked at John in genuine bafflement.

John smiled. "Where do I start? Because I don't really see things in that light at all. The victory, the sense of achievement, for me comes from seeing things integrate and knit together. To watch one man—or one abbey or one family—streak ahead and win, making losers of all the rest, brings me no delight. I like seeing the flow of things looping around and feeding back into their origins, building up momentum, gradually increasing: love creating more love, kindness creating gratitude, and gratitude creating kindness; mercy creating trust and hope, trust and hope expanding the soul to be capable of compassion. It's a different kind of victory, I guess. Everyone wins."

William shook his head, perplexed. "I don't see how you can run an abbey along those lines."

"*Verti me alio vidique sub sole nec velocium esse cursum nec fortium bellum nec sapientium panem nec doctorum divitias nec artificum gratiam sed tempus casumque in omnibus.* King Solomon had it about right. But to time and chance, we add grace and Christ's kindness, and the miracle is accomplished. Meanwhile, forgive me if this sounds trite, don't be afraid of your fear, and don't be afraid to let the brothers see it tomorrow. This will be your only hope, brother. Let them see your heart. At the moment they aren't sure you have one. In this community at least, weakness will draw forth neither contempt nor attack but only compassion."

THE

THIRTY-FIFTH DAY

After Prime, in the heavy mist and uncertain light of dawn, Brother Benedict and Brother Boniface, hunched against the cold, hurried across from the novitiate to the infirmary, where they had been asked to provide cover, releasing Brother Michael to attend the Chapter meeting.

They found Michael methodically checking his charges in every room. He had tidied everything, even the stores, the linen shelves, the physic shelves, and the packs of herbs. Everything stood labeled and trim. The washing had been hung to dry; the few old men who lived there permanently now sat neatly beside their beds, tucked in with blankets.

A tray of bowls stood ready for the gruel that would be brought across later from the kitchen, and a great kettle of water hung over the fire in preparation for hot drinks.

"Whatever time did you start all this?" asked Brother Benedict in astonishment. "Holy Queen of heaven! You must have been up half the night!"

Michael smiled but seemed to Benedict not his usual self. "Are you all right, Brother Michael? What's amiss? There's something going on, isn't there?"

Michael shook his head. "All is well. If these old rogues leave you any space to think at all this morning, say a Hail Mary for us in Chapter. We have decisions to make today. Now, do you know what you're doing? Is there anything you're not sure about? You'll remember that Father Gerald likes chamomile tea with honey in it, and Brother Denis needs wrapping up warm against the cold or he gets earache."

Brother Benedict was laughing at him. "I know you don't get out much, but you're only going to Chapter! You'll be back before Terce. I think your little brood will survive until then—even in our tender care! Off you go, and you'll still be in time for the tail end of the Mass. We'll be just fine."

"All right then." Michael hesitated. "All right."

He took off his sandals and put on some warm woolen socks and his winter boots and took his cloak from the peg by the door, Brother Benedict watching him with curiosity. It was surely raw, chilly weather, but he did not recall that Brother Michael usually took such careful precautions before he dashed across to the cloister.

"Good-bye then," said Michael, his eyes very bright. "Take good care of them." And he was gone.

He did not go into Mass but went straight to the chapter house. He wanted to sit alone for a while and pray. It was dark and cold, with just one light burning: they would bring the lanterns through with them when they came from the morrow Mass.

"*Veni Sancte Spiritus*," whispered Michael, watching the glistening halo in the damp air about the candle flame. "*Veni Sancte Spiritus, et emitte caelitus lucis tuae radium. Veni, pater pauperum . . . veni, lumen cordium . . . Flecte quod est rigidum, fove quod est frigidum, rege quod est devium . . . veni Sancte Spiritus . . . veni . . . veni.* Come." He fell silent.

Eventually he heard the muted sounds of robed men and sandaled feet. The soft radiance of candle lanterns and the body heat of many brothers warmed the austerity of the room. The dawn light filtered diffidently through the small windows; the lanterns were still welcome.

Brother Michael watched William's quiet tread into the

chapter house, saw him take his place at the lowly seat near the door. His face looked drawn and pale. His expression remote, his close-cropped silver hair fringing the tonsure, his eyelids lowered in curtailment of his gaze, he looked like the personification of winter. But Michael was not wholly convinced that his heart was as cold as at first appeared.

The appointed chapter about disciplining latecomers to meals and divine office stretched out tediously—familiar and hard to concentrate on today. Their abbot had little comment to make upon it, except to remind them that during the Easter feast, when the abbey overflowed with visitors, the peace and order of daily life would be assured by more attention to punctuality, not by letting it slip.

After their confession of faults, the novices withdrew, and but a few confessions of little consequence came from the professed brothers.

"Then, if you are ready to hear his plea," Abbot John said steadily, "Father William de Bulmer is seeking admittance with us."

William stood. He walked with no sound to the central place.

"Before I kneel," he said, his eyes lowered, his body completely still, "your lord abbot has advised me, I must let you see my heart.

"I think you know—you must, for you have made me know it—I am not a good man. There is an integrity in my methods, perhaps; but it has been grievously flawed. I have neither loved nor been loved very much in my years on this earth. Brother Thomas has undertaken to teach me to love. Hope does not burn strong in me that his enterprise will succeed. But to my surprise I confess, yearning does.

"If I have not been a good man, I have at least been a practical man. If I may abide in this house, I dare suppose I may be of practical use here, if not a shining example of sanctity." The dry, reserved voice paused. "I am not doing well. I ask your patience. My heart, Father John said, let you see. Here it is, then, my heart: I am filled with terror lest you turn me away. I long for the beautiful Gospel that has always puzzled me but that I know has a beacon in the life of this house. For the forgiveness and gentleness I have found, I should like the chance to show my gratitude. For the hurt and the anger I have caused, I should like time to try and make amends. And I have glimpsed the face of Christ here. Before that glimpse dims and is smutched and bleared by the sordid life of the world, I should like to try if I might to touch for myself the vision of that fair loveliness . . . compassion . . . faith . . . peace."

He paused for a long moment, and then he said, "When you look at me, I believe what comes to your minds is all you have heard about my reception of Father Columba some years back. Brother Thomas spoke of that to me two days ago. He said that the wound I twisted my knife in was deep and bloody and that I had known it to be so, known exactly how much I would hurt him." He fell silent. Then, gazing steadfastly at the stone flags of the floor, he continued, "Brother Thomas, Columba's faithful man, spoke truth. Whatever you decide about me, I shall remain grateful for the chance to tell you that I am most deeply ashamed of what I did. I wish I could change it and wipe it away. But I cannot. So . . . that is my heart. Look well. It is a casement that does not open with ready ease."

He knelt before them.

"I most humbly beseech you for the love of God to admit me as a brother of this house, that I may learn to love and follow Christ according to the most holy Rule of St. Benedict, to do penance, amend my ways, and serve Christ faithfully here until death."

Then he prostrated himself on the flagged floor, his body insubstantial in the black folds of his robe.

"Those in favor?" asked Abbot John. "And those against?"

"Thank you. My brother, you have a welcome in this house."

THE
THIRTY-SIXTH DAY

*N*ow that he had been received into the community, William could be allocated a cell to sleep in and move out of the infirmary where he had been staying in recent days.

John ignored William's self-assessment of complete recovery, made him strip, and checked the healing of every burn and abrasion. Especially he wanted to ascertain that there was no sepsis or foul smell in any place of broken skin; the fever and lung infection had made him extra-cautious. In John's opinion, it was not sophistication of therapeutic technique but scrupulous attention to cleanliness and meticulous care that laid the foundation for healing. And kindness. John thought people got better more quickly if they felt loved.

He palpated William's larynx and listened to his chest; he looked critically at his color and noticed that his already sallow face seemed paler than ever, and his ribs stood out sharp under his shivering gooseflesh skin. "You're cold? It's warm in here, my brother. I think you are not all the way to where you should be yet. Let's cover you up—yes, dress yourself; I've seen all I need to for now. I see no reason for you to stay here in the infirmary any longer, but you are not to get up for the night office for at least another week, and you are to keep warm. Wear an extra layer when you go out of doors, and stay close to the fire when you are within. You must have a cup of wine every day. If it's fine and dry, you can come over here for that; if it's raining, someone will bring it across to you. In a week's time I'll have a look at you again. Meanwhile, if *anything* goes amiss—if your cough gets worse, if those scabbed-over burns are oozing, if you feel feverish or otherwise unwell, anything at all—you are to tell me; my brother, you must promise me this. We nearly lost you, right to the edge. You are doing well, but the healing is still fragile. William, do you promise me?"

The lazy insolence of William's eyes weighed up John's serious face and earnest expression. It occurred to John to wonder of what value William's promises might be. But William nodded in assent. "'Tis well that one of us thinks I am worth the trouble," he remarked.

Then with a dismissive gesture he waved aside the look of concern these words awakened. "No; 'tis well! 'Tis well! I hear you! The cosseting embarrasses me is all. I'm not ungrateful. I will not undo your good work."

As William stood buckling his belt and putting on his sandals, John noted the tremor of his hands and his shortness of breath. The abbot observed him thoughtfully. "Gently does it," he said. "You have been through hell this last month. A man can only take so much. But wait for me here now. I must go and wash my hands, then I need to talk with you."

After only a brief absence John returned. He sat down on the low stool beside the hearth and contemplated the thin, drained being sitting, facing him, on the edge of the bed.

"William, I am so glad we got it through this time; I'm so thankful you will be here with us for good. Our task now is to discern the right employment for you. In finding the obedience where you can serve contentedly, we have to think about both temperament and status. Whatever work we each of us take up here is no more than an obedience. Whether chopping wood or scribing letters, scrubbing floors or making earthenware pots or saying Mass or dressing the altar—it is all one, prayer and work, work and prayer. But you've been accustomed to authority, and I have no wish to humiliate you in allotting your place. Also we must work with your temperament and natural gifting, for so is Christ best served.

"Each one of us has his own intelligence, his own genius. People think the intellectual work requires intelligence and the men who labor on the farm and in the kitchen are simpler souls of lower ability, but that is wide of the mark. Father James, now, stitching our robes—he has such intelligence in his hand and eye. The stitching is so fine, the work so strong and fit for purpose. James will never be our prior or precentor or novice master; he is not sufficiently scholarly. The word *idiot* was more than once heard on the lips of his novice master—who was *not* Father Theodore!—in reference to Father James. But who could be clothed in one of his habits and fail to appreciate his craftsmanship? This is one of Father James's. You see this small stitching, these details strengthening the corner of the pockets, these belt loops, these perfectly straight seams? What more intelligence could a man need than to fulfill his calling with artistry, good conscience, and finesse?

"You see it work the other way when you let your mind rest upon our meals in community. Brother Cormac, God bless him, is faithful and dedicated, but he is not gifted. We have been waiting and patiently praying for someone with culinary intelligence to come alongside him in the kitchen; and Brother Conradus has come to be with us as a pure gift of grace. So help me find work where *you* can gladly serve God. What can you do?"

William did not take long to ponder the question, having given it some private thought already. "You need a better prior. But that is not for me, though I could serve you right well in that place. The community would not wear it. They will not trust me, and I think they will need to punish me a little too—see me take a lowly seat. I understand. But I am not fitted to dig and hoe and husband the beasts: and I'll wager my life (that contemptible thing) that you of all men will not turn me loose on your aged and sick!

"I think I might best find a use assisting your cellarer. He is old, I see. I have no comment to make on his work until I see the account books, the inventories, and his list of suppliers. But I never was anywhere yet that I could not try a little here and a little there to make the whole prosper better."

Abbot John nodded thoughtfully. He liked the sound of this proposition. Brother Ambrose was a mature, steady soul, not easily upset and full of common sense. He would not be flustered by William's erstwhile seniority nor by his caustic humor and his unnerving manner. The work of cellarer required sound intelligence and breadth of experience. A demanding job, it would keep William out of mischief, which John thought was important. Yet it had a low profile. The novice master, the precentor, the prior, the guest master—they were ever on view. The cellarer worked out of the public eye, keeping everything ticking along. It was a post that had great influence, but in a community of fewer than fifty men, what post had not? And John saw a certain damage limitation in restricting William's activities to the custody of things rather than the care of people.

"That sounds perfect," he said.

Brother Ambrose proved not eager but accepting of the suggestion when his abbot sought his mind on the matter later in the day. What he had seen and heard so far did not add to the appeal of this new member of the community, but he understood why this occupation would seem appropriate. Having reached seventy-eight years of age, he also recognized that a second mind becoming familiar with the community's finances and resources could only be wise. With a good grace he agreed to the abbot's decision, though John thought it might be overstating the case to say he welcomed it.

THE
THIRTY-SEVENTH DAY

You don't think I've made some kind of appalling mistake then? I thought it was received a bit frigidly in Chapter."

Abbot John glanced anxiously at his novice master. Theodore smiled.

"I well remember the resounding silence that met Father Peregrine's announcement he was appointing me novice master after Father Matthew died. Never did faces say 'who?' more eloquently! It was no worse than that. I see why you did it."

"Do you? Why?"

"He is a shrewd manager of material things and presumably understands now that a charitable attitude counts as profit, not loss. Brother Ambrose is steady in character and old in years. Working among the provisions allows William time for formation in our life without too much latitude for leading the weak astray and scandalizing the easily offended. And it makes use of the skills he brings with him. Am I right?"

"You are, as ever, on the nail. I guess some may fear the cellarer's position is too powerful, and with Brother Ambrose so old that power may come too quickly into William's grasp. But you know, when he spoke to us in Chapter, I believe he really meant what he said. I think he really does want to make amends and start again."

"Oh, yes, I agree with you. I think he truly intends to make a new beginning. I can see that we shall not have to be too amazed if his ideas of right and wrong turn out to be a tad at variance from ours from time to time. But what else were you to do with him? I certainly don't want him helping me! Rest easy with it, Father. It was a sensible decision."

✠   ✠   ✠

"You've accounted this twice. Nay, look—you have. It's here under payments fallen into arrears and then again on this page under the rents for Piers Turton of West Applegarth Farm in Osmotherly. Unless there's more than one Piers Turton tenant farmer in our demesnes at Osmotherly? No? Then you have accounted it twice. I'll strike it out. Where d'you want to keep the record? Which list? Yes, 'rents' is kinder, but 'arrears' may jog our memories later on. Time somebody went and paid a visit to Piers Turton of West Applegarth Farm to find out what's going on. What's he farming? He must have more than just an applegarth with that amount of rent owed. He can clear some of his arrears with payments in kind.

"These rents go into payment in arrears here. Why's that? Do they have livestock? Hens? Well, they can pay in eggs and pot-boilers then, to catch up. Nay, I'm not being hard; it'll concentrate their minds—look at all that land they have, they must be able to turn it to some profit somewhere.

"Five oaks fit for timber at the king's gift! That was a wind-fall worth having! What were you building?

"Sale of stock: wool . . . wood . . . what wood?

"Receipts here for *corodies*? What? At whose bidding did you start selling corodies? Oh, Father Chad. Yes, I would never have put that down for a notion from Abbot Columba!

"Why are we paying this much for almonds? Nay, it is indeed *not* the going rate. We can do better than these, even for the finest quality. Was that your reckoning, or did the merchant tell you it was a fair price? Then he was cheating you a-purpose and will do so again. We should take our custom elsewhere.

"Why do they need pewter dishes in the infirmary? I thought we made our own pots. Oh. Fair enough.

"What? You haven't checked the kitchen utensils in two years? That should be done each week. Trust Brother Cormac? If you say so, but the check is to cover him too. If we take a look now after two years, and he has five spoons missing, I'll wager he won't be able to account for them either.

"Is it for us to arrange the provision of towels and warm water for washing the feet of the poor on Maundy Thursday, or will the sacristan do that? What's the name of our sacristan anyway? Father Bernard? Yes, I've noticed the face, but I didn't know the name.

"That was a good price you got for sheepskins! But what's this? How much incense are we getting through? Father Bernard cooking up a storm with the thurible? Has he got a great pile of it left, or is he just using too much?

"*What* is this written on—this record here? *Donkey* vellum? Really?"

In the checker—the one-room building, near the porter's lodge, that housed all the abbey's accounts and records and represented the financial hub of the community life—Brother Ambrose's head was spinning. Nearly eighty now, he had been cellarer at St. Alcuin's since five years after his solemn profession, a stint of almost thirty-four years. In the whole of that time, his record keeping and the domestic arrangements of the abbey had never been so meticulously investigated and scrupulously overhauled as they were today. Sometimes when he had listened to readings from the Scriptures about the Last Day when all would be revealed under the awe-full light of God's Judgment, he had imagined something along these lines; it had never occurred to him the visitation could come unannounced, in person, at St. Alcuin's.

A prudent, dependable, and charitable man, Brother Ambrose had applied himself to his obedience with common sense and diligence these many years. His approach was neither tough nor imaginative, and though he got the job done, once Peregrine's unremitting focus on the financial condition of the community had been replaced by Father Chad's looser grasp on the issues, the balances had started to look less healthy, and future security seemed certainly imperiled.

Wavering between gratitude and defensiveness, Brother Ambrose suddenly began to feel his age.

THE
THIRTY-EIGHTH DAY

*F*ather Gilbert had persuaded Theodore somewhat against his will, the previous autumn, to channel the time and energy of the entire novitiate into producing copies of *Victimae Paschali Laudes* to be sung at the solemn Mass on Easter morning. He already had Jacopone da Todi's *Stabat Mater* up his sleeve for Holy Week.

He had also, during the summer, badgered Father Chad into giving him permission to write away to Paris for a copy of a polyphonic Mass by Pérotin. This had duly arrived, and copies had been made, but Father Gilbert felt disappointed in his brothers' attempts to get to grips with it so far. He had successfully recruited a number of men into a creditable effort at producing the loud insistent drone needed for the slow shifts of the base chant, but finding the voices with sufficient confidence for the complicated tissue of free, fast-moving sound to be woven in the air above it proved more of a challenge than he had anticipated. And try as he might, he simply could *not* succeed in eradicating Brother Josephus's irritating tendency to vibrato and self-indulgently sliding notes. The rehearsals extended to fill more hours than he had ever imagined could be necessary, and he sensed an increasing reluctance in Father Theodore to allow Brothers Ced, Cassian, and Placidus to devote much more time than they had already given to the enterprise. This worried Father Gilbert because not only did the three novices have the best voices in the whole community, but they were also intelligent; and polyphony was still sufficiently avant-garde to mystify and alienate slower and older minds, especially in Yorkshire.

He had a few motets by Johannes de Grocheio and, more important, by Philippe de Vitry, under whose creative genius such exciting innovations were emerging at Notre Dame and Avignon; but the indifference to the new developments that perpetuated in his own community proved a constant frustration. Father Gilbert dreamed of the day when St. Alcuin's would be a name spoken with reverence and awe in the world of sacred music, but he had to acknowledge that not even the first gray streaks of the dawn of such a day could yet be seen.

In Chapter last week he had put up a red-blooded defense for prioritizing the music of Holy Week and Easter now, before it got too late and slipped into disaster or had to be abandoned. In bewilderment and private grief, he realized that Abbot John shared his sense of urgency not at all. On reflection he understood that a man whose passion was for eradicating chilblains and defeating chesty coughs could hardly be expected to appreciate the excitement generated by the new vision just flowering in France of what sacred music could become, but it was a bitter pill to swallow nevertheless.

"Can't we just sing something straightforward that we all know this year?" The abbot's distressing question evoked such a deep and obvious disappointment that John had felt immediately guilty and hurriedly retracted the blunder, placating his precentor with the instruction to do whatever he thought best. This turned out to be an error, as work in the garden, the novitiate, the scriptorium, and the guest house almost came to a standstill, and they were left shorthanded even in the infirmary. Today the abbot felt obliged to summon Father Gilbert and impose severe limitation upon the program of preparation.

As John sat recovering alone from the stormy interview

with his precentor that took up most of the afternoon, his relief at having curtailed the rapidly expanding musical ambitions of St. Alcuin's was considerably blighted by his suspicion that he had not handled this adroitly from the beginning. They would sing something, but not very well, and nobody was happy.

A knock at his door roused him from this gloomy reverie. It announced Father Theodore, looking apologetic and bearing tidings of a letter he had been sent. Apparently two young men from Escrick planned to come up for the Easter feast and sought audience with the new abbot in the hopes of entering as postulants at St. Alcuin's. Would Father John have time to meet them to discuss their sense of vocation in the course of the Easter Triduum, which would be the only holiday from work allowed them? "So I'm afraid, Father," Theodore said in tones of plain sympathy, "the answer has to be yes."

As Theo left the abbot's lodge to send a reply to this inquiry, he held the door open for Brother Ambrose, who had been sent by his new assistant to seek permission to purchase three bolts of black woolen cloth for Father James. As the cloth merchant would likely be present for the Easter feast, it seemed sensible to be ready with the order.

The ringing of the bell for Vespers reached John's ears as the most welcome sound imaginable. The only aspect of the day that St. Alcuin's new abbot could find to feel pleased about was that by some miracle he'd had the inspired foresight to ask Father Theodore to lead the *Lectio Divina* studies at Collatio every evening this week.

THE
THIRTY-NINTH DAY

Running in sandals and a habit is not easy, but John wanted to catch Brother Ambrose before he vanished into the guest house. In the past he might have called him or even arrested his attention with the piercing whistle he had spent so many evenings perfecting as a boy. But he recognized that the dignity of his office meant that in addition to such lack of gravitas being frowned upon, he was now the authority supposed to be doing the frowning. Still, he ran, because he wanted to catch him. Ambrose heard his approach and stopped to wait for him.

"Sorry. I meant to speak to you yesterday, brother. I just wanted to make sure all is well with William—from your point of view, I mean, not his. Will he be a help to you, d' you think? Is he making himself useful?"

Brother Ambrose chuckled. "Useful? Yes. If you have a handful of dead leaves littering the greensward, a hurricane would be useful to clear them away. He's that kind of useful. Much as, if a country had a couple of anachronistic bylaws, it would be nothing a revolutionary annihilation of the whole kingdom couldn't fix."

John looked worried. "Has he . . . have I . . . is he going to be a burden to you? Have I done the wrong thing?"

Brother Ambrose considered his abbot thoughtfully. "I'm getting old, Father John. I haven't as good a grip on things as I used to have. If I'm honest with myself and with you, I am no

217

longer serving this community as well as the cellarer should do. He's come blowing in like the east wind and set everything in a whirl until I hardly know if I'm coming or going. 'What's this doing in two lists? Why are we paying that much? Which merchant are we using? Who mills our flour? How are we financing our guests for Easter?' No stone is left unturned, unexamined, unscoured, and unscrubbed or put back in the place it was in before. My head's in such a spin I've almost forgotten my own name. But I can see already that when he's done, he will pull us back from the brink of the mess we were sliding into, which has been more my doing than anybody's, though I couldn't see how to avoid it. In the sense that a raging inferno is a Godsend for stopping a plague, this man will be a Godsend to us."

He smiled and made a small bow of mock appreciation. "Thank you so much for sending him along, Father Abbot. It was kind of you to think of me."

"Glory! I hope you survive. But seriously, I'm comforted to hear he's making such a real contribution."

"Oh, he is. We've noticed he's with us all right."

"Yes, I can believe that! There's a pastoral dimension too, brother, for which I heartily thank you. You saw him in Chapter when he begged admission here that second time. When he got up from his knees, he looked so dazed and haggard, I almost sent him straight back to the infirmary, to bed. He may have been a villain since forever, but the Lord Christ has slapped him around good and hard in the past few weeks. It was fair enough that he got what was coming to him, but watching him lose his arrogance and all that self-possession has tugged at my heartstrings a bit. After a certain amount of it, breaking a man's pride starts to be breaking his spirit, and I surely don't want to do that. He needs a chance, needs a job to do and a way to prove his worth and give something back—a reason for hope and a means to please the men he so offended. From what you tell me, some of the assurance that's been knocked out of him by the events of the last month or so has been more positively restored in being offered a task that he understands and can do with confidence."

Ambrose smiled, listening to this. "Confidence? Aye, I think you can say he's been tackling the cellarer's duties with confidence. But don't you worry, Father John. It was a shrewd choice you made and, if I find the strength to endure the innovation, no doubt I shall be more grateful than anyone."

"So once you've got over the shock, you think he will be a good thing for us?"

"He'll consolidate our trading position and fill up our coffers again, of that I'm entirely certain! Some of our tenant farmers who've been used to leniency and plenty of slack over the matter of payment of rents due are in for a rude awakening, I tell you without doubt! And no one will be getting any of our fleeces at a knockdown price anymore!"

John scanned Ambrose's face in concern. "Is this good for us? Are you content he is pushing in the right direction? Heaven help us, we don't want our own house besieged by furious tenants bent on arson in five years' time! He took *his* house into the most awful trouble!"

Brother Ambrose laughed. "Aye. He did indeed. But though I'm old, Father, I'm good for a few years yet, and I know the way the world works. If I see his ardor needs cooling before our neighbors decide to torch the whole abbey, I'll think to have a quiet word with you. Nay, he'll be good for us. You have won yourself a formidable champion. You've made a good start here, is my belief."

THE
FORTIETH DAY

In the delirious sunshine of the day, birds feverishly gathered twigs for nests taking shape in every hedgerow. The wood doves, who had their dovecote supplied, occupied their hours in ostentatious courtship, throats puffed to the huge maximum, sidling and bowing in pursuit of desirable favors.

The primroses had all opened, and the windflowers were scattered among the trees above the burial ground, where also wild daffodils had advanced to full bud.

Over the bare hilltop of the moor, the lark flung into the wide arch of the sky, a dizzy, exulting blue. Brother Stephen, on his way up the farm track to look over his lambs before the Palm Sunday liturgies began, paused for a moment just to feel the day. "O God, it's *warm*," he whispered. "*Deo gratias*. Thank you, thank you, thank you."

On this one day the wind dropped, and it felt like a different world. Everything, even summer, seemed possible. Hope had woken up.

THE
FORTY-FİRST DAY

I'm so tired, Tom." Sitting at his table, faced by a heap of Tenebrae psalm chants, special annotated liturgies, and lists for his approval from the cellarer, John gazed sightlessly at nothing, his face as still as a death mask.

This brought back memories to Brother Tom. He knew well the cost imposed on a man by the burden of the abbacy. John needed him. It was time for his standoff to end. "Comes as part of the bundle I think, my friend," he said gently. "You have no guests tonight. You don't have to eat in the frater. Let me kindle a fire for you and fetch you a cup of wine and a bite to eat."

A smile of gratitude and amusement animated John's exhausted features. "Get thee behind me. It's Lent."

"Aye and it'll still be Lent in the morning, when you've been too weary to sleep and have everything still to do, with a hundred visitors pouring in through the gates. I had this trouble with our last abbot. He found it hard to grasp the fact that he was only a human being."

John nodded. "For the fire and the solitude, I would be grateful, and for some supper. But not wine in Lent. The sheep follow the shepherd. A man can't teach what he does not practice."

Brother Tom lit the fire and brought the abbot his supper. A wave of thankfulness flooded through John as he beheld the appetizing plate of vegetable fritters and bread that looked like bread and nothing else. He inhaled the aroma of a dish of frumenty, made with almond milk, sweetened with honey and spiced with cinnamon, and a beaker of apple juice. John began to believe in life again.

He glanced up to thank his esquire, then looked again, his attention caught. Tom evidently had something on his mind.

"What?"

"I won't keep you. Eat your supper while it's hot. I just wanted to say I'm sorry."

"For what?" John's apprehension was so apparent, it made Tom laugh.

He shook his head in reassurance. "Nothing new! Don't worry, I haven't begun another battle while you weren't looking. I'm sorry for making everything so hard and for spending most of Lent in a giant sulk. Forgive me quickly, Father, or your supper'll go cold."

John winked at him. "Go in peace," he said. "I think we're friends."

THE
FORTY-SECOND DAY

John had counted on having these last few days with no visitors to speak of before the pilgrims arrived in droves for the climax of Holy Week and the Easter feast.

Walking over to the checker in the early afternoon, to ascertain for himself how Brother Ambrose was bearing up under rigorous inquisition from his new assistant, he observed with dismay Father Chad crossing the abbey court flanked by two visitors, whom he recognized immediately.

"Oh, no. No, no!" He stopped dead in his tracks, wondering how he could possibly avert the necessity of this meeting, and then a touch on his arm surprised him. "Oh! William! I was coming to the checker, but I see Father Chad is looking for me." He shook his head, lost for a moment. "I should have anticipated . . . that is, I'd hoped . . . well, I thought until Maundy Thursday at least . . . you cannot imagine . . . oh, dear, not them! Father Peregrine used to come limping over for sanctuary in the infirmary with the most splitting headache after playing host to these people."

"They are . . . ?" asked William quietly as the party drew nearer.

"Sir Geoffrey and Lady Agnes d'Ebassier." John groaned softly. He looked in sudden appeal to William's years of experience as the superior of a monastic community: "D' you think I can leave them to Father Chad?"

223

"D'Ebassier?" William shook his head emphatically, recognizing the name immediately and speaking softly and rapidly as the trio approached. "D'Ebassier put up the money for the new big gates: timbers, ironwork, and everything. He paid for our extension to the stable block; last year he gave the chalice, paten, and candlesticks for the high altar. Their gifts are massive. We cannot offend them. You *must* receive this man. May I be of service?"

As John hesitated, William's eyebrow lifted in sardonic inquiry, and his mouth twisted in sudden amusement. "Do not be afraid. What you know of me has been filtered, I guess, through the lens of Brother Thomas's perceptions. I am ruthless sometimes, and Abbot Columba had no use for me, but I am not fickle, and you have surely earned my fealty. The devil looks after his own."

He coolly appraised John's disconcerted expression. "Make haste; they are here. Do you want my help or not?"

With one swift glance in the direction of his visitors, now almost upon them, John made up his mind. "Oh, yes, please. Stay with me!" he whispered.

Father Chad seemed only too relieved to off-load the aristocratic guests onto his abbot, but as he courteously bowed his departure, William said, "Father Chad, before you go, will you search out Brother Thomas and send him this minute to light the fire in Father's lodging; and he must provide whatever refreshment sits well with this house for guests in Lent. Now. Do not delay. Then find Francis and send him to find us too."

Father Chad's reaction to this tersely spoken aside seemed mixed. Discernibly put out to receive such direct orders from a newcomer merely trying his vocation for a year at St. Alcuin's, he nonetheless found himself submitting to the authority of William's command with a reflex of complete obedience.

John, meanwhile, pleasantly and diffidently received the

newcomers' felicitations upon his appointment as abbot and then paused, wondering what he should say next. William turned to them again. Startled, John watched his face transformed by luminous geniality as he made a modest bow of welcome, waiting for his abbot to introduce him.

"Oh—this is Father William, new to our community. He came to join us from a house near Chesterfield just a few weeks ago."

"Chesterfield? Chesterfield?" Sir Geoffrey's face creased in a torture of difficult recollection at this information. "Wasn't there some frightful abbey in Chesterfield? Or priory? Augustinians? Appalling prior—really wicked man—place burned right down just a matter of weeks ago. Know the place I mean? What was his name, that man?"

John did not suffer from headaches. He could not remember the last time he'd had a headache; but now he felt the first bands of tension begin to tighten around his brow, down to his neck. He shot a glance of horror at William.

"Ah!" William's eyelids flickered momentarily as he suavely purred, "Yes, I know the place you mean. It was as you say— burned right down. St. Dunstan's is the name you are looking for. They are in our prayers, Sir Geoffrey. My Lady Agnes, what a delight to meet you—do you like flowers? It is cold standing here in the open, but before my lord abbot finds us warmth and refreshment in his lodging, I wondered if you would like to take a glimpse at our cloister garth; it is so beautiful. The tiny jonquils and crocuses are in full bloom; should you like to see?" His eyes held hers in amiable gallantry, a captivating smile playing lightly on his lips, the thin, hard, wintry face suddenly metamorphosed into a most compelling magnetism. John beheld him in astonishment.

"Indeed, I *do* love flowers," she responded eagerly. "And yes, I should so like to see them!"

In the cloister garth Father Francis materialized, and

William murmured in his ear, "Talk to d'Ebassier. I need to speak to Father Abbot."

As, without question, Francis advanced, smiling upon his guest, calling to his notice the nook on the right angle of the cloister roof where the wrens had begun to build, and Lady Agnes crossed the garth exclaiming in delight at the profusion of early spring flowers, which she knelt to examine more closely, William spoke quietly into his abbot's ear. "You must pay court to this woman. Make her feel special. Nay, truly—don't worry— she's not after your body, but she is hungry for cherishing and is married to an oblivious idiot. The man holds the purse strings, but the favor of the woman steers the heart of the man. We need these people. My lord, don't look at me like that! We are hard up and rely on you to spearhead our fiscal endeavor. Be sweet, make her feel good. Leave the man to me." He stepped away from John to stand at the side of the nobleman squinting in vain to see the nest where Francis was pointing.

Rooted to the spot by William's advice, his thoughts in turmoil, Abbot John saw Lady Agnes turn to him with childlike and slightly coquettish appeal. "May I pick just one, Father John? Just *one*?"

In one moment of gathering dismay, he took in the wistful entreaty of her lifted gaze as she knelt in the damp moss of the cloister garth . . . the penetrating ray of his cellarer's assistant's eyes boring into his head . . . and the exuberant booming of his guest's response to a question from William: "Stag, you say? Yes, I hunt stag! Yes, his royal highness has been with us some weeks through last season. Some magnificent beasts we have now; keep 'em in the forests, you know. Get some wondrous big beasts that way, bigger than the ones up on the open moorland above the abbey here. We should have good increase this year. You could hear those randy bucks roaring right across the valley. Why, some of the those big stags can take on fifteen or twenty hinds during the rut and sire enough young on 'em to keep us in as much sport as we want—not that you monks want to hear too much about rutting, what? Ha! Get behind me Satan, eh?"

John's eyes felt as if someone was squeezing them. He heard William softly clear his throat.

"By all means!" the abbot said hastily. "Er—yes, pick them all, have what you like!"

William handed Sir Geoffrey back to Francis in one swift, understood glance and stepped lightly across the cloister garth, bending down to Lady Agnes. Delicately slipping his hand under her wrist, he raised her to her feet. "They are yours, my lady. We shall make sure you have some in your chamber every day that you are here." He stooped and picked half a dozen jonquils with a couple of leaves and a stubborn stalk of wet, dead grass, twisting it to secure the flowers into a little nosegay, which he offered her with a small, shy smile and the slightest bow. She took them, laughing.

John was beginning to feel the reality he had known and faithfully loved slipping helplessly through his fingers and wishing he had never heard of William and never entertained the idea of serving this community as its abbot, when William spoke again. "My lord, my lady, 'tis bitter cold, and I think our brother will have lit us a fire. Can I invite you to step into my lord abbot's lodging? You will know the way?"

He stepped back in considerate deference to allow their distinguished guests, followed by Father Francis, to move into the cloister. His quizzical, gently mocking gaze met John's appalled face. Lightly, he cupped his hand under his abbot's elbow as Francis paused on the cloister step, looking back for them.

"*Avant, mes braves!*" murmured William, his touch exerting a pressure that gently propelled John forward.

Like a man in a dream, Abbot John passed along the cloister. He felt sick with worry, and his head pounded relentlessly. Other than that, it was as though he had no body; he could feel nothing at all. He saw Francis move ahead of their guests in a swift, graceful movement to open the door of his lodging and invite them to enter. He heard William's low voice in his ear: "You must invite them to eat at your table tonight, my lord. Only them; their servants will find hospitality in the guest house, but ask them you must, there is no choice." Then John stood on the threshold of his lodging. It was simple and plain, for the quarters of an abbot. Just this one substantial room served for his daily work, his pastoral counsel of the brethren, and the reception of his visitors, and beyond that a dining room that held up to twelve guests, and his chamber with his bed and nightstand, and the chest for his clothes. He had no reception hall separate from his atelier, as many superiors did, but Peregrine had liked it this way, and so did John.

As he paused in the doorway, he saw first the fire blazing merrily in the hearth, then that the chairs into which Father Francis was solicitously settling his guests now boasted cushions, the ones that normally graced the ceremonial chairs in the sanctuary of the high altar. Brother Tom stood unobtrusively against the wall, ready for whatever might be required of him. John's great oak table had been cleared of documents and books, of music, quills and seal and ink and every other bit of paraphernalia. Instead of these, a large plate of delectable little pastries, savory and sweet, waited for them, and a steaming jug of something that smelled deliciously like spiced fruit punch, beside a collection of the beakers from the abbey's pottery—in this case, none of them chipped at all.

As he watched Francis further entrance Lady Agnes with the captivating sparkle of his smiling eyes (there was no cynicism or even self-consciousness in this; Francis smiled at everyone he met, and they were all entranced—except his erstwhile novice master had not been, but that was long ago), Father John doubted his own capacity to accommodate himself to this gracious political world full of seeming and pleasantry.

"Be yourself, my lord, for you are very lovable; let them see," came the quiet murmur in his ear again, and then William was plying their guests with dainty food and hot drinks.

Abbot John looked across the room to Brother Tom, who still stood alert to his abbot's needs and responded with a questioning lift of the eyebrows. "Thank you!" John mouthed silently, and Tom's face softened in a smile as he inclined his head in acknowledgment.

All of a sudden, in that moment, things clicked into place for Abbot John, and he saw what his brothers were doing for him. As he surveyed his room, he thought of the needs of the infirmary, where Brother Michael would be bending, smiling over the old and the frail, serving them drinks, seeing their needs were comforted, where Brother Boniface would humor them, saying what they needed to hear, cajoling them into compliance with firm kindness, and John saw that this was different but the same. Not a sham, simply necessary—the appropriate work of the abbey's hospitality and gratitude for the generosity of these folk who liked to give lavishly of their plenty for the work of God.

"Has your journey been straightforward?" he asked kindly as he stepped fully into the room, hearing Tom close the door behind him. "Are you very weary? It's a cold time of year to be traveling."

William straightened up with his plate of pastries, his face relaxing as he watched his abbot in approval. "Surely you will need to rest when you are refreshed," said John in honest concern, "but I hope you may like to dine with me tonight."

"Well done, my lord abbot," said William quietly as three-quarters of an hour later Father Francis, still chatting easily (another gift for which he was renowned) escorted John's aristocratic guests out of his lodging in the direction of the guest house and Brother Tom removed the empty plate and drinking vessels ("I'll be back in a moment, but anything you need urgently you'll find piled on your bed, Father John.")

"What's all this 'my lord abbot'? 'Father John' is fine—no need for pomp and ceremony!"

But William shook his head. "You *are* my lord abbot, and I think you need to hear it said a little to begin to believe in yourself. You did good work today. Brother Michael tells me they hardly know how to find enough linen for the everyday needs of the infirmary. The sheets are all sides-to-middled and even then are worn thin and ripping. Linen is expensive, Father John. But today, with a little kindness to a lonely woman—and why not? Was not Christ kind?—you will have bought six new sheets for the infirmary; aye, I guess you will! It is your service, and it is not hollow. Why should you scowl at them and spurn them because they are rich? On Thursday Ambrose and I will stand with a pile of towels and warm scented water at your side as you wash the feet of the poor. Today you have washed the feet of the rich. What's the difference? They all have calluses and stink. They are all merely human. They are all moved by kindness.

"Anyhow, the office of None is not yet, and you look wrung out. Let me leave you in peace by your own fireside, though not with these cushions; you're a humble monk. I'll take them back to where Brother Thomas filched them from. Take a few minutes to find yourself again."

He stood with the cushions in his arms and watched as John, glad to be obedient, sat down by the fire. "We did a good job. We were glad to serve you. You are much loved," William commented, and then the latch clicked shut.

Abbot John found himself alone, slightly bemused but unexpectedly happy.

THE

FORTY-THIRD DAY

At Brother Martin's request, Father Theodore sent Brother Cassian down to mind the porter's lodge while Martin went in search of Abbot John. The two young men from Escrick, feeling that it would be more helpful to the abbot if they could find audience with him before the bulk of the faithful appeared on his doorstep, had managed to beg a day free and hitch a ride with a carter bringing some barrels of ale for the guest house. The community mostly drank Brother Walafrid's dubious brews, but there were times when these needed to be given a lower profile in the abbey's daily fare.

Brother Martin took the two young men across to the guest house, where they could wait more comfortably, and walked over to the cloister. He was not sure his abbot would be as delighted with the thoughtfulness of the two lads as they had hoped, but they were here now.

Theodore did send Cassian, but resolved to have a discreet conversation with Brother Martin. Nobody considered it prudent to have a novice left with the porter's responsibility, but neither was it diplomatic for the novice master to refuse a direct request from one of the brothers when that request was made in the hearing of all the novices. So he dispatched Cassian, a sensible young man, but did not feel best pleased.

Brother Martin ran his abbot to earth in the sacristy, where Father Bernard had been briefing him for his central part in the Easter Vigil and was now taking him through the correct folding of the humeral veil and reminding him that he must wait until the Blessed Sacrament had been censed three times before leading off the procession to the altar of repose. Abbot John had watched this done every Holy Thursday of his life, but he felt very nervous at the prospect of being the one relied upon to get it right. He had spent most of the morning with Father Gilbert, trying to sing the *Exsultet* to his precentor's satisfaction, and felt very conscious that his attempts so far did not pass muster. The intonation of the three *Lumen Christi* versicles of the *Lucernarium* caused him no trouble, provided he didn't pitch the first one too high, but the *Exsultet* was on a different level entirely. In the end he had persuaded Father Gilbert to add it to his duties as cantor and sing it himself. Father Gilbert assented to this meekly, in the demure tones of one acquiescing compliantly to a necessary burden. Not even to himself did he admit the triumph of bagging the *Exsultet* when he had thought all he would be able to count on was the long Gospel *Alleluia*. Abbot John knew himself heartily relieved to pass on the responsibility, but it still made him feel a failure.

"Ah, there you are, Father Abbot! A couple of lads from Escrick have asked to see you—they said you would be expecting them." Father Martin stood smiling encouragement in the doorway as his abbot turned and looked at him blankly, the humeral veil still in his hands. "What?" he said. "*Today?*"

"Well, yes, Father, it is today, and they are here" came the jocular response from Brother Martin, which he saw did not find favor with his abbot, so he composed his features into an especially respectful expression. "They are in the guest house, Father. They thought it would be helpful to you if they came at a less busy time."

"It would," replied John shortly. "I wish they had. Very well, yes, I'll go. Bernard, I think I've got the hang of this, but you'll be there beside me to give me a prod if I don't get it right, won't you?"

In the porter's lodge, meanwhile, Brother Cassian opened the door to two people approaching the abbey on foot: a middle-aged woman with an open, pleasant, gentle face and a much older woman he could immediately discern to be her mother. One glance told him they had no wealth, but they both had great dignity, a quiet natural authority that intrigued Brother Cassian. He had the odd sensation of having met them before. They reminded him of someone, but he couldn't think who. The more he looked at them, the more familiar they seemed, but he still couldn't place them at all. They both smiled at him, and the younger of the two women swung the heavy pack she carried down onto the floor.

"God give you good day, brother," she said amiably. "Is Brother John about?"

"Brother John? You mean Father John? Abbot John?"

It took Cassian by surprise that this made them both laugh, but they assured him that, yes, the abbot was the man they had meant.

"I'm not sure where he is," said Brother Cassian. "I can go and have a look for you when Brother Martin gets back. Why don't you go across to the guest house where they can make you comfortable, and I'll have a look for him the minute I'm free to do so?"

The women agreed to this, and the younger one hefted her bag onto her shoulder again.

"Who shall I say is looking for him?" asked Cassian.

"His sister Madeleine," answered the older woman, "and his mother."

☩   ☩   ☩

The two would-be postulants from Escrick returned to the guest house in a state of barely suppressed excitement. They liked Father John. Their aspirations had been heard patiently and respectfully, and they both felt that their questions had been carefully considered and helpfully answered. Having satisfied himself of their earnest intent, the abbot had told them they could both return to the abbey novitiate after Easter to try the Benedictine life at St. Alcuin's. His only stipulation was that they see their home circumstances responsibly finalized.

"I like that man," said Colin to Bernard. "That's a body I could trust. What did you think? Do you still feel the same?"

"I think I would have wanted to come whatever he was like. I want to be Christ's man, not the abbot's man. But I did like him, yes. He seemed a peaceful soul, not too rushed. I like the idea of this gentle way of life: time to meditate, time to listen to people; just staying here quietly with nothing to do but pray."

Colin was silent for a moment. "I'm not sure that's always quite how it is," he ventured tentatively. But Bernard had the stronger personality, and Colin's views did not always count.

Back in the cloister they had just left, Abbot John let himself out of his lodge with the intention of going along to the chapel. He needed five minutes' peace to put some thoughts together for his homilies for Holy Thursday and Good Friday. As he turned from the door, he almost collided with Brother Cassian.

"Sorry, Father! I thought you'd seen me. Your mother's here!"

The abbot blinked, startled, then bemusedly raised a hand to his brow. "My *mother*?"

"Aye, and your sister Madeleine." Cassian smiled. "They seemed very entertained by the idea of your being the superior of an abbey!"

John looked at him, and Cassian had a sudden sense he had perhaps said the wrong thing. But his abbot replied only, "Aye, I can imagine they would. Where are they then?"

"I sent them on to the guest house." Cassian hesitated, then added, "I thought they seemed like really nice people, Father."

And John's face relaxed in a smile. "Thank you for saying that. I'll go and find them."

✠   ✠   ✠

"We brought you yellow archangel." Madeleine had lifted her bag onto the guest house table and rummaged in it for the neatly bound packs of dried herbs from their garden.

"That'll be good for your old men—achy joints and back pain and so on. Lavender and rosemary you have a-plenty, I know, and calendula and chamomile, I should imagine, and tansy and all the usual things. But I didn't see feverfew when I was here in the summer, so I dried you some of ours. Herb bennet— I'll wager you have some! How could you live in a Benedictine house and not? But we had so much, I dried some roots for you anyway. Ready for use? Certainly! What d'you take me for? I wouldn't bring you roots with the mud still on them! They're ready to pound or soak or whatever you want to do, straight from the pack as they are. Mullein flowers too, because they're good for so many things. And some royal fern because it grows down our way, but I don't think you have it here. Oh look! Mother put in lady's smock; I told her you'd have some, but she said you might not have had time to gather it, and it's a good pick-me-up, isn't it—anyone who's lost their appetite or got generally low. And Mother wanted you to have a little bag of her orrisroot. Be grateful, she's had to buy that! I don't suppose you need it really, but it smelt so lovely, and she thought if you have anybody with a skin rash—incontinent people maybe—it would be good to soothe sore places and make them smell sweet."

Abbot John sat listening to this eager flow, watching her place the carefully tied bundles in a pile on the table.

"You've used your good linen to wrap these," he observed.

"Well—it was for you."

"Adam." John looked up at his mother as she spoke his baptismal name. He smiled. "'Adam.' That feels like a long time ago."

As his eyes met hers, he felt her searching of his soul: brief but thorough. "Adam, should we not have come? I never thought of anything but how proud we were of you. We heard you'd got back safely from Cambridge, and we wanted to receive the Blessed Sacrament from your hands. But now we're here, I see you must have barely a minute to call your own. I think we may have judged it wrong. This was not the time, was it?"

John smiled. "Vocation comes in layers," he said. "It builds from the middle like an onion. The last layer is that I am an abbot now. And yes, you're quite right, I'm rarely idle. But underneath that, I'm an infirmarian: John, a simple monk who loves to heal people, which I learned from you, and thank you both for this precious, precious store of herbs. Brother Michael will be gloating over these with great satisfaction! And the orrisroot is a gentle touch, Mother—making someone who is sick smell fragrant and sweet is an uphill task; it will be just what we need. Underneath John, maybe something of me is still Adam, picking the wildflowers in the midmorning, when the dew has dried but the heat of the sun has not wilted the plants. A boy searching for violets in the hedgerows, and for meadow rue—not because it was much use but because they called it the herb of grace. Madeleine's brother, your son, taking the goat along the track to browse where the vetches grow. All these things I was called to be, and they all belong to who I am, and if I lose any of them, part of me will be lost. How could you have judged it wrong? How could you ever not be welcome? Only I must ask you to forgive me that this time of year you'll have to share me with everybody else."

The bell began to ring for the office.

"Have supper with me tonight?" John looked at them anxiously. "I have so many things to remember, so many duties and people to see. Will you forgive me? I can't—"

"Ssh." His mother leaned forward and lightly pressed her finger to his lips. "We came because we love you, not to make your life difficult! Will we still be allowed in the infirmary, to see Brother Michael and what he's doing there? And in the gardens—the herb gardens? And up on the farm—to see the lambs? Then after Mass tomorrow, we'll make our way. We'll come back and see you again in the summer maybe."

"You'll not stay for the Easter feast?" John was rising to his feet.

"It will be Easter everywhere, my son. We didn't come for all the pomp and ceremony: we only came to see you. Off you go then; that bell has stopped! See you for supper!"

As Abbot John slipped into his stall and waited a moment before giving the knock for the community to rise, he thought about how many different things a person is, how many different threads weave the story of every single life—and how hard it is to know people really, to see the layers of vocation and life experience that form their point of view. And he gave thanks for his mother . . . his sister . . . his boyhood memories . . . the unconditional love that had held the growing years of his life.

THE
FORTY-FOURTH DAY
Holy Thursday

Brother Cormac had the honesty to admit to himself that he felt deeply threatened by the tubby figure of Brother Conradus bustling purposefully around his kitchen. His honesty even stretched to an awareness that "my kitchen" is how he thought of it and that this was the source of the problem, not Brother Conradus.

He stepped deliberately upon his resentment to at least hold it in place if it could not be eliminated and said humbly to the novice busily gathering on the table the items he needed for his soup, "Is there anything you would like me to fetch, brother?"

"Ooh! That is such a kindness!" Brother Conradus beamed at him. There was something about his rosy cheeks and dark eyes—his unaffected enthusiasm and good humor now he had found his way to his proper environment—that exuded a most infectious cheerfulness. Brother Cormac was surprised to find himself instinctively returning the smile.

"I need some chervil, a great big bunch!" Caught in the glow of Brother Conradus's ardor for the task at hand, Cormac obediently took a basket and a knife and set off for the kitchen garden as he was bid.

"Onions," murmured Brother Conradus to himself. "Leeks

... pepper ... salt ... " He hummed a psalm chant happily to himself as he fetched the broth he had set aside from yesterday to assist with the flavoring and the large bowl of dried green peas he had left to soak overnight.

"Bay ... coriander ... cardamom ... celery seed ... carrot seed ... just the tiniest touch of dried mint for the memory of summer."

As he passed through the cobbled yard to the garden, Brother Cormac encountered Brother Thomas, drawing a jug of water for the abbot's table.

"I am dispatched to gather chervil," he remarked.

Tom identified the problem.

"Aha! Deposed!" he responded with a sympathetic grin.

Cormac nodded. "Deposed, resentful, and feeling a bit ashamed of myself." There was something about relationships forged in the formative time of the novitiate. The bonds endured. His sense of comradeship with Tom and Theodore, Francis and Thaddeus never really died away. He could talk to Tom. "I shall not find this easy. I've always thought it would be the hardest thing to do—if I should be asked to give up this obedience, I mean. And like everyone else, I can't help but see that Conradus was born to this work, and I'm not."

Brother Tom nodded understandingly. "It's the memories, the old loyalties; they are so precious," he said. "Things that meant so much, that stay present in the wood and stone of a place. If you let go of the place and the things that belong to it, you feel afraid that you'll lose hold of the memory."

Cormac looked at him, his eyes dark wells of emotion. "Indeed," he said.

"Yes." Tom picked up the jug from where he had set it down beside the well. "Same with me. It's just the hardest thing to do—to let personal loyalties and old ways of thinking go, for the sake of the deeper principles underneath that matter more. I mean, they matter more than the treasures of memory, but because the principles aren't personal, they feel so austere. It's easier to make life be about the small, personal things—the people, the place, and the memories. If you see what I mean."

He inclined his head to direct Brother Cormac's attention to the kitchen door that stood open behind him, where Brother Conradus had appeared in hope of his chervil. His hands clasped together in uncertainty, sensing a not altogether happy mood in this meeting of professed brothers, he hesitated on the step.

"I'm sorry!" Cormac couldn't help but laugh at him: he had such an uncanny resemblance to a beaver at that moment. "I'm going for the chervil, brother, I am! You've caught me wasting time here gossiping with Brother Tom, but I'm on my way!"

"What are you cooking?" asked Tom genially as Cormac stepped briskly toward the garden.

"Chervil soup, Brother Thomas, because it's Holy Thursday. And I have some small sourdough barley loaves set to rise; and I've made some gingerbread, and the rice in almond milk is seething slow over the fire."

Tom shook his head in wonder. "Have you any idea—*any* idea—what a Godsend you are to us?"

Brother Conradus beamed in pleasure. "Thank you kindly! And this new cellarer, Father William, he seems most knowledgeable and helpful: he even knows where to get vanilla! But," his face dropped in consternation, "I feel uneasy about Brother Cormac. It means so much to him, I think—his place in the kitchen."

"It does." Tom nodded. "It does. But alas, he's a rotten cook. So he'll have to get over it. Which he will do. Don't let him . . . don't let anything . . . put you off. Cormac has to eat as well. He gets the point. And you be careful of that new cellarer; he's a scoundrel and a half! Nay, not really, I'm only teasing. Right: water to my lord abbot's house. And I shall be dreaming of gingerbread all morning!"

✠ ✠ ✠

As his guests began to arrive, Father Bernard went over with Abbot John for the last time the arrangements for the washing of feet after the special solemn Mass that would take place in the afternoon. He reminded him of his part in the procession with the Blessed Sacrament to the altar of repose that would conclude the Good Friday Vigil. He showed him again where each holy vessel would stand and went over again the orders of precedence and the stations of prayer around the chapel with the Paschal candle. As he tried to absorb and commit to memory all of the detail, Abbot John felt even more deeply conscious of the magnitude of the task that rested upon him.

During the morning, he walked across the abbey court to the guest house to greet some of the pilgrims before they became too numerous for that to be practical. Among the people milling about in the spring sunshine, he noticed William moving unobtrusively, pausing for conversation here and there. John came alongside him in time to hear the tail end of one of these exchanges.

"We need some good salt too—none of this filthy stuff that's coming in from the Bay of Bourgneuf. And yes, in answer to your question, our fleece is excellent, and we can do you a good price in exchange, if you will promise to give us first refusal— oh, good day, Father John! This is our new abbot, my friend. Father, this is Wat Bridger, who supplies many of our spices and some very high-grade rice. He has other rice too—I know this, I've had it—but the clean grain with no mites in it is what we're after; nothing else. He has a ship coming from Arab lands later in the year, and he can bring us some wonderful fragrant bundles of Eastern delights. Our abbot has a particular fondness for ginger, my friend; see you find us the best that you can."

Abbot John found himself alone with the merchant as, with

a charming smile, a courteous bow, and a murmured farewell, his cellarer's assistant slipped away among the knots of visitors, stopping with a friendly bow of greeting by a tall, stout, bearded man with a very flamboyantly dressed wife.

Never in twenty-eight years of monastic life had it occurred to John to see Maundy Thursday as a commercial opportunity, and this new perspective added an entirely different dimension to his understanding of the purpose of this gathering. He wondered if Father Peregrine would be turning in his grave at such hard-nosed opportunism or if he would applaud the shrewd common sense of it. He wondered if it consolidated their stability and protected their mission or if it perverted their path of simplicity into something cynical. Then he realized that Wat What's-his-name had been speaking to him for some while now and was politely and expectantly waiting upon his reply.

"I am so sorry," he said humbly, bringing his scattered wits to the interaction. He remembered William's whisper of two days ago, *Be yourself; you are lovable*. To make amends for his discourteous absence of attention, he pretended that this was a patient in a critical stage of illness, requiring the full strength of John's heart and intelligence to pull him through. "I am not yet used to my new role as abbot of this community." John allowed his soul to look trustingly into the man's eyes for a moment. "And I find this gathering a little overwhelming. What did you just say to me? Please forgive me."

When the boats came in at Hull later on in the year, Wat Bridger personally supervised the selection of rice and spices consigned for delivery to St. Alcuin's Abbey. He knew that the quality of what he sent would be critically inspected. He had been promised a very good deal on their fleeces, which he knew were good; and his heart had been won entirely by the gentleness and humility of their abbot, who could look at you as if you were the only person in the world.

THE
FORTY-FIFTH DAY
Good Friday

Abbot John listened to the chapter, watched the reader return to his stall, and began to speak.

"On Good Friday I have nothing original to say. This seems to me not a time to be clever or innovative—to try to improve the tradition with audacious new thoughts of my own. I have no new thoughts. All my sight is filled with Christ upon the cross, nailed in stark suffering, waiting through agony for a glory he has almost lost sight of: *'Eloi, eloi, lama sabachthani?'*

"Of all the Good Fridays I have sat in this chapter house, keeping watch with you, my brothers, the one I remember most was five years ago. Before Father Peregrine was taken ill.

"I remember him talking to us quietly, the way he always did. He spoke about how Jesus opened wide his arms for us on the cross—an embrace, Father said, that was big enough for everyone in the world. He said that the thing about being nailed to a cross, wide-open like that, is that you are brought to a place where you can no longer change your mind. Do you remember that homily?

"Father got a bit scholarly at this point! He spoke about the holy name of God in the Scriptures: I Am That I Am. He drew our attention to the numerous times in the Gospels—especially the Gospel of John—where Jesus takes to himself the *ego eimi*, the holy name of God: '*I am* the Good Shepherd. *I am* the Way, the Truth, and the Life. *I am* the Bread of Life. *I am* the Light of the World.' Father said Christ was consciously aligning himself—for our benefit—upon the pattern of God's nature and identity. He was conformed to the being of God the Father by his choices, by his attitudes, and by who he essentially was.

"But then Father Abbot said that the heart of all this, the perfect living icon of God-in-Christ, becomes clear to us when we gaze upon Christ on the cross. Helpless, hurting, his arms spread wide, no longer able to even see or feel the presence of his God, no longer able to teach or choose, to challenge or heal, he is just nailed there. And his body announces the real presence of God, saying, 'Here I Am.'

"Father said Jesus had stopped choosing for himself; he said when Christ opened wide his arms for us on the cross, that was anyone's hug: friend, brother, enemy, betrayer. Christ was just *there*; it was over to us now to respond. This was the finale, the moment we decide whether we are religious sightseers, pausing to look and then moving on, or whether we will stop and hug him back. He reminded us, Christ is *nailed* to that cross. Those who jeered at him to come down from it saw no miracles. So anybody who accepts that embrace, who hugs him back, has to accept the cross as well as the Christ.

"Father said that we are the body of Christ, and we go the way of the cross. If we are drawn to him, if we are in love with him, what we do is embrace one another, without question, exception, or reservation. In embracing one another, we find we have embraced the cross, but also the Christ.

"He said, 'Jesus opened wide his arms for you on the cross. It's up to you. In each other, you have the chance to hug him back.'"

"I always remembered that. I can't put it any better. It's what seems to me to be true."

✠ ✠ ✠

Abbot John turned toward the community, his arms open in blessing. "Our Savior Christ said to his disciples, 'Peace I leave with you, my peace I give unto you': therefore let us share with one another a sign of Christ's peace."

At that time in the wider church, the kiss of peace had fallen out of fashion. In many churches the faithful passed around a wooden pax-board, and they kissed that instead of one another. But Father Peregrine would never have it so. He thought that the only chance anyone had of finding Christ was if they searched for him in reconciliation and tenderness in their relationships with one another. When the time came for the kiss of peace in the Mass, they followed the custom of turning to those on their right and left and exchanging a simple token gesture of peace. But on Good Friday every year, despite the considerable throng of visitors in the nave, he made the brothers in the choir take the time to exchange the kiss of peace with one another.

And so they did this day.

All the brothers, both novices and professed, moved quietly about the choir. "Peace be with you. . . . Peace be with you. . . . Peace be with you, Brother Clement. . . . Peace be with you, Brother Benedict. . . . Peace be with you, Father John . . . "

And then Tom and William found themselves face-to-face with one another. For a moment they both stopped. Tom saw cautious trust in William's eyes, but uncertainty too. Tom had thought all was well between them, forgiveness sought and offered, but on reflection he saw that the initiative had not been his; and the history had been stormy.

"Peace be with you, Brother Thomas," said William tentatively in that light, soft voice Tom had once so loathed. He did not look as sure of himself as he used to do, Tom thought. He did not look quite sure of anything.

These impressions and thoughts flashed through Tom's mind in an instant, but Brother Theodore waited patiently behind him, and Tom realized he was holding up the orderly progress of things.

"The past is too heavy to carry," he said quietly. "Let's start again. Peace be with you, my brother, my friend."

He took William into his arms, held him tenderly, held him close, felt the return of his embrace. When he released him, William looked away, breathing through his mouth as a man does when he can stave off weeping that way. And Tom passed on quickly. "Peace be with you, Father Chad."

THE
FORTY-SIXTH DAY
Holy Saturday

Brother Michael entered the chapel thronged with visitors, keeping custody of the eyes and walking with peaceful tread the length of the aisle to the choir. As he passed his own stall and approached the abbot's seat, John's heart sank. *Oh, no. What now?* He watched Michael with apprehension, but Michael's face remained sealed in composure, giving nothing away.

He reverenced the altar, his face serious and serene, and bent to speak to Abbot John as he drew level with his stall.

"You owe me ten Hail Marys and a pot of Brother Walafrid's really good muscle rub," he whispered. Then he turned and walked with lowered eyes and calm monastic decorum to his place between Brother Stephen and Brother Thaddeus.

Men in community miss very little. They all saw the sudden schoolboy grin that lit their abbot's face as he bent his cowled head in prayer.

Brother Tom felt a sense of something that had somewhere been made complete.

EASTER DAY

*T*om watched William make his way to the lectern. He looked older now, thin and tired, his face wearied into deeper lines. Eyes that knew what to look for could still see the faded line of discoloration around his throat. Other than that, he seemed the same—almost. The same irony of expression, the same don't-mess-with-me detachment. But underneath that, something frigid and inaccessible had relaxed. Tom thought he saw peace: a soul that had come through fire and found its way to the light.

He watched William's fine, long hands find the page in the beautiful Gospel that lay open on the lectern, ready for anyone who came to read to find his place.

ASHES ✠ FIRE ✠ LIGHT

GLOSSARY OF TERMS

Ambra: measure of salt.

Benedictine Rule: the document guiding daily life, written by St. Benedict.

Breviary: monastic prayer book.

Cellarer: monk responsible for oversight of all provisions; a key role in the community.

Chapter: daily meeting governing practical matters, where a chapter of St. Benedict's Rule was read and expounded by the abbot.

Choir: the part of the church where the community sits.

Cistercian: order of monks, reform of Benedictine tradition.

Cloister: covered way giving access to main buildings of a monastery.

Collatio: Bible study.

Corody/corrody: purchased right to food/clothing/housing from a monastery for an agreed period, which could be for life.

Desmesne: modern equivalent would be *domain*.

Dorter: dormitory.

Eucharist: Holy Communion meal, the Lord's Supper.

Frater: refectory.

Garderobe: toilet.

Garth: garden quadrangle enclosed by the cloister.

Grail: chalice, the sacred cup holding the wine of the Eucharist.

Hours: the services of worship in the monastic day.

Lay: not ordained.

Liturgy: structured worship.

Missal: book with the words for the Mass.

Nave: the body of the church occupied by the public in worship.

Obedience: the occupation allotted to a monk.

Obedientiary: monk with a particular office.

Office: the set worship taking place at regular intervals through the day.

Ostler, also hostler: man who looks after horses.

Palfrey: high-bred riding horse of the Middle Ages.

Pater Noster: the Lord's Prayer.

Pilgarlic: literally someone who is bald; a term of contempt.

Porter: doorkeeper.

Postulant: new member not yet made a novice.

Precentor: worship facilitator.

Prie-dieu: a kneeling desk for saying prayers.

Prior: in an abbey, the deputy leader; in a priory, the leader.

Raw: northern English word to describe cold, damp weather.

Reredorter: latrines situated convenient to sleeping quarters.

Rood screen: wooden structure with the cross (rood: Old English) on the top, dividing the choir from the nave.

Sacristan: monk with responsibility for the vestments and vessels, etc. of the altar.

Tenebrae: special Good Friday service marked by gradual extinguishing of lights.

Thurible: container in which incense is burned in worship.

Viaticum: literally, *food for the journey*; Eucharistic bread and wine of the Last Rites.

Villein: peasant legally tied to the land where he worked.

Monastic Day

There may be slight variation from place to place and at different times from the Dark Ages through the Middle Ages and onward: e.g., Vespers may be after supper rather than before. This gives a rough outline. Slight liberties are taken in my novels to allow human interactions to play out.

Winter Schedule (from Michaelmas)

2:30 A.M. Preparation for the nocturns of matins: psalms, etc.
3:00 A.M. Matins, with prayers for the royal family and for the dead.
5:00 A.M. Reading in preparation for Lauds.
6:00 A.M. Lauds at daybreak and Prime; wash and break fast
       (just bread and water, standing).
8:30 A.M. Terce, Morrow Mass, Chapter.
12:00 noon Sext, Sung Mass, midday meal.
2:00 P.M. None.
4:15 P.M. Vespers, Supper, Collatio.
6:15 P.M. Compline.
The Grand Silence begins.

Summer Schedule

1:30 A.M. Preparation for the nocturns of matins: psalms, etc.
2:00 A.M. Matins.
3:30 A.M. Lauds at daybreak, wash and break fast.
6:00 A.M. Prime, Morrow Mass, Chapter.
8:00 A.M. Terce, Sung Mass.
11:30 A.M. Sext, midday meal.
2:30 P.M. None.
5:30 P.M. Vespers, Supper, Collatio.
8:00 P.M. Compline.
The Grand Silence begins.

Liturgical Calendar

I have included the main feasts and fasts in the cycle of the church's year, plus one or two other dates that are mentioned (e.g., Michaelmas and Lady Day when rents were traditionally collected) in these stories.

Advent: begins four Sundays before Christmas.

Christmas: December 25th.

Holy Innocents: December 28th.

Epiphany: January 6th.

Baptism of our Lord: concludes Christmastide, the Sunday after January 6th.

Candlemas: February 2 (Purification of Blessed Virgin Mary, Presentation of Christ in the temple).

Lent: Ash Wednesday to Holy Thursday; start date varies with phases of the moon.

Holy Week: last week of Lent and the Easter Triduum.

Easter Triduum (three days) of Good Friday, Holy Saturday, Easter Sunday.

Ascension: forty days after Easter.

Whitsun (Pentecost): fifty days after Easter.

Lady Day: May 31st.

Trinity Sunday: Sunday after Pentecost.

Corpus Christi: Thursday after Trinity Sunday.

Sacred Heart of Jesus: Friday of the following week.

Feast of John the Baptist: June 24th.

Lammas (literally *loaf-mass*; grain harvest): August 1st.

Michaelmas: feast of St. Michael and All Angels, September 29th.

All Saints: November 1st.

All Souls: November 2nd.

Martinmas: November 11th.

Next in The Hawk and the Dove series:

The Hour before Dawn

Coming in January 2012

If you've enjoyed *The Hardest Thing to Do*,
be sure to check out the first three
books in the series!

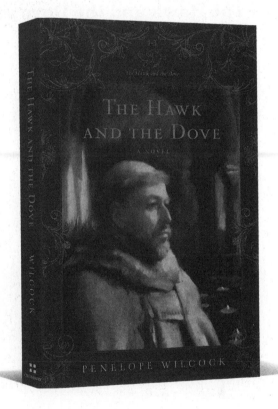

This 3-in-1 volume includes:
The Hawk and the Dove
The Wounds of God
The Long Fall

Coming in January 2012

The Hour before Dawn

Book 5 in The Hawk and the Dove series